Peter
LOVESEY

READER, I BURIED THEM

AND OTHER STORIES

SPHERE

SPHERE

First published in Great Britain in 2022 by Sphere
This paperback edition published by Sphere in 2023

1 3 5 7 9 10 8 6 4 2

A CIP catalogue record for this book is available from the British Library.

ISBN 978-0-7515-8588-9

Typeset in ITC New Baskerville by Palimpsest Book Production Ltd, Falkirk,
Stirlingshire
Printed and bound in Great Britain by Clays Ltd, Elcograf S.p.A.

Papers used by Sphere are from well-managed forests
and other responsible sources.

FSC
www.fsc.org

MIX
Paper from
responsible sources
FSC® C104740

Sphere
An imprint of
Little, Brown Book Group
Carmelite House
50 Victoria Embankment
London EC4Y 0DZ

An Hachette UK Company
www.hachette.co.uk

www.littlebrown.co.uk

Dedicated to my son, Phil, ideas man and short story Dagger winner, and my upbeat daughter, Kathy, who reads every word and asks for more. Together with Jax, my ever-inspiring wife, they keep me going.

Contents

Foreword by the Author

Let me tell you a story about a short story. It was called 'The Bathroom' and was my first in print, almost fifty years ago, in *Winter's Crimes*, an annual collection from Macmillan, who had published my first novel. Soon after publication, a letter arrived from Ruth Rendell. As a novice author, I was thrilled to learn that a crime writer I admired but had never met had actually read my story and liked it enough to get in touch. The theme, a house with a sinister past and its influence on the current occupants, had interested Ruth and she wanted to see it for herself. The house was a real one and still existed, but the street had been given another name and I knew where to find it. Ruth, who lived in Highgate at the time and drew inspiration from long walks in London, went specially to see it and wrote back to tell me about the impression it made on her. Houses and the dark forces within them were a recurring theme in her writing. She had already written *The Secret House of Death* and later titles would include *The House of Stairs* and *Thirteen Steps Down*. We met and she generously encouraged me to write more short fiction and gave me a lovely quote for the cover of my next book.

I couldn't have asked for a better start and I haven't stopped since. This new collection reaches the landmark of my hundredth short story. Writing them is a treat I give myself between novels, trying out fresh ideas and new ways of developing them. Some approaches will work only in this short form, but others provide the impetus for longer books. For years my novels were set in the Victorian era because I wasn't sure I could write about the modern police. Thanks to getting up confidence exploring contemporary themes in short stories, I finally made the switch to a modern-day Bath police series featuring Peter Diamond. He has bulldozed his way through twenty books and into this collection in 'A Three Pie Problem'.

I looked for a common factor in the latest stories and found it. Almost all of them are about groups or individuals with an interest or a way of life that is unexpectedly visited by crime. Mostly they are unlikely protagonists: a romantic novelist, a dressmaker, a beekeeper, a brotherhood of monks, a bookseller, the cast of a play, an obituary writer, an entrant for a fancy hat contest and a lady seeking advice for a personal problem. In each, you will learn a little about their activities just as I did and I hope you will be surprised and entertained by discovering how the crime emerges.

One of the stories takes us right back to Edgar Allan Poe, who is generally regarded as the writer of the first modern detective story, 'The Murders in the Rue Morgue', which was itself a short story. The history of crime writing shows how the earliest popular writers from Poe onwards concentrated mainly on short fiction. Conan Doyle, the creator of Sherlock Holmes, is the obvious example, along with G.K. Chesterton (Father Brown), and E.W. Hornung (A.J. Raffles). In America, *Black Mask* magazine was a huge influence on writers like Dashiell Hammett, Raymond Chandler, Erle Stanley Gardner, Cornell Woolrich and John D. MacDonald. *Black Mask* ran from 1920 for about thirty years and after it ceased publication, *Ellery Queen's Mystery*

Magazine and *Alfred Hitchcock's Magazine* became the main outlets for short mystery fiction, and continue to be so – which brings me back to my story.

Buoyed up by Ruth Rendell's encouragement, I submitted 'The Bathroom' to *Ellery Queen*. My jubilation ended when they sent me a polite letter of rejection. Maybe it was too British for American readers, I decided.

Every writer must learn to accept disappointment. Six years after 'The Bathroom', I wrote another story reworking the theme of a house and its past and sent it off to New York and this time it was accepted by the editor, Fred Dannay, one of the duo who wrote so many ingenious novels and short stories under the pseudonym of Ellery Queen. Mr Dannay actually encouraged me to write more. I was on a roll. I became a regular contributor. Then I did something that makes me cringe when I think of it. I dusted off my eight-year-old copy of 'The Bathroom' and resubmitted it to him in the hope that now I was getting known, he would take it.

I heard nothing back. That's the end of your flirtation with *EQMM*, I told myself. How could you have been so stupid?

That same year of 1981 I registered for a crime writers' conference in Stockholm. To my horror when I got there and saw the list of delegates they included Fred Dannay. How embarrassing! I was tempted to take the first flight home.

I spent the first two days keeping at a distance from my nemesis. He was easy to spot in a crowd because he was bald and bearded with thick, dark-rimmed glasses. But he was also a short man who disappeared from view behind more substantial figures like Julian Symons and Christianna Brand. I was doing remarkably well at avoiding him until late on the Saturday when I stepped into the hotel lift. Two people were already inside: Fred Dannay and his wife, Rose.

The doors closed behind me.

No escape – and I was wearing my name-tag. I tried not to appear as alarmed as I felt. He leaned forward for a closer look at the label.

He said, 'Peter Lovesey. I know your name.'

Top of your blacklist, I thought.

'We published some of your stories.'

I forget my stumbling reply. I waited for him to tell me only a scumbag would resubmit a story after it had already been rejected.

The eyes twinkled behind the heavy specs. He just said, 'Keep them coming, won't you?' Then the doors opened and he and Rose stepped out.

I'm certain he knew.

Later that year, a letter arrived from Ellery Queen accepting 'The Bathroom'. It was published in the August issue, but with a different title.

And here I am, forty years after that reprieve, still writing short stories. As a tailpiece to this new volume, I have taken the liberty of including 'The Bathroom', together with 'The Tale of Three Tubs', my telling of the true story behind the story.

Gaslighting

To say that Luther was unprepared for what he found when he switched on the stage lights is an understatement. He was the first to arrive for the final dress rehearsal and he had the worst shock of his life. Upstage left, a body was hanging from the end of a rope.

An overturned card table was beneath, evidently kicked aside. It was part of the set for the Manninghams' first-floor living room. The Matchless Theatre production of *Gaslight* was due to open on Friday.

His heart thumping, Luther hurried from the control room down the centre aisle to the stage. He was overweight and unfit, but he got there as speedily as he could and hauled himself up. The suspended figure was motionless.

He knew who she was – Georgia, who was playing Bella Manningham, the lead role. She wasn't in costume. She wore the white jeans, black top and boots he'd got used to seeing at rehearsals. But her copper-coloured hair was still drawn up and pinned in Victorian style, leaving no doubt who she was, even though her face was angled away from him, forced upwards by the tension on the rope, which made an inverted V-shape under her chin.

It seemed she had rigged up this gallows herself. The rope looked thick and solid, probably a hand-line normally suspended from the fly loft and tied out of sight on a pin-rail.

Luther's first impulse was to cut her down and try resuscitation. People who hang themselves generally die from pressure on the arteries. But he'd need to get up to her head level – eight or nine feet above the stage – and he'd want a professional cutting-tool for rope that thick. Most of the ropes used in rigging systems are steel-reinforced. A hand-rope may have been solid hemp, but it would be a devil to cut. Maybe the best plan was to find a set of steps from somewhere, climb up to the level of her head and try to loosen the noose. Even so, this couldn't be a one-man task. He'd need someone else to take her weight while he worked on the knot.

He'd already taken out his phone when a voice hailed him. 'Up bright and early as usual, Luther. Oh, Jesus!' Stuart, who was playing the husband, Jack Manningham, had come from backstage and was standing in the wings, taking in the horror of the scene. 'Is she . . . ?'

Luther took hold of Georgia's right hand to feel for a pulse. There wasn't the faintest flicker. The hand was limp and cold. He shook his head. 'Some hours ago, I think. She must have done it last night after we left. Looks like she moved the table here and kicked it away to leave herself hanging. God knows why. I had no idea she was suicidal.'

'Nothing we can do for her, then?'

'I think not. I was trying to work out how to get her down, but now I've changed my mind. We should leave things exactly as they are and call the police.' He dialled 101 and jammed the phone to his ear.

*

The rest of the cast arrived soon after. Oscar, who was playing Rough, the ex-detective, shook his head and went silent. Sally, cast as Elizabeth, the Manningham's housekeeper, sank into a chair with her hand across her mouth. And Muna, with the part of the teenage maid, Nancy, turned very pale and outstared anyone whose eyes met hers. Wardrobe, make-up, lighting and stage management, four individuals who did other jobs in the production as well, hadn't known Georgia so closely, but the spectacle on the stage horrified everyone.

When the police officer arrived, he treated the gruesome scene with calm, as if he was well used to actors hanging themselves onstage. He was PC Lilywhite, a uniformed constable with the air of a chief inspector. 'Is anyone in charge here?'

'Me, I suppose,' Luther said. 'I'm the director and I was the first to find her.'

'Who is she?'

'Her name is Georgia Flanagan and she had the leading role.'

'She's wearing a ring. Is that for the play?'

'She's married in real life to a guy called Anton, who has an IT business, a very successful one. You'll need to inform him, I expect.'

'Only if you're certain it's her.'

'It can't be anyone else.'

PC Lilywhite took the details and made a call to the police station. He told the actors a patrol car would be on its way to Anton Flanagan's address and the officers would break the news to him and bring him to the theatre. 'Any idea what time she did this?'

'It must have been last night,' Luther said, as an ugly

possibility gnawed at his brain, 'after I gave notes on yesterday's rehearsal. I think she was the last to leave.'

'But she didn't leave, did she? She's still here.'

Luther felt the blood rise in his cheeks.

'What time did you leave?'

'About ten-thirty. It was a long day. We had a tech rehearsal first and then a break for a meal and then the dress rehearsal. Then they got out of their costumes and sat in the audience seats for my notes.'

'Was Mrs Flanagan distressed in any way?'

'I didn't notice she was.'

'These notes you say you gave . . . can I see a copy?'

'"Notes" is a theatrical term, officer. Sometimes they're written down, sometimes not. It just means I mention points from the rehearsal that need extra work.'

'In short, you don't have a copy.'

'Most of it was off the cuff.'

'Could she have been upset by something you said?'

'I can't believe she was.'

Oscar, the member of the cast with enough years of acting behind him to challenge a statement like that, butted in. 'That isn't quite right, Luther. She ended up in tears.'

'Oh, come on,' Luther said. 'You're not blaming me for this.'

'Each rehearsal call I attended, you told her she wasn't getting it right.' Oscar turned to the other cast members. 'Isn't that true?'

After a stunned silence, Sally said, 'But she needed telling. She wasn't much good.'

'Doesn't matter any more what a rotten actor she was, does it?'

'How did she get the main part, then?' PC Lilywhite asked.

Embarrassment descended like the safety curtain.

The constable looked Luther up and down. 'Casting couch?'

'Nothing like that,' Sally said.

'If you want the truth of it,' Luther said, 'her husband Anton is our principal sponsor.'

'He put up the money?'

'Yes. And when Georgia wanted to audition for the part, I could hardly refuse. Sally would have done it better.'

'I'm her understudy,' Sally said. 'I play the housekeeper.'

'I see,' PC Lilywhite said. 'You'll take over the leading role now.'

'I haven't given that a thought.'

'You'd better, ma'am. The show must go on. Isn't that the rule? And my show goes on as well. I must invite the police surgeon to take a look at her.'

After making his call, PC Lilywhite asked for a stepladder, saying he wanted to inspect the noose. One was fetched from the wings and he climbed up. 'I'm thinking the average woman – no insult intended, ladies – doesn't get much practice at tying knots.' He put his hands on Georgia's shoulders and rotated her for a better look. 'Now this is remarkable, as good a noose knot as any of your stagehands could tie. Where did she learn that?'

A question nobody could answer.

He stepped higher and seated himself on top of the ladder, a position of authority. 'Has anyone found a suicide note?'

'We haven't looked for one,' Luther said.

'It would help me if you made a search now. Why don't you take a section each? There's a lot of clutter here.'

'It's a Victorian living room,' Sally said. 'They loved their ornaments.'

The search got under way with PC Lilywhite directing the operation from the top of the ladder. 'So there's only one scene, is that right?'

'Three acts, in point of fact,' Luther said, 'but they all take place on the same set.'

'What's the play?'

'*Gaslight*. The one about the poor woman almost driven out of her mind when her husband plays on her fears, hiding things and claiming she must have hidden them and dimming the lights and telling her she must be going mad.'

'Not nice. Not nice at all.'

'But in the end, she comes out the winner.'

'With the help of my character, Sergeant Rough, a police detective,' Oscar chimed in from where he was looking for the suicide note.

'One of us. That *is* nice. I like that.'

'A retired cop, I'd better add,' Oscar said, 'but famous in his day. It's a plum part for a mature actor.'

'Obviously. Do you know anything at all about the real police?'

'Quite a lot, in fact,' Oscar said without hesitation. 'Luther makes sure we prepare for our parts by researching them. Before we did the first read-through, I studied a book called *Scotland Yard Casebook*. I visited the Black Museum with a neighbour of mine who kindly got me in. He worked as a detective for twenty years.'

'We all did our homework. It's supposed to help,' Sally said from upstage where she was opening drawers in the bureau. 'I researched Victorian servant life and all the duties a housekeeper carried out.'

Muna, the youngest of the cast, said, 'And I learned how to light the gaslights and lay a fire.'

'And lay the master of the house,' Oscar said.

'Don't be so coarse,' Sally said.

'It's in the script, you know it is. The maid flirts outrageously with her boss.' Oscar smiled at Muna. 'You did some role-play with Stuart and I thought he rather enjoyed it, what we saw of it. What you got up to in private is anybody's guess.'

Muna stared him out and said nothing.

Stuart tried to make light of the comment. 'I'm sure the officer doesn't want to hear about the finer points of method acting.'

'Finer points!' Oscar said, laughing. 'I've heard it called a few things in my time. That's a new one.'

'I only want to know why this lady hanged herself,' PC Lilywhite said. 'How did she prepare for the part of this unfortunate wife? Was she unhappily married?'

'Far from it,' Luther said. 'She has a very supportive husband.'

'As she kept reminding us,' Oscar said. 'He's our angel.'

PC Lilywhite blinked.

'A bit of theatrical jargon,' Luther explained. 'An angel is an investor who backs a production.'

'The money,' Oscar said.

'Right. I understand. Coming back to the question I asked, how did this happily married lady prepare for her part?'

'She didn't,' Oscar said. 'She was still bumping into the furniture.'

'That's so unkind,' Muna said, seizing her chance to get back at Oscar.

'But true.'

The search for the suicide note came to an unsuccessful end.

Luther was making a huge effort to remain coherent. Inside, he was mired in desperation. 'I've been thinking about what you said, officer, about the noose. She may not have needed to tie the knot herself. The previous production here was an Agatha Christie, *And Then There Were None*. I wasn't involved in any way, but I came to see it. All the characters die and one of them, a woman called Vera, is hanged. Not literally, of course. This is theatre. The actress will have been wearing a body harness unseen by the audience, but the noose goes round her neck and is real. It's the end of the play.'

'I suppose it would be, with everyone dead,' PC Lilywhite said.

'But it fitted the title. That's how the novel ended. When it was first adapted for the theatre, Agatha Christie wrote a happy ending which doesn't work with a modern audience. Most productions since have used the book version with the hanging.'

'So you think the noose was left over from the Agatha Christie play?'

'Quite likely. Tied to the pin-rail with other ropes not being used.'

'That would explain the knot.' PC Lilywhite had a way of stating the obvious and making it sound like a brilliant deduction.

Luther couldn't keep down the guilt that by now was piercing his soul. 'I'd like to get something off my chest.'

'What's that?' PC Lilywhite said from the top of the ladder.

'When Oscar said I gave her a hard time, there may

8

be some truth in it. Where possible, we try to bring realism to our acting, from personal experience, as Sally was saying, and I felt from the beginning that Georgia had nothing to draw on. She was happily married to a good man. Her character is supposed to be "haggard, wan, frightened, with rings under her eyes which tell of sleepless nights and worse" – I'm quoting Patrick Hamilton, the playwright, here – and she just wasn't cutting it. Make-up can put the rings under the eyes, but she needed to find the despair in herself. When I gave her my note, I wanted a response. If I'm honest, I thought it would help her to know how it feels to be on the receiving end of some criticism.'

'Gaslighting,' Muna said.

'Nothing so mean as that.'

'You're losing me,' PC Lilywhite said.

'It's a buzzword these days,' Stuart said.

'It's much more than that,' Muna said, glaring at him. 'It's real and horrible. It happens in personal relationships, or at work, or in the theatre. Psychological manipulation. I despise it in any form.'

'That goes for me, too,' Sally said.

Muna told PC Lilywhite, 'Our play was written in 1938, but the same emotional abuse goes on, when a person deliberately makes someone else, generally a woman, doubt herself. Her confidence goes and she becomes more dependent, more malleable. It's cruel, insidious manipulation.'

'Sick,' Sally said in sisterly support.

'Gaslighting,' PC Lilywhite mouthed the word again. He seemed to enjoy speaking it.

Muna now turned her contempt on Luther. 'Are you telling us your note was intended to help Georgia?'

'Something drastic was needed,' Sally said, suddenly switching to Luther's defence. 'She was way off beam in the rehearsal. She wasn't lacking in confidence and she knew the words, but none of it was coming across as it should. She sounded more like Mary Poppins than Bella Manningham.'

'So she had to be humiliated in front of us all and driven to suicide,' Muna said. 'That's the ultimate in gaslighting. I've never liked method acting and I wish I'd said so before this.'

'Oh, come on,' Sally said. 'It was nothing like so bad as that. I'd rather have a critical note from Luther than a bad press review that the whole world can read.'

PC Lilywhite asked whether anyone could remember the actual words Luther used to Georgia.

'I can't remember verbatim,' Luther said. 'The gist of it was that she should show more emotion when she spoke the lines. I remember saying she'd done well to remember them, because hers is the main part with some long speeches, but acting was more than a feat of memory. It was about becoming the character speaking the words. She hadn't fully embraced the role.'

'If that's all that was said, it doesn't sound like grounds for suicide,' PC Lilywhite said.

'You're not an actor, so you wouldn't know how she felt,' Muna said. 'Those words told her she was a failure. Her dream was over.'

The tension among the actors was threatening to ignite. PC Lilywhite checked his watch. 'The police surgeon should be here any minute.'

'Oh, my God.'

The voice from the auditorium caught everyone off guard. Instead of the police surgeon, it was a guy with thick black hair to his shoulders, about thirty, in a black leather jacket and white chinos, standing in the aisle with his hand clapped to his face.

'Georgia's husband, Anton,' Oscar told PC Lilywhite in a lowered voice.

The policeman got down from the ladder.

Anton was striding towards the stage. 'I didn't believe it when they told me. Why have you left her like this? Can't you cut her down?'

'We're waiting for the police surgeon, sir,' PC Lilywhite said. 'That's the way things are done. Why don't you sit down and I'll come and speak to you?'

'No need,' Anton said. 'I'm coming up.'

Under the stage lighting, the scene that was now enacted was either touching and tragic or overplayed and mawkish, depending on one's point of view. Anton crossed the stage, wrapped his arms around the legs of his dead wife and pressed his face into her thighs. 'Georgie, darling, how could you do this? What possessed you?'

Most of the cast looked away in embarrassment.

'Better leave her alone, sir,' PC Lilywhite said, putting a hand on Anton's shoulder.

The grieving husband didn't seem to have heard. Moaning loudly, he was pawing at her hips under the loose T-shirt.

'You're dragging on her,' PC Lilywhite said. 'I must ask you to stop.'

Persuasion didn't work. In the end, the policeman took hold of the grieving husband's arm and managed to detach him.

And now Anton's despair turned to rage as he faced the actors. 'You people are to blame for this. She wanted so much to make a success of her acting and you ganged up on her and destroyed her confidence. You knew she was inexperienced and you hounded her to death with your sarcasm and your spite.'

'That isn't true,' Sally said. 'We treated her kindly. She was a part of our team and we all wanted the play to be a success.'

'She couldn't sleep,' Anton said. 'Couldn't eat properly. Couldn't think straight. She was in turmoil and got no support from any of you. I was getting texts from her saying everyone wanted her to fail.'

Surprised looks were exchanged among the cast.

'Why would we do that?' Stuart asked.

'You tell me,' Anton said. 'What was the hidden agenda – force her out of the play so that someone else could take over?'

'Absolutely not,' Sally said, flushing scarlet. 'That was never our intention.'

'The rest of you know each other well. You've done scores of plays. She'd had a couple of walk-on parts and now she was top of the bill. That was tough.'

'She wanted the role,' Oscar said.

'You're telling me she did. She learned the words perfectly. And she could have triumphed if she'd been treated right and given some support.' He pointed an accusing finger, first at Luther and then each of the others. 'You'd better examine your consciences, each of you. There's sure to be an inquest and I intend to speak out and say where the blame lies.'

With that, Anton turned away and quit the stage, as dramatic an exit as any ever made in this theatre.

Georgia's body was eventually seen by the doctor, cut down by two attendants he brought with him, removed from the stage and driven to the mortuary. The police left and the company did their best to regroup.

'I feel dreadful,' Sally said. 'I've got the shakes. What do we do now?'

'We go for a drink,' Luther said.

In the pub, they tried to process what had had happened and been said. Stuart made the reasonable point that Anton had been in shock and was looking for an outlet for his emotions. 'We happened to be there, so he turned his anger on us.'

'I didn't notice her sending texts yesterday,' Sally said. 'She was on stage most of the time.'

'Later she did when Luther was giving his notes,' Muna said. 'I was sitting next to her. She had her pink phone out and was texting right through.'

'To Anton?'

'I didn't look. I'm not that sneaky.'

'Let's move on from all that,' Luther said. 'What are we going to do? I don't suppose anyone feels any more like rehearsing this afternoon.'

'But we're due to open on Friday,' Oscar said. 'Do we cancel out of respect?'

'The respectful thing is to carry on,' Sally said.

'Show of hands,' Luther said. 'All in favour of cancelling.'

No hands went up.

'Like the policeman said, the show goes on,' Oscar said. 'But can you handle the part, Sally?'

'I damned well should. I understudied it.'

'I can find someone to play the housekeeper,' Luther said. 'What if we run the dress rehearsal tonight and take this afternoon off as a mark of respect and get our heads right?'

It was agreed that Sally and whoever played the housekeeper would bring their scripts on stage and otherwise

13

it would be a full-scale rehearsal. Sally left for home straight away.

'How are you feeling, Luther?' Stuart asked. 'That was a tough few moments when Anton turned his fire on you – well, on all of us.'

'It bothers me, of course. I obviously came down harder on Georgia than I intended. I really felt after yesterday that she hadn't got into the role. Nowhere near. I decided some strong words were needed and then she might get an inkling of what it means to be under criticism. In a month of Sundays I didn't think what I said would drive her to hang herself.'

'Don't be hard on yourself,' Stuart said. 'All of us who were there agree she had to be told. There could be some other reason none of us knows about.'

'Like what?' Luther said.

'Like her marriage was on the rocks.'

'That's absurd. We all know they were fine together. You only had to see the state Anton was in. He was devastated.'

'He would be, wouldn't he, if his wife hanged herself, even if they had been fighting.'

'Personally,' Oscar said, 'I thought his reaction was overdone, almost as if he was play-acting, all that hugging of her legs and groaning. We could have been watching some third-rate melodrama.'

'Weren't you convinced by it?' Luther said.

'He's no actor.'

Muna spoke. 'Actually Anton has done some acting. Georgia told me. As a child, he was sent to a crappy stage school.'

'Pushy parents?'

'Yes, but he loved every minute of it and did some commercials and got into drama school.'

'Really? A wannabe actor?'

'Only he thought he knew it all already and was kicked out after a couple of months, so he did a crash course in IT and the rest is history.'

'Can't knock him for being filthy rich,' Oscar said. 'We all benefit. I hope he isn't having second thoughts.'

'We banked the cheque two weeks ago,' Luther said.

'Nice work.'

'For God's sake, this isn't about money,' Muna said. 'Georgia killed herself and we're responsible.'

'You mean I'm responsible,' Luther said.

'That's not what I said.'

'If any of us needs to shoulder the blame, it's me.'

'Think about what Stuart said a moment ago, then,' Oscar said. 'What if their marriage wasn't all we were led to believe? What if Anton was jealous she'd started acting and wanted her to fail big-time. He puts up the money for our production, making sure she gets the plum part and will screw up.'

'That's evil,' Muna said. 'Only a twisted mind could come up with something so horrible.'

Oscar didn't rise to that. He seemed to have inside knowledge. 'Jealousy can make anyone evil. We've only got Anton's word that she was texting to say we all expected her to fail. He could have been gaslighting her himself, texting her to say she was no good and ought to face up and pull out.'

'I don't know where you get these vile ideas.'

'I'll tell you where, Muna. Some of you were too embarrassed to look when he tried to embrace her, carrying on like that with a dead body, but I wasn't. I watched the entire performance and when the cop pulled him away I saw something the rest of you seem to have missed. Anton had a pink object in his hand – her phone. He must have

15

removed it from her back pocket when he was fumbling under the T-shirt.'

'Why would he do that?'

'You tell me. I'm thinking he plans to wipe the messages he sent her. He didn't want that phone being taken away by the police and having his texts read out at the inquest.'

Everyone had gone quiet, digesting this.

'Can you do that – delete everything?' Luther said.

'Right back to the factory settings. He's an IT expert.'

Stuart said, 'I heard that even if you think you've deleted everything, it isn't really removed. It's marked for deletion by the operating company, but it's still in there somewhere. Anton would know that.'

Oscar shrugged. 'So he destroys the phone, hammers it to bits and chucks it in the river.'

'He'd have to do the same to his own phone,' Luther said.

'He will if he wants to shift the blame onto you.'

'Why didn't you speak out when you saw the phone in his hand?'

Oscar spread his hands. 'You were there. You saw the state he was in. Would you have spoken out?'

'I suppose not.'

'If PC Lilywhite had been any use, he would have noticed and got suspicious,' Oscar said.

'He had no reason to be suspicious,' Luther said. 'Besides, he isn't a detective. He was an ordinary bobby sent to deal with an incident.'

'We should report this as soon as possible,' Muna said. 'Whatever texts were sent, they're evidence and the phone must be handed to the coroner.'

'Is it a crime to undermine someone's confidence?'

'In its extreme form it is. It's called coercive and controlling behaviour.'

'Leave it with me,' Luther said. 'I'll see that it's investigated.'

After the first night of *Gaslight* the reviews were generous enough to ensure full houses for the rest of the run. Nothing was written about the late changes in the casting. Sally was widely praised for her playing of Mrs Manningham, 'a rich reading, with all the heart-rending bewilderment of the exploited and abused wife developing into self-awareness and confidence through the support of the ex-detective Rough, played robustly by Oscar Smith'.

Another drama was played out a week later when Luther called unexpectedly at the country estate where Anton Flanagan lived in a Lutyens mansion with a modern annexe at the back. As soon as he set eyes on the woman who opened the door, he suspected a secondary motivation for the gaslighting of poor Georgia. It was obvious that this was the new lady of the manor, dressed in a figure-hugging cream-coloured outfit. She looked Luther up and down, took stock of his wrinkled shirt and faded cords, and asked if he had an appointment.

'No,' he said, 'but I think he'll want to see me.'

'Yeah?' She made it sound like a rebuke.

'Tell him it's Luther, from the Matchless Theatre. Say I've found something of interest.'

She sighed and used her phone.

Then she gave an even heavier sigh. 'He has a few minutes to spare. I'm supposed to show you to his office – as if I'm his receptionist.'

Teetering on high heels that made her movement

laughable, she led him through the main house and into the annexe, much of which was open plan, with banks of computers manned by geeks with beards and ponytails.

Anton ran his empire from a large office upstairs adjacent to a board room, where Luther was told to wait. Pictures of cityscapes lined the walls. He recognised Sydney, Hong Kong and New York. He could hear Anton speaking on the phone next door.

He was kept waiting almost twenty minutes and there was no apology from Anton when he appeared. 'This had better be quick. I'm expecting another call from the coast.'

The coast wasn't Southend-on-Sea, Luther decided. 'I'm doing you a favour,' he said. 'I don't know if you're familiar with the law. I was told you trained as an actor.'

'That's immaterial,' Anton said.

'Immaterial to what? I haven't started. I'm talking about what will emerge when the inquest is held. I don't know if you still intend to blame me and my colleagues for Georgia's suicide.'

'I most certainly do,' Anton said. 'I was emotional at the time for obvious reasons, but I haven't changed my opinion.'

'Interesting,' Luther said, 'because I have a different take on it. I know Georgia was troubled by a series of texts she got while she was rehearsing. Anonymous texts. They really got into her head and affected her acting.'

'Who told you this?'

'Georgia did.' Untrue, but justifiable, Luther had decided. Anton reddened and frowned. 'I don't believe you.'

'She didn't say anything to me, I admit, but you know how it is when women get together and share their secrets.'

'She spoke to one of the others in the cast?'

'It doesn't matter who,' Luther said.

'You can't prove this.'

18

'Another of the cast saw you take Georgia's phone from her pocket while you were hugging her.'

So?' Anton said, less troubled, as if he'd expected this and had his answer ready. 'She wouldn't have wanted her private messages being read by the police. As her husband, I had a right to take it back.'

'I thought you would say that,' Luther said, 'so I went to see them.'

'The police?'

'I told them there was a danger you would destroy the phone to hide vital evidence.'

'I don't buy this. I don't buy it at all. They haven't been to see me.'

'So are you willing to hand it in?'

'Too late.' Anton produced a smile. 'I carelessly dropped it and accidentally drove over it.' The smile became a laugh. 'Crushed it completely.'

'That's what the police said you would do if you had something to hide. Did you do the same with the phone you used to send the thirty-four messages she received from you on the day she died?'

The hilarity was over.

'It turns out that Georgia knew how to deal with nuisance texting. As an IT man, you'll know better than I do that all text messages have to go through a gateway at the carrier's.'

'True, but they don't store them all. The sheer number of texts going through the system would defeat them.'

'Your wife was smarter than you think. When the texts started, she called the carrier and asked them to put a trap on any further messages she got. They were able to tell her the messages were coming from you.'

He'd turned white. 'How do you know this?'

'The police did what they do in these cases, issued a

subpoena and now they have transcripts of all the messages she received in the twenty-four hours before she hanged herself.'

Anton's face was a mask, petrified by guilt. 'Have you seen them?'

'No, but the coroner will. And so will the court that deals with you.'

Sweet and Low

The thief came at 2.30 a.m. on an October night dressed in a white protective suit like an invader from another planet, not a scrap of flesh visible. Large hood with dark visor. Gauntlet gloves. Calf-length boots. Carrying what looked like a firearm, he strode across the turf towards the area behind the farmhouse where Shirley Littledale's twelve hives were sited.

A bee rustler.

The stealing of beehives is hazardous but rewarding. Each hive contains a colony of up to fifty thousand bees and the vast majority collect nectar that is processed into honey. The value of honey has increased as the bee population has declined. Bee rustling has become a profitable crime.

The sensible time to steal beehives is by night, when bees and humans are supposed to be dormant. The object carried by the raider wasn't in fact a firearm, but a defensive weapon known in the trade as a smoker. Fumes wafted into a hive will confuse the colony by masking the bees' internal communication system. They are unable to rally and make a united response.

After the bees were subdued, the rustler moved the box-shaped hives by hand-trolley across the yard to where a flatbed truck was parked. In a little over twenty minutes all twelve were taken and the getaway vehicle moved off.

Inside the farmhouse, Shirley Littledale slept on.

'Bee rustling? Get away,' Helen Morgan said.

'It's true,' her friend Gaye said. 'They drove off with her entire stock, her apiary, or whatever it's called.'

'I've never heard of bees being rustled. Sounds like something out of an old cowboy film.'

'They're livestock, same as cattle, when you think about it. Anyway, it had a terrible effect on Shirley. She's bereft.'

'It'll have a terrible effect on us all.'

Gaye was president of the local branch of the Countrywomen's Guild, but not because she was pushy or ambitious. She had been shoe-horned into the job by Helen, a strong personality who was secretary and mainstay of the branch. Without Helen, they would have folded years before. Their main objective was to support good causes and honey was the top seller on their market stall, more of a money-spinner than home-made jam or even home-made cakes. The guild also had its social side enjoyed by all the members, but the fund-raising always came before the partying.

'When did this happen?' Helen asked.

'At least a week ago,' Gaye said.

'Some rogue beekeeper.' Helen was never without an opinion.

'How do you know?'

'Bees aren't any use to anyone except a beekeeper. You need the know-how, or you get stung to bits. Vicious little things.'

'Vicious?' Gaye said in surprise. 'I thought everyone liked honey bees.'

'Not me. Have you ever gone near a hive?'

'Now you mention it, no. Everyone knows you have to respect their territory. Have you had a bad experience with bees?'

'Not specially. I've been stung a couple of times. Most people have. But I do have some idea what goes on in the hive. They're ruthless with each other and I'm ashamed to say it's a female society – a queen bee and thousands of workers, all female. The males – the drones – have a short life. They have only one purpose, to mate with the queen, and that kills them.'

'With a smile on their little faces.'

Helen didn't often get jokes. 'They're the lucky ones. All the rest are forced out of the hive when the weather turns cold and they quickly die.'

'Poor things,' Gaye said.

'What goes on with the queen is even more savage. As soon as she emerges from her cell she kills any other potential queens. Unlike the workers she can use her sting time and time again. It's serial murder.'

'I'm rapidly revising my opinion of bees. You seem to know a lot about it.'

'My ex was a beekeeper. Still is, as far as I know. It takes all sorts. I'm sorry about Shirley, but bee people are a small community. The police will know who to ask.'

'Shirley hasn't called the police,' Gaye said. 'She doesn't want them involved.'

'Why ever not? It's theft. Those bees must be worth hundreds, if not thousands.'

'She's in a state of shock.'

'Yes, but . . .'

'She made it very clear she isn't going to make an issue of it.'

'What does her bloke say?'

'Him?' Gaye's eyes rolled upwards. 'You know what Ben's like, the fat slob. Does nothing except prop up the bar in the pub each evening and ogle any woman who comes in. He's useless at running the farm.'

'Is that what she told you?'

'No, but it's common knowledge. Shirley's in denial about him. She gets what she wants in bed and doesn't realise there's more to life than that – or ought to be. He's a stud, that's all.'

'A drone.'

Gaye laughed. 'That's him exactly, leaves all the running of the farm to Shirley. She's far too sweet-natured. She ought to get tough with him. It's so unfair.'

'I've never heard her complain. I thought she was reasonably content.'

'She likes the beekeeping, certainly. She thinks of her bees as family. Positively dotes on them. That's why she doesn't want the police involved – in case it panics the thief into destroying the hives. I feel so sorry for her.'

'If she's so attached to them she must want them back.'

'Ideally, yes, but she seems resigned to losing them, poor soul. She's talking about keeping chickens instead. It won't be half as satisfying.'

'Or productive. A few hens don't bring in much income. We can't sell more eggs on the market stall. We've got our supplier already.'

'There's nothing we can do . . . is there?'

'We have a duty to help,' Helen said as if she was addressing the branch committee. 'It's in the interests of the guild. All the income from the sale of honey.'

'We can't use our funds.'

'I don't mean that. We can do what Shirley doesn't want the police to do – investigate.'

'How?' Gaye asked, turning pale. Investigating crime wasn't in the charter of the guild.

'By asking around. There's a beekeepers' club in the village. Shirley doesn't belong to it, but they ought to know something. They should be pleased to help, if only so it doesn't happen to one of them.'

'One of them may be the rustler, going by what you said.'

'Quite possibly,' Helen said as if it was of less importance than what she was about to ask. 'If I went along to meet them, would you come with me?'

There was a pause for thought.

'As our president,' Helen added.

'What can we say to them?'

'Appeal to their better nature.'

'I can't see the thief tamely handing back the hives.'

'Well, no. Get the word around that all Shirley wants is her bees returned and whoever is responsible might come to his senses and leave them in a field somewhere where they'll be found.'

Gaye had learned to be wary of Helen's scheming, but this seemed reasonable. 'All right. If that's all it is, spreading the word, I'll join you. Where do they meet?'

First, Gaye insisted Shirley must be told what they were planning. They needed her agreement.

'Is this the turn coming up?' Helen asked, at the wheel of her Range Rover.

'Not yet. Haven't you been here before?'

'Between ourselves, I keep my distance. I can't tell you why, but she makes me feel inferior.'

Gaye was surprised. Helen wasn't the sort to feel inferior to anyone. 'I've known her a long time and always found her friendly. My boys were at school with hers. We agreed to take it in turns to drive them to football training.'

'I bet you ended up doing most of it.'

Gaye laughed. 'Now you mention it, yes, but she's terribly busy running the farm.'

'She makes that very clear. The queen bee, I call her. If she has sons, you'd think they'd help in a crisis like this.'

'They live miles away. Three of them went abroad.'

'How many did she have?'

'Five, and two daughters.'

'Quite a brood.'

'With the bloke she's got, it's a miracle she didn't have twice that number.'

'Oh, Gaye, you break me up.'

The farmhouse came up on the right. After they had parked in the yard, Gaye pointed to the place beyond the kitchen garden where the beehives had been sited. A stack of plastic sacks containing fertiliser now occupied the area.

'Doesn't look as if she's expecting to get her bees back,' Helen said.

'Do they have a homing instinct?'

'Not as you mean it,' a voice broke in from behind them. Shirley Littledale had come unseen from the back of the farmhouse, a tall, regal-looking woman in her fifties with silver hair coiled and held in place with combs. 'It's a nice idea, but their home is the hive. They won't leave it unless the queen takes flight and she won't budge unless the rest of them choose to evict her in favour of a new queen. How nice to see you both. Obviously you've heard about my loss.'

'That's why we came,' Gaye said.

Presently they were seated at the square wooden table

in the farmhouse kitchen drinking coffee. Helen explained their plan.

'The beekeepers' club?' Shirley said. 'Some of them know me, but I'm not a member. I don't want them to think I'm accusing any of them of stealing my bees.'

'That's why it's better coming from us,' Helen said. 'Well, we wouldn't point the finger at anybody, nothing as crude as that. We'd gently but firmly make it clear that all you want is your bees back. We'd ask them to spread the word among the beekeeping community. Then when the rustler gets to hear and understands that beekeepers everywhere are on the lookout for your hives, he'll want to be shot of them. If he's got any sense, he'll leave them out one night for you to find.'

Shirley looked wistful. 'It's a nice idea.'

'Speaking for the guild, it's in all our interests,' Gaye said. 'Your delicious honey is the most popular item on the market stall.'

'You won't tell the police? Promise me that. I don't want them involved.'

'Absolutely not,' Helen said. 'We're giving the rustler a chance to put things right.'

'I'm glad Ben didn't put in an appearance,' Helen said on the drive back. 'I've never liked the way he looks at me in the pub. He's probably spent the night with some little tart from the rough end of the village.'

'I doubt it,' Gaye said. 'Shirley keeps him in check. He does a lot of ogling, and that's all.'

Helen wasn't so sure. 'It only wants one woman to give him the come-on. He wouldn't hesitate, an oversexed man like that.'

'I bet he would. Remember the Australian barmaid at the Plough?'

'That Raelene with the bright blue hair and the cleavage? She didn't last five minutes.'

'This is the point. She made a play for Ben one evening in the pub and Shirley got to hear about it from one of her scouts straight away. You know how it is with texting. Raelene was gone the same week and Ben didn't show his face in the pub for weeks after.'

'Nice work. I remember – and we've had men running the bar ever since. See what I mean about the queen bee? Don't underestimate Shirley.'

'Does she choose the pub staff, then?'

'Haven't you noticed? The Littledales have been running the village since the year dot.'

'In that case I'm surprised they aren't doing something about the missing hives.'

'Shirley's decision. She wants it handled sensitively, like we're doing.'

'Are we? Let's hope so.'

The beekeepers' club met on the first Tuesday each month in the function room at the Plough. Most members bought a drink first and took it upstairs with them. Helen and Gaye managed to take Ian Davis, the chairman, into the snug for a few private words before the meeting started. He didn't need telling about Shirley's missing hives.

'Shocking. We've heard stories about bee rustling, but I never expected it to happen so close to home. Are the police investigating?'

'This is the problem,' Helen said. 'They aren't. Shirley told us she'd rather give the culprit the chance to put things right and return the hives before it gets to that stage.'

'How restrained. That's kinder than I would be.'

'The main thing for Shirley is to get her bees back unharmed. She's very attached to them.'

'I can well understand that. Bees are charming creatures, endlessly fascinating.'

Unseen by the chairman, Gaye raised an eyebrow at Helen, the despiser of bees.

Ian Davis added, 'They could teach us a lot about making our own lives more productive.'

'Why would anyone do a thing like this?' Gaye asked him.

'Occasionally things go wrong in this hobby,' he said. 'You find your colony is under-producing, or affected by some disease, or suffers an attack from a predator like a woodpecker. Then you may well look with envy at someone else's healthy bees. It would be a temptation.'

'I can understand.'

'Why don't you come into the meeting and speak to the members?' he suggested. 'Somebody may know more about this than I do. We'll make it clear you're not accusing anyone. This is a crime that concerns us all.'

When they went upstairs Gaye was introduced as the president of the guild, so it fell to her to do the talking. Helen, after putting her up to this, was notably silent. The members listened politely, even though they could offer little in the way of suggestions except for installing surveillance cameras.

'Words like stable door and horse spring to mind,' Davis commented. 'However, you may be sure, ladies, that we'll all be on the lookout for anything suspicious.'

'That wasn't easy,' Gaye said when they were driving away. 'I don't know if it was my imagination, but I felt some hostility coming from the audience.'

'You're wrong about that,' Helen said. 'The long faces showed they were worried about being raided themselves. You did brilliantly. Some good will come of it. Mark my words.'

'Thanks.'

'Ben should have been up there, not you. What sort of husband is he, letting her suffer and doing nothing to help?'

'He isn't her husband. They're not married.'

'Her man, then. Father of all those children. He owes her some kind of loyalty whether they're man and wife or not. Where is he when she needs him?'

'Good question. I don't recall seeing him for some time. I got the impression he wasn't about when we called on her.'

'Has he jumped ship, do you suppose? Come to think of it, he wasn't in the pub the last few times I was there for a meal. He used to be a fixture, like the horse brasses.'

'I haven't heard of them breaking up,' Gaye said. 'They've had their differences over the years, brief separations even, always because of his flirtations. It never lasts long.'

'Let's hope you're right.'

'I expect he's moved to another pub where there are barmaids and none of Shirley's friends to spy on him.'

'Or she murdered him,' Helen said.

There was a telling pause before Gaye said, 'I hope you're joking.'

'Many a true word spoken in jest.'

'Yes, but . . .'

'I know you think of her as every bit as sweet as the honey she provides, but from my perspective she's one very tough lady, strong enough to beat the living daylights out of a drunken letch when he rolls in late one night.'

30

'You are serious.' Shocked, but unable to dismiss it totally, Gaye said, 'What would she do with the body?'

'Bury him. Put him in a silo to rot. Feed him to the pigs. There are plenty of ways on a farm. She made it very clear she doesn't want the police involved.'

'But that's because she thinks it will panic the rustlers into destroying her hives.'

'That's what we're supposed to believe. And now we've spoken to her, I've got strong doubts. You said a moment ago Ben hasn't been seen for a while. What if she decided he's surplus to requirements?'

'She found some other man?'

'I'm not saying that. But if Ben stopped providing what she wants from him, or she lost interest, I wouldn't put it past her to put him down like some farm animal. There's no room for sentiment when farmers slaughter their livestock.'

'Don't,' Gaye said. 'You're giving me the creeps.'

Two days later, Gaye had a phone call from Ian Davis of the beekeepers' club. 'This may be a false dawn,' he said, 'but do you know the derelict cottage on the back road to Aveton Gifford?'

'Where the fire was a few years ago?'

'That's it. Well, one of our members is Vic Mackenzie who teaches at the school. There was a story going round yesterday about two boys who claimed to have seen a ghost there.'

'Oh, yes?' she said, faintly amused.

'Let me tell it as it was described to me. They were out on their bikes and they looked across the field from the lane and saw a strange, spectral figure come out of the front door and glide around the back. It appeared to be carrying a white bucket.'

'A ghost with a bucket?'

'Can you tell what I'm thinking? We beekeepers use plastic buckets to take the feed to the hives and also to collect the supers with the honey. And bee suits are usually white. I thought of those missing hives. It might be worth a check.'

'I'll call my friend Helen,' Gaye said at once.

Within the hour they were motoring through the narrow lanes. 'I told you spreading the word would get a result,' Helen said. 'Won't it be splendid if we've found the rustler?'

'Marvellous – as long as he doesn't get nasty with us.'

'No chance. My experience of beekeepers is that they respect each other. Deal with him in a civilised way and he'll respect us.'

'Stealing beehives isn't respectful or civilised.'

'True, but I bet he regrets it now.'

They pulled off the road in front of a farm gate and looked down the slope of a field where sheep were grazing. For years the cottage on the far side had been abandoned.

'Okay,' Helen said. 'Let's stake it out.'

Gaye wasn't usually aware of her blood pressure. She could hear a pulse pounding in her ears as they strode across the field. Wouldn't you know it: Helen seemed well in control. Gaye tried to appear calm. She had only herself to blame for getting involved in this reckless mission.

They were within shouting distance when a door opened and a white figure stepped out. After a moment of panic Gaye saw that this was no ghost. It still looked unearthly, more like a spaceman. But as they had anticipated, the outfit was a bee suit and black mesh veil – which of course made it impossible to identify the wearer.

'It's all right,' Helen said, untroubled. 'He hasn't seen us. He'll be concentrating on the job.'

Gaye was less confident, but this seemed to be true. The figure was carrying a bucket in one hand and a smoke machine in the other. And – settling any doubt – from this angle a row of hives was revealed behind the cottage.

'What's he going to do? Collect the honey?'

'Possibly.'

'I won't be comfortable anywhere near bees,' she said.

'Very wise. We'll let him do his stuff and wait on the other side of the cottage.'

They took a wider approach that kept them out of the beekeeper's line of vision. The end of the cottage they chose to hide behind had taken the worst of the fire damage. All the windows were broken and bits of masonry had shifted, shedding slates from the roof. This ruin couldn't be anyone's regular home. The current occupant had to be a squatter.

The two women sat on a low wall and waited. Twenty nerve-testing minutes passed before they heard footsteps along the blind side of the building.

'Time to make ourselves known,' Helen said.

Gaye didn't trust herself to speak, but got up and followed.

They rounded the corner and met the squatter, still in his protective suit and veil. At the sight of his visitors he dropped the bucket and smoker and turned to run.

'No you don't,' Helen shouted, all intentions of respectful, civilised behaviour forgotten. She was better equipped for a chase than the beekeeper and she sprinted after the departing figure, grabbed his shoulder and thrust him against the cottage wall. 'Let's see who you are.'

She pulled the tab on the zipper under the veil. A pale, paunchy, terrified face was revealed.

Shirley's partner.

'Ben!' Gaye said.

Helen pressed both hands against his shoulders. He was big enough to have pushed her away, but he didn't. 'What's this all about, Ben?'

He didn't answer, but it was obvious he wasn't going to put up a fight. The only threat was coming from several bees swooping on the bucket he'd dropped.

'They've smelt the honey. We'd better continue this inside,' Helen said.

Gaye reached for the cottage door.

Inside the derelict building they found a camp bed, a sleeping bag and a pathetic collection of beer cans and packets of biscuits and cake.

'It's temporary,' Ben said, 'until I find somewhere better.' On the last word he broke into a fit of coughing.

'You've made yourself ill, by the sound of you,' Helen said. 'What are you doing here?'

'She slung me out.'

'Shirley?' Gaye said.

'Doesn't want any more to do with me. Called me a drunken slob, a freeloader and other things. She doesn't care what happens to me. She's got no mercy. I can die for all she cares.'

Gaye found this hard to believe of Shirley. 'But why? Why is she so angry?'

'You don't want to know.' He produced a series of deep, gut-wrenching coughs.

'So it was you who stole the hives?'

'Borrowed them.'

'Without permission,' Helen said. 'What for? Revenge?'

'I'm getting desperate here. It's freezing at nights. And I miss her, believe it or not. I thought she might come looking for her bees.'

'She's not going to want you back after this.'

'You don't get it, do you? She'll be in a panic over the bees. I'll say I found the guy who nicked them and scared him off. She's going to be so grateful. I'm caring for them. This is my own bee suit I'm wearing. I was giving them a feed just now. They need a supply to get through the winter months.'

'So do you, by the look of you.'

He shivered and said nothing.

'And you really want to go back to her?'

'Wouldn't you, living in this pigsty?'

'You were taking a risk. She could have sent the police.'

He shook his head. 'That's one thing I do know. She won't want that lot crawling all over her farm.'

'You were banking on her finding you here?'

'There was a good chance. People talk. I thought she'd have come before this.'

What a spineless man, Gaye thought. 'It hasn't worked, has it? Face it, Ben, she doesn't want you back and if you stay here much longer you'll die of hypothermia if pneumonia doesn't get you first. Let me see if I can get you into a better situation. We belong to a club that supports a hostel for the homeless. That would be a start.'

'Would you?' he said, his eyes glossing over with self-pity.

'I'll make a phone call now. And don't worry. We'll get those hives back to where they belong. We know someone experienced who'll take it on. We won't tell Shirley who took them. We can say it appears the rustler left them here in the expectation they'd be found and returned to their owner – which is broadly true.'

After Ben had been admitted to the hostel and served with his first cooked meal for weeks, Gaye phoned Ian Davis and asked for his help in returning the hives to Shirley Littledale. He said he'd get Vic, the schoolteacher, to help.

'We'd like to come, too,' Gaye told him. 'While you and Vic replace the hives we can smooth things over with Shirley. It's unfair to ask you to deal with her.'

He chuckled. 'Yes, being economical with the truth isn't my forte. I wouldn't want to be caught out by the queen bee.'

'Funny you should call her that,' Gaye said. 'My friend Helen used the same words.'

'She does act that way.'

'And Helen said poor old Ben is just her drone.'

'Ha,' he said. 'I see where this is going. Pushed out in the cold to die when he's no use to her majesty. There's no room for sentiment in a hive.'

Shirley was overjoyed to see her hives on the truck. 'I can't tell you what a weight off my mind this is, you lovely people. Come in and have a drink.'

'I think the men would rather get on with the unloading,' Gaye said. 'Where exactly do you want the hives?'

'Where they were before is the perfect place,' Shirley said, 'but I'll have to move those sacks of fertiliser to make room. I dumped them there because I couldn't bear to look out of my kitchen window at the empty space.'

'The men will lift them if we ask,' Helen said.

'Would they? How kind.'

In the kitchen, coffee and biscuits were soon on the table.

'I can't tell you how grateful I am to you ladies,' Shirley said.

'We sell your honey, so it was in our interest to locate the hives, even if we didn't entirely solve the mystery,' Gaye said.

'The men probably know who did it, but they aren't saying,' Helen added without making eye contact with Gaye.

'And I won't ask,' Shirley said. 'I'm with you on this. But I think we should take a couple of mugs of coffee out to them, don't you?'

Gaye offered to take out the tray. In the yard, Ian Davis and his colleague had already dragged the sacks aside and were getting into their bee suits.

'Before you start on the hives, have some coffee,' she told them. 'Shirley couldn't be more delighted. Where shall I leave the tray?'

'On top of the sacks will do.'

She carried it across to where they had made a neat stack of the plastic sacks. They formed a good flat surface, but there was some mud on the top sack where it had been face down on the ground. And there was something else.

She dropped the tray.

'What happened out there?' Helen asked after the job was done and they were back in the car and about to drive off. 'Was it a bee that frightened you?'

'What makes you say that?'

'The tray. The smashed mugs. I know Shirley didn't make a big deal of it, but you looked like death when you came in and told us.'

'The other day, after we visited the beekeepers' club, you said something about Shirley that shocked me. You said she may have murdered Ben.'

'Did I? Well, I get things wrong sometimes.'

'You said she was strong enough to have beaten the living daylights out of him. And being on a farm she could have disposed of his body several ways.'

Helen laughed. 'It didn't happen, darling. We both know that.'

'But you were serious at the time.'

'Forget it.'

'She's the queen bee.'

'Unkind of me. I've seen another side of her now.'

'And Ben is just a drone. Drones get evicted from the hive and die of the cold.'

'He's all right. He's being looked after now.'

'But you also told me the queen kills off her rivals. It's serial murder, you said.'

'My big mouth. I'm like that.'

'If you think about it, the ground below an apiary is the ideal place to bury bodies. No one except the beekeeper goes near. Shirley was in a terrible state when her hives were taken, but she refused to call the police. She covered up the ground with those sacks.'

'Gaye, my pet, your imagination is getting the better of you.'

'Is it?' Gaye reached for her bag and took out her credit card case. Secured in the window pocket was the damning piece of evidence that had acted like an electric shock. 'This is why I dropped the tray. It was sticking to one of the sacks they'd moved.'

'What is it? A thread? Show me.'

Gaye lifted it up and held it to the light.

A long, fine human hair, tinted blue.

Lady Luck

You would never have guessed the adviser in the job centre was Lady Luck. True, there was something otherworldly about her, like one of the strange stone heads on Easter Island staring fixedly at the horizon, except her gaze was on the clock. In front of her was the form Danny had been told to complete. She must have read it because she told him he'd been unemployed for far too long.

After several untroubled weeks of signing on, Danny had been ordered to attend for a work-search review. He didn't need one. Unemployed by choice, he was living a contented life in a council flat in Twickenham on state handouts and burglary.

He tried his winning smile, but there was no meeting of minds. At this stage in their relationship Lady Luck's charm eluded him.

She said a new supermarket had just opened on the edge of town and was looking for night stockers.

At first Danny thought she'd said 'night stalkers'. He was tempted to give that a try. It would fit in nicely with the house-breaking.

She explained that it was stacking shelves on an eight-hour shift starting at 10 p.m. Danny turned white. He didn't fancy that at all. He needed to keep his nights clear.

He was told there was no physical reason why he couldn't

do the work and he'd better go for the interview at 3 p.m. sharp or face a cut in his jobseeker's allowance and questions about his flat.

Lady Luck meant what she said.

Later the same day Danny went to meet the recruitment manager. The supermarket was only ten minutes from the flat. With every step he racked his brain for a get-out, something like an allergy or a phobia that would allow him to fail the interview.

A deep-rooted fear of shelving? A habit of dropping things?

Too obvious.

He could say he was affected by the moon. That might worry them. 'I can't help myself. I have an uncontrollable urge to howl and run about on all fours. It's harmless – I think.'

But he didn't need any of the excuses. The moment he stepped through the supermarket door a remarkable thing happened. A young woman dressed like a cheerleader in the shortest of bright red skirts, silver tights and a glittery top and carrying a string of balloons came from nowhere and linked her bare arm in his.

If there is such a person as Lady Luck, Danny thought, this ought to be how she looks. But deep down he knew he was here thanks to the stone-faced woman in the job centre.

A trumpet fanfare sounded from the public address followed by an announcement.

'Ladies and gentlemen, to celebrate the opening of our brand-new Twickenham store we are presenting an amazing free gift each day this week to one of our customers randomly chosen as they step through the door. We decided today's winner would be the first customer to come in after three o'clock and he – lucky man – receives a week's free holiday in the wonderful city of Marrakesh with all expenses paid.'

His new friend said, 'You'd better hold the balloons. I'm supposed to tie them to your trolley, but you didn't bring one in.'

Danny decided it was best not to explain why. He'd forget about the night-stocking interview. Holding the balloons high, he allowed his glamorous escort to lead him past the long row of checkouts to the far end of the store where some people with champagne glasses were waiting to greet him. An important-looking man in a bow-tie and suit shook his hand and handed him an envelope. Cameras flashed and there was another public announcement about his lucky win.

Within the week he was in Morocco.

He'd never been abroad except for a couple of stag-party trips to Benidorm, so this was an adventure. Finding his hotel bus was the first test. As soon as he got past immigration he was bombarded by locals offering taxi-rides. With a sense of purpose he made a beeline across the terminal to the shuttle bus area.

The bombarding was to become the staple feature of his week in the city. If it wasn't for taxis it was for Berber rugs, leather goods, spices and offers to show him belly-dancing and snake-charming. He quickly learned how to say no to these people with a firmness that would get you a punch in the eye in Twickenham.

The Marrakesh experience was all a bit much at first, the crowded streets, the noise, smells and strange sights, but as the week progressed he started to get the hang of it. Part of his prize was a pocketful of dirhams – the local currency – and he learned to haggle in the heaving souks and find places to eat and take time out from all the noise and relax with mint tea and sweetmeats.

But as a professional burglar he took an interest in the architecture. Not the Koutoubia minaret – which you could glimpse from almost any part of the city – but the private dwellings of rich Moroccans. Villas mostly, pink or ochre, nicely spaced in their own grounds in the Nakheel district just off the tourist beat. Streets wider than motorways, and almost deserted. Danny did see one Rolls-Royce glide by with a silver horseshoe tied to the front. These people believed in their good luck. They couldn't get enough of it.

The most appealing thing about the millionaire homes was their construction. True, the exteriors appeared like fortresses, flat, unforgiving stone walls. But they had one thing in common that would appeal to any burglar.

Flat roofs.

Even better, they were limited to a couple of storeys because of some local decree that the only tall buildings in the city were minarets. Get up there and you'd be laughing. You'd be spoilt for choice. The villas were evidently planned around enclosed courtyards where the good life was enjoyed in private.

Security? The owners didn't seem to bother. There wasn't an alarm to be seen, or CCTV.

One residence in particular was an open invitation. This wasn't the largest, but it had a well-kept exterior surrounded by shrubs and trees, which don't come cheap in the desert. Among them was a handsome palm tree in a graceful curve that overhung the roof.

Danny went back to the hotel and thought long and hard about that palm and how it might be used. He'd seen film of barefoot boys shinning up palm trees with the aid of rope tied loosely around their ankles. They made it look easy.

He weighed the options.

Lady Luck had got him to Marrakesh but it was up to him to make the experience pay. This night would be his last in the city. Tomorrow he'd be back in Twickenham living on the social and the small rewards he got from burglary. These Arabs were so rich they wouldn't know if anything was taken. Why not make the most of his luck and collect some souvenirs? He'd happily settle for small stuff like banknotes, jewellery and designer watches.

Soon after midnight he set off for Nakheel equipped with a torch and a strip of towelling, the belt of the complimentary bathrobe from his hotel room.

Climbing the tree was harder than he expected because he had to learn the knack of getting a purchase against the trunk and bracing his legs with his bare feet held in place by the flannel belt while pulling with the arms.

Eventually he scrambled onto the roof and rubbed his aching biceps. Luckily he'd made no sound. If there was a guard dog here, it was asleep – or smart enough to know it couldn't reach him.

He crept to the edge and peered over. The heady scent of orange blossom mingled with stale cigars and cannabis wafted up to him. As he'd guessed, the moonlit courtyard was a rich man's hideaway. Statues, a pool, sunshades and loungers strewn with empty bottles and intimate items of clothing. But no people. They would be out to the world.

All the windows of the villa were within this enclosed part and some were open. Danny had no difficulty descending from the roof to a ledge and inside.

His torch beam showed him some kind of dining room with a large oval table low to the floor and surrounded by cushions. In the centre on a tray was a gleaming silver tea-set of the sort he'd seen in the souks, tall, ornate pots and small cups without handles – but too large to steal. He couldn't take items as big as that and he'd never know where to fence them in this alien city. He wanted smaller stuff.

Move on, he told himself. Find the private rooms. The good thing about this stone-built house was that there were no creaking floorboards.

At the far end of a passage was an open door. Danny purred. He'd found some sort of boudoir, with multi-coloured drapes from the ceiling and huge silk cushions. First he checked that no one was in the bed. Then he started opening drawers in an exquisitely carved sandalwood unit that stretched right across one wall.

Sexy underwear, fine to the touch, enough for an entire harem. Thongs, bras, basques, camisoles and skimpy night-dresses in profusion.

High quality make-up and perfume on open shelves under hinged mirrors.

There ought to be jewellery, but where was it? A safe?

Maybe hidden inside the wardrobe. Danny jerked open a door and almost suffered a cardiac arrest.

A pair of beautiful brown eyes was staring at him from between the hanging clothes.

'Oh, shit,' he said.

His luck had run out.

He had no idea whether she understood, but he started talking, as much to get control of his own shattered nerves as hers. 'I won't hurt you. It's not you I'm after. I just dropped in, like. Thought the place was empty. Really, ma'am, I'm not going to touch you. I don't do violence.'

The woman was crouching at the bottom of the vast

wardrobe. As far as Danny could tell, she was dressed in a T-shirt and jeans, definitely an Arab woman, but in western clothes. She, too, was alarmed. She'd started hyperventilating.

'I'm backing off,' Danny said, making a calming gesture and taking a step back. 'You can come out if you like.'

She wasn't willing to do that, but she seemed to respond because the breathing slowed a bit.

'Okay, I'm out of here,' Danny said.

She spoke – and in English. 'Who are you?'

As if it made a difference.

'Just a visitor,' Danny said. 'Tourist. Well,' he added, deciding some honesty might be no bad thing, 'everyone calls me Danny.'

'These rooms are kept locked,' she said. 'How did you get in?'

'Over the roof and through a window. Are you alone then – like a prisoner in here?'

'It is the way my husband decides.'

Husband? A warning bell sounded in Danny's head. 'Is he about?'

'He won't come in now,' she said.

'Aren't you allowed out?'

'Please. I don't wish to speak of this.' As if to discourage more questions, she pulled one of the hanging garments partially over her face and Danny noticed a bruise on her forearm.

'Does he hit you?'

She was silent.

'That shouldn't be allowed. That's out of order.' The reason she had been hiding in the wardrobe was now obvious. She was hiding from her brutal husband. 'Listen, you don't have to suffer this. You could escape.'

She shook her head, but her eyes showed the suggestion had some appeal.

'I'm serious,' Danny said – and he was. He felt genuine sympathy for this abused woman. For the moment, her situation mattered more than the burglary. 'Listen, this is your lucky day. I can climb out of a window and unlock the door from the other side.'

'It's no use,' she said. 'I have nowhere to go.'

He took his room key from his pocket. 'Hotel Splendide in rue de la Liberté. It's not far. Do you know it?'

She nodded. 'Do you really mean this?'

'Hundred per cent.'

She took the key and emerged from the wardrobe. She was larger than Danny had expected. Probably doesn't get much exercise, he thought, walled up here. Not that her size mattered, but her eyes and voice had made him picture someone frail.

'I can help you through the window and down to the ground,' Danny offered, not without uncertainty whether it was physically possible. 'Is the main door locked?'

'Yes, but from the inside,' she said. 'I can open it if I get down.'

'Let's go for it. You'd better put a few things in a bag. Do you have money?'

She shook her head.

'Doesn't matter. I have some back in the room. I'll join you later.' He still hoped to find something of value here.

She stuffed some clothes into a backpack and Danny dropped it from the open window. 'You next. It's not far down.'

'I can't jump.'

He still had the bathrobe belt. 'Can you hang on to this? I'll lower you down.'

'Are you sure?'

Easily said. Achieving it would be a challenge. She couldn't lift her leg up to the window ledge.

'Do you mind?' Danny said. He put his hand under her thigh and helped.

By slow stages and a stomach-wrenching, arm-straining effort from Danny, the descent was completed. If there was a gallantry award for helping ladies in distress he would have earned it, no question.

'On your way now,' he gasped.

She needed no second bidding.

After recovering his breath, he got back to the main purpose of his visit. More of the villa waited to be inspected. Was Lady Luck still plotting his destiny from her control room at Twickenham job centre?

He left the boudoir, pushed open another door and got his answer.

This was a sitting room of some kind, with cushions of many colours. Face up on the floor was a dead man with a dagger in his chest. There was no question that he was dead and his murder hadn't happened long before because the blood that had seeped from the wound was still wet. In his right hand was a phone.

Danny had never been slow to size up a situation. He'd seen for himself that this was a patriarchal society where women were subordinate to men. The so-called Arab Spring had brought many reforms and a whole new constitution, but it had not been mainly about changing the status of married women. The dead man was the jailer–husband, stabbed by the woman before Danny arrived. She had bruised her arm in the struggle. She had hidden in the wardrobe and escaped thanks to Danny's help. He felt quite pleased with himself.

Not for long.

From outside came the heart-stopping wail of a police siren. The victim must have called them on his phone before expiring.

As Danny's lawyer explained after the trial, 'It could have been a whole lot worse. The cops really believed you were the killer. You were well advised to stick to your story and as you didn't actually steal anything you aren't technically a thief. Three years for trespass and helping a murderer escape is a light sentence.'

'Did she really escape?' Danny asked.

'They believe she made her way to the Hotel Splendide and found your money and your return ticket. She knows England, I was told. When she was younger, her parents sent her to a language school in London. How she got through security posing as you is anyone's guess, but the seat on the plane was filled.'

'And I get three years in a sweaty Moroccan jail?'

'It could have been life. You've done a year already on remand. You're a lucky man.'

Back in Twickenham someone allowed herself a slight smile.

Reader, I Buried Them

Yes, I was the gravedigger, but my main job was over-seeing the wildflower meadow. I'd better correct that. My main reason for being there was to worship the Lord and most of my hours were spent in prayer and study. However, we monks all had tasks that contributed to the running of the place and I was fortunate enough to have been chosen long ago to be the meadow man. If that sounds a soft number, I must tell you it isn't. Wildflower meadows need as much care as any garden, and this was a famous meadow, being situated at the back of a Georgian crescent in the centre of London. The monastery had once been three private houses. The gardens had been combined to make the two acres people came from far and wide to admire. My meadow had been photographed, filmed and celebrated in magazines. Often they wanted to include me in their reports and I had to be cautious of self-aggrandisement. I had no desire for celebrity. It would have been counter to the vows I took when I joined the brotherhood.

Closest to the monastery I grew rows of vegetables, but nobody except Brother Barry, the cook, was interested in them. My spectacular meadow stretched away beyond, dissected by a winding, mown-grass path. In the month of May we were treated to a medieval jousting tournament, the spring breezes sending the flagged wild irises towards the spikes of purple-helmeted monkshood, cheered on by lilies of the valley and banks of primroses. Summer was the season of carnival, poppies in profusion, tufted vetch, ox-eye daisies, field scabious and foxgloves along the borders. Even as we approached September, the white campion, teasel, borage and wild carrot were still dancing for me. At the far end was the shed where my tools were kept and where, occasionally, I allowed myself a break from meadow management and did some contemplation instead. To the left of the shed was the apiary. If you have a wild-flower meadow you really ought to keep bees as well. And to the right were the graves where I buried our brothers who had crossed the River Jordan. When their time had come I dug the graves and after our Father Superior had led us in prayer I filled them in and marked each one with a simple wooden cross. You couldn't wish for a more peaceful place to be interred.

And that was my way of glorifying God. The others all had their own tasks. Barry, I have mentioned, was our cook, and had only learned the skill after taking his vows. A straight-speaking man, easy to take offence (and therefore easy to tease), he had done some time in prison before seeing the light. Between ourselves, the meals he served were unadventurous, to put it mildly, heavily based on stew, sardines, baked beans and boiled potatoes, with curry once a week. Although my stomach complained, I got on better with Barry than any of the others.

A far more scholarly and serious man, Brother Arnold, was known as the procurer, ordering all our provisions by phone or the internet, including my seed and tools. Being computer-literate, he also communicated with the outside world when it became necessary.

Brother Luke was the physician, having been in practice as a doctor before he took holy orders. A socialist by conviction, he combined this responsibility with humbly washing the dishes and sweeping the floors.

Then there was Brother Vincent, a commercial artist in the secular life, who was painstakingly restoring a fourteenth-century psalter much damaged by the years. Between sessions with the quills and brushes, he also looked after the library.

Our Father Superior was Ambrose, a remote, dignified man in his seventies who had been a senior civil servant before he received the call.

You may be wondering why I'm using the past tense. I still live the spiritual life and manage a garden, but it is no longer at our beloved monastery in London. One morning after matins, Father Ambrose asked us all to remain in our pews (for your information, the chapel had been created out of two living rooms by knocking down a wall and installing an RSJ. Not everyone knew this was a rolled steel joist and we had fun telling Barry we were expecting a Religious Sister of St Joseph). 'I want to speak to you about our situation,' our Father Superior said. 'It must be obvious to you all that our numbers have been declining in recent years. Three brothers were called to higher service last year and two the year before. I won't say our little cemetery is becoming crowded, but the dead almost outnumber the living now. None of us are in the first flush of youth any more. Tasks that were manageable ten years ago are becoming harder now. I watched Jeffrey cropping the meadow at the end of last summer and it looked extremely demanding work.'

As my name had been singled out, I felt I had a right to reply. 'Father, I'm not complaining,' I said, 'but if I had a ride-on mower instead of the strimmer, it would ease the burden considerably.'

'Jeffrey,' he said, 'I am discussing much more than your situation. I might just as well have used Barry and his catering as an example.'

'What's wrong with my cooking?' Barry asked.

'The curry,' Luke muttered. 'Oh, for an Indian takeaway.'

'Did you say something?' Father Ambrose asked.

'Trying to think what could be done, Father,' Luke said.

Ambrose moved on with his announcement. 'In short, the Lord in His infinite wisdom has put the thought into my head that we should move to somewhere more in keeping with our numbers. This beautiful building and grounds can be used for another purpose.'

He couldn't have shocked us more if he had ripped off his habit and revealed he was wearing pink Spandex knickers.

'What purpose might that be?' Luke asked eventually.

'I know of a school in Notting Hill in unsuitable accommodation, much smaller than this, and in a poor state of repair.'

'A school?'

'A convent school.'

'You're suggesting they move here?'

'It's not my suggestion, Luke. As I was at pains to explain, it came to me from a Higher Source.'

'Our monastery converted into a school? How is that possible?'

'It's eminently possible. This chapel would double as the assembly hall. The spare dormitories would become classrooms, the refectory the canteen, and so on.'

'What about my meadow?' I asked.

Ambrose spread his hands as if it was obvious. 'The playing field.'

I was too shocked to speak. I had this mental picture of a pack of shrieking schoolgirls with hockey sticks.

'And my studio would become the art room, I suppose?' Vincent said with an impatient sigh.

'I see that you share the vision already,' Ambrose said. 'Isn't it wonderfully in keeping with our vows of sacrifice and self-denial?'

'Where would we go?'

'I'm sure the Lord will provide.'

'Do we have any say?' Barry asked.

'Say whatever you wish, but say it to Our Father in Heaven.'

This is one of the difficulties with the monastic life. There isn't a lot of consultation at shop-floor level. Decisions tend to be announced and they have the authority of One who can't be defied.

We filed out of the pew dazed and shaken. If this was, indeed, the Lord's will, we would have to come to terms with it.

I returned to my beautiful meadow and tried to think about self-denial. Difficult. I vented my frustration on a patch of brambles that had begun invading the wild strawberries. After an hour of heavy work, I remembered I had recently put in an order for seed for next year's vegetable crop. If Father Ambrose's proposal became a reality, there wouldn't be any need for vegetables. So I went to see Arnold, the procurer. He has a large storage room with racks to the ceiling for all our provisions. There's a special section for all my gardening needs and beekeeping equipment.

I said what was on my mind.

'Good thinking,' he said, looking up from his computer screen. Eye contact with Arnold was always disconcerting because he had one blue eye and one brown. 'I'll see if it isn't too late to cancel the order.'

'Did you know what Father Ambrose was going to say this morning?'

'Not at all,' he said. 'Has it upset you?'

I knew better than to admit to personal discontent. 'I don't like to think about our departed brothers lying under a hockey pitch.'

He shook his head. 'Those are only mortal remains. Their souls have already gone to a Better Place.'

He was right. I wished I hadn't spoken. 'Are you in favour of this?'

'It's ordained,' he said. As the second most senior monk, he probably felt compelled to show support.

I heard the slap of sandals on the floorboards behind me. We had been joined by Vincent, the scribe. He was a more worldly character than Arnold, always ready with a quip. 'What's this – a union meeting?' he asked. 'Are we going on strike, or what?'

'Brother Jeffrey is here to cancel his order for next year's seeds,' Arnold said. 'We have to look to the future.'

'A future without a meadow? That's going to leave Jeffrey without a garden shed for his afternoon nap.'

'We don't know where we'll be,' I said, ignoring the slur about my contemplation sessions. 'Wherever it is, I expect we'll have a garden.'

'No problem for me,' Vincent said. 'All I need is a small room, a desk and a chair. And my art materials, of course. Do we have some more orpiment in stock?'

'Plenty,' Arnold said.

'What's orpiment?' I asked.

'A gorgeous yellow,' Vincent said. 'The old scribes used it and so do I, but modern artists prefer gamboge.'

'If it's so gorgeous, why isn't it used more?'

'Because it's the devil – if you'll pardon the expression – to grind the natural rock into a pigment. In fact, the variety I use is man-made, but based on the same constituents. I'll take some with me, Arnold. Chin up, Jeffrey. I'm sure there'll be a little patch of ground for you at the new place. If we leave London altogether, you could find yourself with acres more to grow things on.'

But you never know what the Lord has in store. The concerns we had over moving from the monastery were overtaken by a shocking development. Our Father Superior reported to the infirmary with stomach pains, vomiting and diarrhoea. Some of us suspected Brother Barry's cooking was responsible, but Brother Luke diagnosed an attack of gastroenteritis brought on by a virus infection. All that could be done at this stage was to make sure the patient drank plenty of fluids. Normally the infection will subside. But poor Father Ambrose didn't rally. His condition worsened so quickly that we barely had time to administer the last rites.

Was it a virus, we asked each other, or food poisoning? The latter seemed unlikely considering all of us had eaten the same food and no one else had been ill. A post-mortem would have settled the matter, but, as Luke remarked, it wouldn't have altered anything. Being a qualified doctor, he issued the death certificate and nothing was said to the local coroner. I dug a grave and we buried Father Ambrose the following Monday.

After a period of mourning, we resumed our worship and work. Life has to go on for the survivors. Vincent returned to his restoration work. Barry got on with the cooking, and assured us all that he was using fresh ingredients and regularly washing his hands. Luke, with no patients to tend, scrubbed the infirmary. And I made a wooden cross for Ambrose, carved his initials on it, placed it in position and then went back to caring for my wildflowers. The ever-changing, ever-beautiful meadow was a source of solace. Already the bee orchids were appearing.

There was no debate about installing our next Father Superior. Arnold, through seniority, was the obvious choice. And he had gravitas. We held a token election and he was the only candidate. A well-organised monk I haven't mentioned, called Brother Michael, took on the mantle of procurer and computer operator.

One afternoon I was in my shed having a few minutes' contemplation when I was startled by someone tapping on the window. It was Michael.

'Did I wake you?' he asked when I invited him in.

'I was fully awake,' I said. 'Meditating.'

'I've been doing some thinking myself,' he said.

'What about?'

'Father Ambrose's sad death.'

'He was getting on in years,' I said. 'It comes to us all eventually.'

'But not so suddenly. He was gone in a matter of hours. I was wondering whether he was poisoned.'

I was aghast. 'Food poisoning was mentioned, but we all eat the same and no one else was ill, so the virus seems more likely.'

'I don't mean food poisoning. I'm speaking of murder by poison – as in arsenic.'

'Oh, my word! You can't mean that.'

'I'm sorry,' Michael said, 'but I have some information

that I feel bound to share with somebody. When I took over the store I decided to do an inventory and there was one item that was new in my experience, called orpiment.'

'It's paint,' I told him. 'Brother Vincent needs it in his work. It's a shade of yellow the medieval scribes used.'

'So I understand. But have you seen the packet it comes in? There's a warning on the side that it contains poison. I checked on the internet and it's produced by fusing one part sulphur with two parts arsenic.'

Shocked by this revelation, I tried to answer in a level voice, not wishing to turn our peaceful monastery into a hornets' nest. 'I didn't know that,' I said. 'Presumably Brother Vincent is aware of it.'

'I also looked up the symptoms of arsenic poisoning,' Michael said. 'Nausea, vomiting, abdominal pain, diarrhoea – easily confused with acute gastroenteritis.'

'What exactly are you suggesting, Michael?' I said, still trying to stay calm. 'None of us had any reason to poison Father Ambrose.'

'The motive may not have been there, but the means was.'

'Let's not get carried away,' I said.

'It's tasteless,' he said.

'You took the words out of my mouth.'

'No. I'm saying that arsenic has no taste. And if you remember, it was a Friday – curry night – when Father Ambrose died. The orpiment wouldn't show up in curry.'

'But no one else was ill. We all had the curry.'

'If someone meant to poison Father Ambrose, they could have added some of the stuff to his bowl.'

'But when?'

'As you know, Barry spoons the curry into the bowls with some rice and then one of us carries the tray to the table.

57

Then we bow our heads and close our eyes for the grace. The opportunity was there.'

Clearly, he'd thought this through in detail and believed it.

'Are you accusing Brother Barry of murder?' I asked.

'Or whoever carried the tray. Or whoever was seated beside Father Ambrose, or whoever was opposite him.'

'Any of us, in fact?'

'Well, yes.' His eyes widened. 'And when I said just now that there was no motive, I was trying to be charitable. If one thinks the worst, there is a motive – Father Ambrose's master plan to remove us all to another monastery. No one likes change. Let's face it, we were all shocked and distressed when he announced it. By getting rid of Ambrose, we would save the monastery.'

I shook my head sadly. 'Michael, if this were not so silly, it would be a wicked slander. Do I need to remind you of the vow of obedience we all took? It's unthinkable for any of us to question our Father Superior, let alone cause him harm.'

He appeared to see sense. 'I hadn't thought of it like that.'

'Then I suggest you put it out of your head and don't mention it to anyone else. I'm going to forget you ever spoke of it.'

A year went past. I cropped my meadow late in August after the seeds had spread and Michael's alarming theory was as weathered as the bronzed hay. I'm bound to admit I had been unsettled by it. Despite my promise to forget about the conversation, I couldn't stop myself casting my brother monks in the role of poisoner. Once the seeds of suspicion are sown and growing, they are as difficult to root out as ground elder. Take Arnold, for example. He had attained the highest position in our community through Ambrose's death and as the procurer he had easy access to the orpiment. Equally, Vincent was in possession of the deadly stuff and although he professed to be indifferent to a move, he'd reacted strongly when it was first mentioned. Luke, with his doctor's training, probably knew more about the dangers of poisoning than any of us. Barry, as the cook, was best placed to administer the poison, and had been deeply upset by the criticism of his culinary skills. And Michael had benefited from Ambrose's death and risen to the position of procurer. What was his reason for spreading suspicion of everyone else? Uncharitable thoughts come all too readily when you're gardening and most of them are best ignored.

Late in October, when the last butterflies had gone and autumn mists were appearing over the meadow, the harmony of our community received another jolt. Arnold, our new Father Superior, had made almost no significant changes to our routine since being called to lead us. Then he announced he would be leaving the monastery for a week on a small mission. From time to time, the calls of family disturb the even tenor of our existence, so we thought nothing of it. In Arnold's absence, our services were led by Brother Luke. But when Father Arnold returned, he addressed us in chapel and my heart sank, for he stood to one side of the altar, just where Father Ambrose had been when he announced his ill-omened plan.

Arnold cleared his throat before saying anything. 'You may not all appreciate what I have to say, but hear me out, and when you have had time to absorb it, you will be better able to consider the matter without personal feelings intruding. A year has gone by since our dear departed Father Ambrose raised the question of vacating this building so that the school could move in. As his successor, I feel bound to give consideration to his last great idea. It had been revealed to him, as he made clear, in the nature of a divine vision. After much prayer, I was moved this week to take the process a step further and I am pleased to tell you I have been to see a building that with the Lord's help we can transform into a monastery better suited to our numbers.'

After a moment's uneasy silence, Luke asked, 'What is it, a private house?'

'No, a lighthouse.'

'God save us,' Barry said in a stage whisper.

'These days, the warning lamps are automatic, using solar-powered batteries, so there's no need for a keeper, but the living space is still there,' Arnold said. 'The rooms are wedge-shaped, most of them, smaller than the dormitory you're used to, but they will actually provide more privacy.'

'I don't think I'm hearing this,' Vincent said in a low voice.

'There are kitchen facilities,' Arnold went on, warming to his theme and sounding awfully like an estate agent, 'and a telegraph room that we can convert to the chapel. The building isn't just a glorified cylinder, you see. There's a keeper's house attached and most of our communal activities would take place in there.'

'Where exactly is it?' I asked.

'Off the north-west coast of Scotland.'

'*Off* the coast?'

'It's a lighthouse, Jeffrey.'

'Some lighthouses are on land.'

'This is an island a mile out to sea, a crop of rocks known as the Devil's Teeth.'

He wasn't doing much of a selling job to a bunch of London monks. 'So it's built on solid rock?' I said. 'Isn't there a garden?'

'That's one thing it does lack,' Arnold admitted.

I was speechless.

'When you say "kitchen facilities",' Barry said, 'can I run a double oven and two hobs, as I have at present?'

'I believe there's a Primus stove.'

'I don't believe this.'

'Where will I do my restoration work?' Vincent asked. 'I need a north-facing light.'

'Top floor, in the lamp room,' Barry unkindly said.

But there was no question that Father Arnold was serious. 'Brothers, we must be flexible in our thinking. It can only do us good to adjust to a new environment. Try to come to terms with the concept before we discuss your individual needs.'

We had curry as usual on Friday. Brother Barry's curries were notable more for their intensity than their flavour, so nothing was unusual when Father Arnold gasped and reached for the water jug. We always drank more on curry night. We smiled and nodded fraternally when he complained of a severe burning sensation in the mouth and throat, extending to his stomach. There was more concern when he retched and ran from the table.

Four hours later our Father Superior was dead.

Brother Luke, who was with him to the end, could do nothing to reverse his rapid decline. The patient vomited repeatedly, but brought up little. Severe stomach cramps, diarrhoea and convulsions set in. He complained of prickling of the skin and visual impairment. Before the end he became intensely cold and was talking of his veins turning to ice. A sort of paralysis took over. His facial muscles tightened and his pulse weakened, but his brain remained active until the moment of death.

You will have gathered from my description that Luke gave us a full account next morning of Arnold's last hours. A chastened group of us discussed the tragedy after morning prayers.

Barry insisted it couldn't have been the curry. 'It must have been the same virus that killed poor Father Ambrose.'

'Again?' Michael said. 'I don't think so.'

'Why not?' I said. 'The symptoms were similar.'

Michael gave me the sort of look you get from a dentist when you insist you brush after every meal.

Then Luke said, 'I must admit, my confidence is shaken. I've never come across a viral condition quite like this. In fact, I'm thinking I should report it to the Department of Health in case it's a new strain.'

'Before you do,' Michael said, 'let's consider the other option – that he was poisoned.'

I raised my hand to dissuade him. 'Michael, you and I went over this before. Speculation such as that will damage our community.'

'It's damaged already,' he said. 'Aren't two violent deaths in a year serious damage? I was silent before, at your suggestion, but this has altered everything. We know for a fact that a poisonous substance is stored here.'

'What's that?' Barry said.

'Orpiment. The pigment Vincent uses is two-thirds pure arsenic.'

'*Vincent?*'

All eyes turned to our scribe.

Michael added, 'It doesn't mean Vincent administered the stuff. Any one of us could have collected some from his studio or my shelves. I don't keep the store locked.'

'And used it to murder Ambrose and Arnold? That's unthinkable,' Barry said.

'Well, maybe you can think of some other way it got added to the curry you serve,' Michael said, well aware how the words would wound Barry. He wasn't blessed with much tact.

While Barry struggled with that, Luke asked, 'What possible reason could anyone have for murdering Father Arnold?'

'Come on,' Michael said. 'Just like Ambrose, he was about to uproot us. None of us wants to see out his days on a lump of rock in the Atlantic Ocean.'

'So there was motive, means and opportunity, the three preconditions for murder.' A look of profound relief dawned on Luke's features. As our physician, he was no longer personally responsible for failing to contain a deadly virus. 'You must be right. I'm beginning to think we can deal with this among ourselves.'

'What – a double murder?' Michael piped up in disbelief.

'We don't want a police investigation and the press all over us.'

I added in support, 'They'll want to dig up Father Ambrose for sure. Let him rest in peace.'

Barry agreed. 'No one wants that.'

Michael, in a minority of one, was horrified. 'We'd be shielding a killer. We're men of God.'

'And He is our Judge,' Luke said. 'If we are making a mistake, He will tell us. Shall we say a prayer?'

This was the moment when we all became aware that Luke, as the senior monk, was the obvious choice to be elected our new Father Superior. Even Michael bit his lip and bowed his head.

I dug another grave and we buried poor Father Arnold with the others at the edge of the meadow next morning. None of us asked what Luke had written on the death certificate. He was now our spiritual leader and it wasn't appropriate to enquire. I constructed the cross and positioned it at the head of the grave.

The lighthouse wasn't mentioned again. Father Luke had more sense. He wasn't quite as paternalistic as some of his predecessors. He believed in consulting us as well as the Lord and we left him in no doubt that we wanted to remain where we were, in our beloved monastery in the heart of London. Life returned to normal. I managed my meadow and kept the graves tidy. Vincent worked on his psalter. Barry kept us fed. Michael ran the store with efficiency and ordered our supplies online.

It came as a surprise to me one afternoon in January when I was in my shed wrapped in a quilt, indulging in my post-prandial contemplation, to be disturbed by a rapping at the door. Michael was there, hood up, arms folded, looking anything but fraternal.

'Is something up?' I asked, rubbing my eyes.

'You could put it that way,' he said. 'The Father Superior wants to see you in his office.'

'Now?'

'He's waiting.'

The office was in the attic at the top of our building. Michael escorted me and said not another word as we went up the three flights of stairs.

Father Luke's door stood open. He really was waiting,

seated behind his desk, hands clasped, but more in an attitude of power than prayer. 'Come in, both of you,' he said.

There wasn't room for chairs, so we stood like schoolboys up before the head.

'This won't be easy,' Father Luke said. 'It's about the deaths of Father Ambrose and Father Arnold. Michael has informed me, Jeffrey, that he spoke to you after Ambrose died, about the possibility that he was poisoned with arsenic.'

I said, 'I think we all agree that he was.'

Michael said, 'But at the time you told me to keep my suspicions to myself.'

Now I understood what this was about: a blame session. I'd never felt comfortable with Michael, but I hadn't taken him for a sneak. 'That's true,' I said. 'It was the first time anyone had suggested such a thing and it was certain to cause friction and alarm in our community.'

'Go on,' Father Luke said to Michael. 'Tell Jeffrey what you told me.'

Michael seemed to be driving this and enjoying it, too. 'When I took over as procurer, I gained access to the computer and this enabled me to confirm my theory about the orpiment. It is, indeed, a pigment made of sulphide of arsenic that was used by monks in medieval and Renaissance times to illuminate manuscripts.'

I couldn't resist saying, 'Clever old you!'

Father Luke raised his hand. 'Listen to this, Jeffrey.'

Michael went on, 'However, when I searched the internet for information about the effects of acute arsenic poisoning, some of the symptoms Father Luke reported didn't seem to fit. Typically, there's burning in the mouth and severe gastroenteritis, vomiting and diarrhoea – all of which were present – but the second phase of symptoms, the prickling of the skin and visual impairment, the signs of paralysis in the face and body, aren't associated with arsenic.'

Father Luke said, 'Symptoms very evident in Ambrose and Arnold.'

Michael said, 'It made me ask myself if some other poison had been used, something that induces paralysis. I made another search and was directed away from mineral poisons to poisonous plants.'

I was silent. Already I could see where this was going.

'And eventually,' Michael continued in his self-congratulatory way, 'I settled on a tall, elegant, purple plant known, rather unkindly, as monkshood, the source of the poison aconite. Every part from leaf to root is deadly. After the first violent effects of gastroenteritis, a numbing effect spreads through the body, producing a feeling of extreme cold, and paralysis sets in. The breathing quickens and then slows dramatically and all the time the victim is in severe pain, but conscious to the end.'

'Precisely what I observed,' Luke said, 'and twice over.'

'This proved nothing without the presence of aconite in the monastery,' Michael said. 'There are photos and diagrams of the monkshood plant on the internet, so I knew what to look for and where best to search. It prefers shady, moist places. I spent several afternoons while you were taking your nap checking along the edges of the meadow where the water drains, close to the wall. Of course you hacked the tall stems down, so the plants weren't easy to locate, but eventually I found your little crop. The spiky, hand-shaped leaves are very distinctive. Some of the ripe follicles still contained seeds. Are you going to admit to using it, adding it to the curry?'

Father Luke said, 'The Lord is listening, Jeffrey.'

I didn't hesitate long. I'm not a good liar. I hope I'm

not a liar at all. If you read this account of what happened, you'll see that I always spoke the truth, even if I didn't always volunteer it. 'Yes,' I said. 'I used some root, chopped small. I made sure I was sitting beside our Father Superior when he spoke the grace. Then I sprinkled the bits over the curry. I couldn't face life without my beautiful meadow.'

'So you took the lives of two good men,' Michael said to shame me.

Our Father Superior shook his head sadly. 'Now I'll have to notify the police.'

I said, 'I'll save you the trouble.' I walked to the window, unfastened it and started to climb out.

'No, Jeffrey!' Father Luke shouted to me. 'That's a mortal sin.'

But he was too slow to stop me.

I was indifferent to his plea. I'd already committed one of the mortal sins twice over. Here on the roof I was at least fifty feet above ground. Below me was a paved area. When I jumped, I was unlikely to survive. If I had the courage to dive, I would surely succeed in killing myself.

With my feet on the steep-pitched tiles, I edged around the dormer to a place where no one could lean out and grab me. Then I climbed higher, intending to launch myself off the gable end.

Father Luke was at the open window, shouting that this wasn't the way, but I begged to differ.

Up there under an azure sky, on the highest point of the roof, I was treated to a bird's eye view of my meadow and if it was the last thing I ever saw I would be content. Glittering from the overnight frost, the patterns of my August cut were clearly visible like fish scales, revealing a beauty I hadn't ever observed from ground level. This, I thought, is worth dying for.

I reached the gable end and sat astride the ridge without much dignity, collecting my breath and getting up courage. A controlled dive would definitely be best. I needed to stand with my arms above my head and pitch forward.

I grasped the lightning conductor at the end and raised myself to a standing position.

And then I heard a voice saying, 'Jeffrey, don't do it.'

For a moment, teetering there on the rooftop, I thought the Lord had spoken to me. Then I realised the voice had not come from above. It was from way below, on the ground. Brother Barry was standing in the vegetable patch with his hands cupped to his mouth.

I called back to him. 'I'm a wicked sinner, a double murderer.'

'That's not good,' he called back, 'but killing yourself will only make things worse.'

I told Barry, 'I don't want to live. The police are coming and I can't bear to be parted from my meadow.'

He shouted, 'You'll get a life sentence. It's not as bad as you think, believe me. You'll share a cell with someone, but what's different about that? The food is better, even if I say it myself. And with good behaviour you'll be sent to a Category C prison where they'll be really glad of your gardening experience.'

I was wavering. 'Do you think so?'

'I know it.'

What a brother he was to me. I'd never considered the prison option, but Barry had personal experience of it. And he was right. I could pay my debt to society and make myself useful as well. Persuaded, I bent my knees, felt for the lightning conductor and began to climb down.

*

In the prison where I have been writing this account of my experiences, I am proud of my 'trusty' status. Barry was right. I can still lead the spiritual life and I always remember him in my prayers. The governor has put me in charge of the vegetable garden and I have persuaded him to allow me a wildflower section. No monkshood or other poisonous plants, of course. But by May we'll have an explosion . . . of colour. And I built my own tool shed. Every afternoon I go in for an hour or so. Even the governor knows better than to disturb me when I'm contemplating.

Angela's Alterations

Second time around for Marcus, first for Sophie. He was thirty-nine, she three years younger. The wedding was non-religious, held in a seventeenth-century barn with two hundred guests, a jazz band, delicious food and dancing until dawn.

But Sophie was realistic. She knew the wedding had been the fairy tale beginning. The rest of their married life would be more humdrum and she was prepared for the dull routine enforced by the need to earn a living in these tough times. The one shining thing was that she loved Marcus and he adored her. His first wife had not been worthy of him. That was Sophie's opinion. He rarely spoke about her and resisted the chance to blame her for the break-up. But she must have been a rotten wife and a poor mother because the judge had given Marcus full custody of Rick, their son. Everyone knows the woman normally gets priority. It's not sexist. It's practical. She must have been wholly unsuitable as a parent.

Marcus had a steady job at a petrol station. He did a bit of everything there, keeping the pumps clean and functioning, seeing to the deliveries when the tankers arrived, working the till, stacking the shelves in the shop and sometimes mopping out the toilets. He said there was plenty of variety and he was reasonably secure in the knowledge that cars always needed filling up. The hours weren't so good because it was an all-night place and he had to take his turn at the shifts. One week in three was the night shift. But, as Sophie said, she was used to being alone at night. She'd lived all her adult life up to now as a single woman. Being separated from Marcus one week in three meant she really appreciated his company for the other two.

Sophie's job had more sociable hours. She was a barista in the local branch of Costa, the coffee-shop chain. When she'd first gone out with Marcus and he asked her what she did for a living he thought she said she was a barrister. He asked if she worked for the defence or the prosecution and it was some time before she guessed what he was on about. It had become a running joke between them with saucy remarks about silk and briefs and being called to the bar.

With two salaries they managed well enough, renting a small house in Derbyshire that they made into a cosy home. Good neighbours, a garden where they grew their own beans and tomatoes, and a corner shop that supplied almost everything else they needed.

The one problem was Rick, her new stepson. Maybe the divorce had upset him. More likely (in Sophie's opinion) he'd been deprived of the love and attention he should have had from his mother. Certainly Marcus couldn't have been a more caring father. Whatever it was, Rick was a difficult young man, and that was putting it mildly. Fifteen at the time of the wedding – which he refused to attend – he came with a history of antisocial behaviour. Sophie wasn't told for a long time about the childhood misdemeanours. She was certain Marcus kept quiet from the kindest of motives. But gradually things filtered through. The boy had been excluded from nursery school for persistently attacking the other children, headbutting, spitting and scratching. He threw an old lady's cat into a pond. He ran a kind of protection racket at secondary school, demanding regular money from certain children who feared having their bicycles smashed or their backpacks thrown over fences. As he got older and the hormones kicked in, he started pestering girls, touching them at every opportunity. When they objected he spread rumours about them through social media. He was suspended from school for a time for rigging up a camera in the girls' changing room. He tried drugs, got drunk, carried a knife. He was a constant worry for Marcus. And as the incidents grew more serious, he became known to the police. They called at the house twice and spoke to Marcus.

Rick left school at the first opportunity and joined the unemployed. Somehow he managed to fund the lifestyle he wanted, out most of the night clubbing, sleeping through much of the day and arguing with his father whenever they were in the house together. Mostly he ignored Sophie – apart from a few muttered obscenities, which she didn't mention to Marcus. But she had a suspicion he was taking money from her handbag and she took to keeping it within reach at all times.

Her neighbour Paula called one Sunday morning when Rick was still in bed and Marcus at work. They enjoyed coffee and a chat.

'What are you going to do about that stepson of yours?' Paula asked out of the blue.

'What do you mean?'

'Anyone can see he's getting you down. He's trouble. I saw him yesterday shoplifting in Tesco. With that long blond hair of his he doesn't seem to realise he stands out. He took a basket in and collected a magazine and slipped several packets of condoms into his pocket.'

'Oh, don't!'

'Well, at least he's taking precautions. I suppose you ought to be grateful for that. But I wouldn't want a daughter of mine going out with him. He'll end up in the courts if you're not careful. Does Marcus have any idea what his son gets up to?'

'I'm afraid it's the usual story. A broken home, a mother who was never there when she was needed.'

'Yes, but what about Marcus?'

'He's well aware of it. He tries, he really does.'

'My husband wouldn't stand for it. He'd beat some sense into the little perisher and kick him out if he didn't behave. How old is he now?'

'Going on seventeen.'

'A lot of kids his age fend for themselves. Some look after disabled parents as well.'

'We're hoping he'll come to his senses now he's virtually an adult. He's not without ambition. He wants to learn to drive.'

'God help us all when he does,' Paula said, and they both laughed.

Two evenings later, Sophie and Marcus had a visit from a clergyman. He was the vicar at St John's, the local church. They were surprised to see him because they weren't church-goers, but Marcus invited him in.

'You're wondering what this is about,' the vicar said. 'I'm responsible for three churches altogether. Most of my time is spent at St John's, and I conduct the occasional service at the other two, St Matthew's at the end of North Street, and St Barnabas, the little one beside the green at Barn

End. They're lovely old buildings, of much interest architecturally, and people visit them just to look round. We put out leaflets just inside the door and there's a box for contributions. Some people are most generous and pay more than the suggested token amount.'

Sophie's stomach clenched. She could already see where this was going.

'Some time last week, the box at St Barnabas was broken into,' the vicar went on. 'It's made of wood with a padlock and regrettably someone had forced it open and taken the contents. We don't know how much money was in there, but we usually empty it once a month and the contributions can range from twenty to thirty pounds. I expect you're wondering why I'm telling you this.'

Neither Marcus nor Sophie answered.

'There's a lady – you don't need to know her name – who lives in the row of terraces opposite St Barnabas. She does some cleaning in the church and arranges flowers. She was in there one afternoon sweeping between the pews and she was surprised to see a young man come in. He just stepped inside for a moment and took a lot of interest in the box, tapping it with his hand and rattling the padlock. Then he saw her and went away. But an hour later, she was at home and saw the same young man enter the church and come out a few minutes later, looking furtively to right and left before walking quickly away. Suspecting something was wrong, the lady went back and discovered the box broken and emptied of money. I suppose I should have gone to the police as soon as she phoned me, but I didn't. Sometimes the Lord has ways of rectifying transgressions. I spoke to the lady, of course, and promised to investigate. She said she was sure she would recognise the young man if she saw him again.'

'Is this why you're here?' Marcus asked.

'I'm afraid so. I believe you have a son by the name of Rick.'

'I do.'

'The lady identified him as the thief and I don't think there's any question she is mistaken. She's reliable and has no axe to grind. Let me say at once that I believe in second chances. If you can persuade Rick to return the money and give an undertaking that he'll never steal again, I'm prepared to forgive and forget. This, I think, is a watershed moment and he must understand why I'm being lenient. I don't wish any young lad to start on a life of crime. I fear that's what will happen if he goes through the penal system.'

'That's very understanding,' Marcus said.

'I thought perhaps you wouldn't believe me.'

Sophie said, 'If we can't believe a man of God, who can we believe?'

'Shall we see if we can help him between us?' the vicar said.

'You mean, convert him?' Marcus said.

'Not at all. That's far too much to aim for at this stage.'

'You'd just like the money back?'

'Not from you. That would be too easy. I'd like Rick to return it in person to me. He'll surely see the sense in doing that, rather than being up before the courts. Then I'll have a chat with him about his future. If you can do the same, we may set him on a better path. He'll need much support and encouragement from you both.'

'We appreciate this,' Marcus said, 'and I hope Rick will, as well.'

Rick returned from the nightclub too late for a fatherly chat and was still in bed at noon next day, but as soon as he appeared, bleary-eyed and unshaven, in the T-shirt and shorts he'd obviously slept in, and told Sophie he was hungry, she offered to cook for him and left the room as if to collect something from the freezer in the garage and instead called Marcus at work. He took a lunch break and came home.

They had agreed that this would come best from both of them, so Sophie stayed in the room when Marcus told Rick about the visit from the vicar.

At first, Rick appeared to ignore his father, staring at a music magazine as he ate the last of his late breakfast. But when Marcus spoke about the collection box, Rick looked up and said, 'So what?'

'So you could go to prison,' Marcus said.

'Not for that,' Rick said. 'I might get community service.'

'What you're getting is a second chance.' Marcus went on to explain the vicar's offer. 'Considering that you stole the money – you did, didn't you?'

A nod.

'Considering it's a criminal offence, you're being treated with exceptional consideration.'

'He wants the money back?' Rick said. 'He can't have it. I spent it.'

'Then you'll have to find thirty pounds from somewhere else.'

'Only twenty-three fifty.'

'That's not the point. You'll find thirty and go and see him with it. He's got to have the box repaired or buy a new one.'

'Haven't got it. I'm skint,' Rick said.

'Then you can spend a few evenings at home instead of paying to get into the nightclub.'

'I don't pay. One of the bouncers lets me in. I happen

to know he's gay and he hasn't come out yet, so he does favours for me.'

'That sort of thing's got to stop,' Marcus said. 'If you stay at home and do a few jobs round the house, I'll pay you, and then you can go and see the vicar when you've got the money to return to him. It had better be this week. Shall we call him now and make an appointment on Friday?'

Rick shrugged.

Marcus passed his phone across. 'It's pre-dialled. All you have to do is press the key.'

Rick stared at the phone and did nothing.

'But if you'd rather not, I'll phone the police,' Marcus said.

Sophie was proud of him.

Rick pressed the key.

'But has he learned his lesson?' Paula asked when Sophie told her about the incident.

A sigh. 'If I'm completely truthful, I doubt it. The vicar talked to him about mending his ways. But since then I've noticed more money missing from my purse. Dishonesty seems to be ingrained in him.'

'That's awful.'

'It's an awful thing of me to say it, but I see no prospect of him changing his ways.'

'Does Marcus feel the same?'

'He's never said so. The boy's his flesh and blood. But deep inside, he knows, I'm sure.'

'This puts such a strain on your marriage.'

'You don't have to tell me, Paula. I'm in despair.'

Silence took over for a time.

'I don't think I've ever mentioned this,' Paula said. 'It would be a long shot, but there is a local woman who is said to have had remarkable results in turning people's lives around. I'm not entirely sure how she does it. Some home-spun psychology, I suppose, force of personality and a bit of witchery for good measure.'

'*Witchery*?'

'There are white witches, aren't there, who do good deeds? Wise women, they are sometimes called. They have some sort of power that can't be explained.'

'Is that what this woman claims?'

'No, it's more what people say about her. She's a little eccentric. But she seems to know what she's doing.'

'Is she expensive?'

'I don't know about that. You'd have to ask.'

'I bet she's never had anyone like Rick to deal with.'

'Probably not, but I heard she's straightened out several young people going through crises in their lives.'

Sophie wondered what Marcus would think of this sugges-tion, let alone Rick himself. 'What's her name?'

'Angela. I don't know her surname.'

'Nice name.'

'Yes, I'm sure she's on the side of the angels with a name like that. She's only about twenty-six herself, but she has a successful business in the town. She took over that tiny little shop where the cobbler used to be, next to the optician.'

One of the difficulties with working in the High Street was that Sophie didn't notice what was going on in the other shops. 'What sort of business?'

'Altering clothes. You want a hem turned up or a seam put in – let out, in my case – and she does it on her sewing machine, while you wait sometimes. It's a useful service when you can't part with an old favourite.'

'Does the shop have a name?'

'Angela's Alterations.'

'Nice idea, but he'd never agree to anything like that,' Marcus said. 'You saw how difficult it was getting him to see the vicar. I had to twist his arm, really.'

'We'd go and see Angela ourselves, in the first place,' Sophie said, refusing to have the suggestion brushed aside. 'She'd need to know what the problem is.'

'What the problems are, you mean. Thieving, shoplifting, blackmail, pestering girls, drugs, drink and defying his parents. She wouldn't know where to start.'

'Sometimes a fresh approach can make a difference. Let's at least go and see her, Marcus. If she thinks he's a lost cause, I'm sure she'll tell us.'

He agreed to take an hour off work on Saturday morning and so did Sophie.

While waiting in the tiny shop, they watched Angela attach a new zip to somebody's skirt. She completed the job remarkably quickly, handling the garment with total confidence. She looked younger than either of them expected, with a streak of bright green in her dark hair and silver clippings in her nose and ears. She wasn't good-looking in the model-girl sense, but she had an intelligent, open face with wide brown eyes that took in her visitors in a way that made them feel as if they were kids themselves. 'What can I alter for you?'

Marcus explained, with some prompting from Sophie. They didn't actually name Rick, but they covered his story comprehensively.

When they'd finished, Angela said, 'So it isn't a sewing machine job,' and they all laughed. The tension eased.

'I'll need to know his name,' she said. 'I can see why you haven't mentioned it so far, in case I don't take him on.'

Marcus exchanged a glance with Sophie. It sounded as if Angela hadn't been put off. 'He's called Rick. I'm sorry to be so direct, but what would it cost us?'

'The same rate as all my alterations,' she said, 'but you wouldn't have the cost of materials. Ten pounds an hour.'

'I doubt if you'd fix him as quickly as you did that zip.'

'No, but I don't charge unless the job is completed to my customers' satisfaction.'

Marcus did a double-take. 'No success, no fee?'

Angela nodded. 'But you must allow me to go about this in my own way, with no interference. Don't ask Rick to visit me. I'll make sure we meet. If he speaks about me – which is unlikely – treat it as if you hadn't heard about me. And of course don't let him know you're paying me.'

Marcus cleared his throat. 'I'm sorry to insist. We ought to put this on a business-like footing. We're not terribly well off.'

'From all you told me, I would think five weeks might do the trick. I wouldn't charge you all those hours, of course. I have a business to run. To give you a general idea, two hours a day would be the maximum. I work a six-day week.'

'That's about six hundred pounds,' Marcus said.

'Maximum,' Angela said.

Marcus turned to Sophie, who nodded eagerly. She'd been impressed with what she'd heard. Witch or wise woman, Angela radiated confidence.

They left her reaching for another garment and giving it a shake. With the sewing machine on its table, the ironing board and the racks of clothes under alteration, there was scarcely room to shake anything.

*

Three days later, Rick said, 'I'm going to learn to drive. I've applied for a provisional licence. Before you freak out, I won't be paying for lessons. A friend is going to teach me in her van.'

'That's nice,' Sophie said before Marcus could speak, just in case he hadn't cottoned on. 'You've always wanted to get behind the wheel.'

'It's on the level, Dad, I promise you.'

Marcus said, so smoothly that Sophie knew he'd worked out what was happening, 'Go for it, son. When you're ready to take the test, we'll pay for it.'

After Rick had gone out, Sophie said, 'Angela's on the case, then. What a clever way of getting his confidence.'

'I hope he doesn't crash her van.'

'He won't. She'll see to that.'

At the end of the week, Marcus returned from work and said, 'I had a chat with Angela today. She stopped by at the garage to fill up. She has this little white van with *Angel's Alterations* on the side in large lettering. And she has L-plates fitted front and rear.'

'What did she say?'

'It's going well. He's a confident driver and he'll soon pick it up. She thinks the lessons are bringing something positive to his life, a sense of achievement.'

'Did she say how they met?'

'No, and I didn't ask. She seems to have her own way of doing things and prefers not to say much about it. I get more impressed with her each time we meet.'

Paula from next door said, 'Angela seems to have taken your stepson in hand. I watched him reversing round a corner in her little van this morning. He looked different to me, much more at peace with himself and the world.'

'Yes, we're so grateful for your recommendation. She's a miracle worker. He's better at home, gets up earlier in the morning and even helps a bit around the house.'

'Speaking of helping, has he stopped helping himself from your purse?'

'He has. What is more, he's on better terms with his dad. They actually talk about music and football.'

'I'm happy for you all. At what point can you say the alteration is complete?'

'I don't know. She'll tell us, I expect. She promised it wouldn't make paupers of us.'

'I've heard her terms are reasonable. And she takes on all kinds of work. It isn't just the troubled teenagers.'

'Such as?'

'I think she cures warts and chilblains and stuff like that. Folk medicine, she calls it. More alterations really.'

'Things witches are traditionally supposed to do?'

'Right, but I wouldn't mention witchcraft if I were you.'

Sophie laughed. 'I wouldn't dream of it. We want to keep on the right side of her while she's altering Rick.'

Marcus, too, was altering. He was becoming more relaxed as the days went by and his relationship with Rick improved.

'Don't ask me how she managed it,' he told Sophie, 'but it seems to be permanent. He and I are going for a drink on Saturday. The first time!'

'I noticed he tidied his room and threw a lot of old junk away. It's remarkable. There must come a point soon when we settle up with her.'

'She said five weeks. We're not there yet.'

82

'How will you do it when the time comes? We don't want Rick to find out.'

'God, no! She knows where to find me. She'll come to the garage, I expect. I'm going to feel like hugging her.'

'Have we got six hundred in the account? That's the figure she mentioned.'

'I think so. I'll make sure. She may prefer cash.'

The transformation in Rick continued. Instead of being so secretive he announced over breakfast one Sunday morning, 'That woman I mentioned, who is teaching me to drive, is called Angela. We met by chance in the street. Actually I was having a bit of a run-in with a copper who said I'd been shoplifting. She came right up and said it was a misunderstanding and she'd sort it out.'

'Were you shoplifting?' Marcus asked.

'That was then,' Rick said. 'I don't do it any more. Any road, she took me for a coffee and we got on really well. She has a small business in the high street mending clothes and that. She's in her twenties, I think, and she has a van and she offered to let me drive it round the car park. I must have done all right because she offered to teach me. She says when I pass the test she'll let me do deliveries for her and she'll pay me.'

'That's terrific,' Sophie said. 'Isn't it wonderful, Marcus?'

'Brilliant,' Marcus said.

'I'd like you to meet her some time,' Rick said.

'Actually, if she's the Angela of Angela's Alterations, I have met her a few times,' Marcus said. 'She fills up sometimes at the garage. And I agree – she's a super person.'

The five weeks were up and Sophie reminded Marcus. 'As far as I'm concerned, she's turned him round. He's a

83

reformed character. He doesn't swear any more. He's given up the nightclubbing. I feel safe with him for the first time since we married.'

'Do you think we should pay her the six hundred?' Marcus said.

'That was the understanding. We must keep our side of the bargain.'

'Shall we see her together?'

'It looks a bit heavy, both of us. Why don't you call in at the shop with the money and tell her how grateful we both are?'

'Good idea,' he said.

'Be careful, just in case Rick is somewhere in the shop. It would be dreadful if he ever found out the truth.'

'It's such a poky little place he couldn't possibly be hiding there. Just to be sure, I'll go at a time when I know he's somewhere else. He's much more open these days about how he passes his time.'

'It was all a bit strange,' Sophie told Paula when she went in for a coffee three weeks later. 'Marcus withdrew six hundred from the bank and went to the shop and said what a difference there is in Rick and how grateful we both are, and what do you think Angela said?'

'The money wasn't enough?'

'No. She said rather than taking the cash, she'd like to be treated to a day's shopping.'

'I don't follow you.'

'It was "treated" that was the operative word. She could easily have spent the six hundred on herself, but she wanted someone – a man – to take her shopping and buy everything for her.'

'Weird.'

'I thought so at first, but then I saw it from Angela's point of view. She works really hard, stuck in that shop all week and doing things for other people. She's not used to having a man take her shopping. It was a one-off opportunity, so I don't begrudge it at all.'

'What did Marcus say?'

'The funny thing is, he hates shopping. But we were so much in Angela's debt that he agreed. You have to laugh, really.'

'And did it happen?'

'Yes, it's done. We're all square now.'

'Where did she choose to be taken?'

'Paris, by Eurostar.'

'Oh, my God – and you allowed it?'

'It was just for a day. They went early and got the last train back. She had boxes of goodies, he said.'

'I hope that's all she had,' Paula said, and added quickly, 'Sorry, darling. I'm sure it was all very proper.'

'I trust my Marcus and we're both very grateful to Angela. She's more than ten years younger than we are. Poor little soul, why shouldn't she have her treat? She's worked a miracle with Rick. Did I tell you he passed his driving test and now she employs him part time?'

Later that summer, Rick asked his father how much it would cost to buy a van of his own. He was thinking of doing deliveries on a bigger scale, full time instead of the odd jobs he still did for Angela.

'I think we should buy it for him,' Sophie said at once. 'We could get a loan, if necessary. It shows such good intentions on his part.'

'I don't know,' Marcus said. 'It's still early days in his rehabilitation. A few months ago I wouldn't have dreamed of letting him anywhere near a van. I'll tell you what. I'll ask Angela's advice next time I see her.'

Secretly, Sophie was a little hurt that her opinion counted for less than Angela's, but she didn't say anything.

'I saw your Rick driving his new van yesterday,' Paula said. 'He gave me a wave, which he would never have done in the old days.'

'It isn't new. It's reconditioned,' Sophie said.

'Good idea.'

'Angela's idea, in fact. She'd heard about it going cheap. Rick spruced it up with Marcus's help and he's really proud of it. He's found one or two regular delivery jobs, thanks to Angela knowing people.'

'And he's still on the straight and narrow?'

'From all I can tell, he is. Instead of nightclubbing he does potholing.'

'Does *what?*'

'You know. Blokes in helmets with lamps going underground on ropes. There are some really deep holes and mineshafts out there. He puts his kit in the van and drives off and we don't see him for hours and hours.'

'Is it safe?'

'They're very professional about it.'

'Some of those holes are so deep you wouldn't stand a chance if you fell. And the mineshafts are notorious.'

'He's getting to know them all and he knows which ones to avoid. From our point of view it's a lot less dangerous than clubbing, what with the drugs and everything.'

'I'm impressed. I won't go on about it, then. What a relief for you both. Is Marcus at work?'

'Upstairs, catching up on his sleep. He's working nights at the garage this week.'

'All this week?'

Sophie nodded. 'One week in three, nine till seven. I thought you knew.'

'Well, I thought I did. I ran out of milk late yesterday and I always have a cocoa at bedtime or I can't sleep, so I nipped round to the garage. About ten, it was. Marcus wasn't on duty. That Asian guy was serving. I asked if Marcus was about and he said he was on a week's holiday.'

'He's not. That isn't true,' Sophie said, her heart thumping.

'You'd better keep an eye on him.'

'I can't understand it. He was gone all night, for sure.'

'Somebody got their wires crossed, I expect,' Paula said. 'Don't look so worried.'

She was deeply worried. She'd noticed Marcus behaving strangely in the last few days. Tight-lipped and twitchy, he almost seemed to shun her at times. She didn't like to dwell on it, but her beloved husband seemed to be undergoing an alteration.

Of all the people to confide in, she chose Rick. He'd become so much more mature now, running his own delivery business, paying his way and being upfront with people.

'I'm worried about your father. He's been behaving strangely. It's like a personality change.'

'I've noticed,' Rick said. 'I didn't want to interfere.'

'I'm so unhappy, Rick. I think he's having an affair.'

'My dad? Get away!'

'Really. I don't think I've lost him entirely, but it could happen if I don't do something about it. I couldn't bear to let him go.'

'Are you sure about this?'

'There are too many signs. People who know me,

customers in the coffee shop, drop hints that they've seen something going on, something they can't discuss with me. And Paula from next door is more outspoken. She says she's seen them together several times.'

'Seen who?'

'Your dad with Angela.'

'*Angela*? That's crazy.'

'That's what I thought at first, but everything points to it.'

'It's not possible,' Rick said, flushing all over his fair skin. 'I see her all the time. I'm running my business through her shop. We're in partnership now. We share the profits and I'm part-owner. Of course I'd know if anything like that was going on with Dad.'

'I couldn't believe it myself for a long time,' Sophie said. 'He visits her when he's supposed to be working nights at the garage. He pays Sanjit to stand in for him.'

Now the blood drained from Rick's cheeks. 'She's my partner.'

'Business partner. Her love life is another thing altogether.'

Rick was silent, seeming to bite back what he had been about to say. Finally he managed to speak. 'But she was my discovery. I found her and she's turned my life around.'

Sophie, too, bit back the words that were ready to spring from her. She didn't care any more about Angela, but Rick would fall apart if he learned the truth about the arrangement.

Now the words poured from Rick. 'Why would he want to take up with her when he's got you? She's far too young for him. I'm closer to her age than he is and she really put herself out to help me through a difficult time. I was on the skids heading for some kind of hell and she reached out to me and pulled me up. I owe everything to her. She thinks I'm young and still in need of help, but our relationship is changing day by day. We're almost equals now. I'd move in with her if she asked me.'

Sophie was on the verge of tears. 'I had no idea. I wouldn't have mentioned it. Oh, this is terrible. I don't want to hurt you. I shouldn't have told you. I should have had the courage to take it up with Marcus.'

'How could she be so cruel – to you and to me? She knows how I feel about her. She must.'

'I'll speak to him.'

'Don't,' Rick said. 'Leave him out of it. If this is true, I know exactly how to deal with it.'

'How's it all going now?' Paula said towards the end of the year. 'Got your life back together, have you?'

'We're doing fine now,' Sophie said, and meant it.

'Marcus came to his senses, did he? I see he's pulling his weight at the garage these days.'

'It was just a silly little episode and we're over it.'

'Men. They all need pulling into line at some stage.'

Sophie smiled, trying to think of a way of changing the subject.

Paula changed it for her. 'She seems to have left the district, that Angela. Strange woman. Disappeared overnight. I don't think anyone knows where she went. Rick's the one who ought to know, but he doesn't say a word.'

'I don't suppose he knows anything.'

Paula gave a faint, disbelieving smile. 'It hasn't done him any harm, seeing how he was in partnership with her. He can still use the shop for his own business. I see the sewing machine has gone. No use to a man running a transport company. I wonder where it went, with the ironing board and the clothes racks. Down one of those old mineshafts where he does his potholing at weekends, I shouldn't wonder. Has he stopped being a worry to you both?'

'Completely.'

'He's made a success of his life, hasn't he, after such a shaky start? Stunning, I call it. You and Marcus must be proud when you see the vans with his name on the side. And it sounds just right – "Rick's Removals".'

The Bitter Truth

'**D**o me a favour and read this.'

'What is it? Hot news?'

'From *me*?' Tysoe of the *Post* shook with laughter. 'It's an obituary. Take a look while I get the drinks.'

Mark Peters angled the sheet of paper to catch the light over his shoulder.

Judson Perrin: Forensic Toxicologist who exposed the Ladybird Killer

Judson Perrin, who died yesterday, was the forensic scientist whose evidence sensationally unmasked the serial killer Dr Hugo Burke-Miller in 1980. Unrivalled in his knowledge of plant poisons, Perrin suggested to the police that the deaths of up to five of the doctor's elderly patients from multi-organ failure may have been caused by absorption of abrin, one of the most fatal toxins on earth. *Abrus precatorius*, known also as the rosary plant, is common in tropical countries and produces shiny red and black ovoid seeds looking like ladybirds and often strung together to form rosaries. When he heard that the doctor under investigation had lived in Belize, where the plant grows abundantly as a weed, Perrin recommended a search of Burke-Miller's Cheltenham property. A box of the seeds was duly discovered. Even so, proof of murder was difficult to obtain because there were no reliable validation tests for abrin in the body after death. Perrin assembled a dossier based on a close study of the symptoms reported in the final hours of five rich patients who had named the doctor in their wills. The subsequent trial was one of the most sensational of the century and made a celebrity of Perrin. He was steadfast under two days of cross-examination and an unexpected conviction was obtained.

Judson Piers Perrin was born in Bruton, Somerset, in 1935, the second son of parents who between them ran a small private boarding school. He obtained a scholarship to Wellington College and in 1954 enrolled in the medical school at St George's Hospital, London, where he gained valuable laboratory experience as a demonstrator in the pathology department. After qualifying as a doctor, he began to forge a reputation in toxicology, and published several innovative papers on plant poisons including ricin and abrin. He first appeared as an expert witness in a case in 1963.

In 1969, Dr Perrin accepted the Chair of Toxicology at Reading University and lectured widely on plant poisons. He was consulted on the use of ricin in the murder in London of the dissident Georgi Markov by Bulgarian secret service agents in 1978. Toxicology as a field of study has increased vastly in complexity as new compounds are developed and more sophisticated methods of detection employed. Perrin relished the challenge, and his 1985 book, *An International Directory of Poisonous Plants*, is still regarded as indispensable. He received the OBE in 1992. He married twice, in 1962 and 1974. His first wife, Marjorie Pelham, was killed in a motor accident in 1972. He is survived by his second wife, Jane Deacon. He had two sons from the first marriage, one of whom predeceased him.

'What's your reaction?' Tysoe asked when he returned with two pints of lager. The Grapes was crowded as usual with journalists.

'I didn't know the old boy had turned up his toes.'

'He hasn't. He's still about. Cheers.'

Mark had been about to take his first sip. The glass stopped midway to his mouth.

Tysoe said, 'Didn't I tell you they put me on the obits desk last month?'

'Ah. Makes sense now.' Mark sank some of the lager. 'Is that, like, a promotion?'

'Some chance. I'm confined to barracks for my sins, but I'm enjoying it. I've been on the road chasing stories for too long. I'm still busy. People are dying all the time.'

'Not Mr Perrin.'

'He's old. He hasn't got long.'

'Is that inside information?'

Tysoe laughed again. Not a pleasant laugh. 'Be prepared, I say.'

'I'm guessing you know something. Your job would depress me.'

'Come on, Mark. Everyone who's anyone has an obituary waiting. You know that. I have getting on for two thousand of the undead on file. The point is, you're more clued up about famous trials than any of the staffers at the *Post*. What do you think of this one?'

'Want an honest answer? Not much.'

Tysoe wasn't offended. He nodded and waited for more.

'Did you write it yourself?' Mark asked. 'No? Then I can be frank. It strikes me as bland. Perrin deserves a better send-off. I mean, there's sod-all here about his work for the Tobacco Products Directive. I believe I'm quoting him right when he said something like when you get sent rotting guts every day of your life you start to care what humanity is doing to its insides.'

'Nice one. Exactly the kind of quote I need to inject some life into the thing. Obituaries shouldn't be dull. They should reflect the vitality of their subjects. You could give this some pizzazz.'

Giving pizzazz to an obituary was a tough call, but as a freelancer, Mark didn't turn work down. 'What's your best offer?'

'I could run to five hundred plus expenses. You might want to visit him.'

'I can't do it for less than eight. What do you mean, visit him? Tell him I'm writing his obituary? That could bring on a seizure before I get a word out of him.'

'Obviously you won't tell him why you're there. You can say you're doing a piece about the trial. We'll send a staff photographer with you to get some pictures.'

'You did say you'll pay eight hundred plus expenses?'

'Did I?'

'It's still peanuts, but I'd like an excuse to meet him.' Already Mark was thinking he could get a feature article out of this as well and sell it to a colour magazine for thousands, not hundreds. The fortieth anniversary of the Burke-Miller trial was coming up later in the year – a convenient peg to hang the piece on. 'Are you sure you don't want a medical man for this?'

'No, it can't be too technical. Leave that to the *Lancet*. You're the ideal choice, or I wouldn't have asked. Get the personal angle, preferably with plenty of quotes and any gossip that's going. Our readers love a bit of goss.'

'How long have I got?'

The gallows humour kicked in again. 'Longer than Perrin, I hope. End of the month, say, about fifteen hundred words? Oh, and for Christ's sake don't tell him what you're up to or he'll want a preview. Even Winston Churchill wasn't allowed a sight of his when he asked. You will regard this as strictly *entre nous?*'

Mark tapped the side of his nose and winked. He could get to enjoy this assignment.

That evening he phoned all the contacts he knew who were likely to have inside information. He told them he would be interviewing Perrin to mark the anniversary of the much-publicised trial, which seemed to have been a life-changer but was all most people knew about the toxicologist. He said he was hoping to discover how the old man's life had panned out in the years since. The facts about his career, the qualifications and the honours, were easily found online and in *Who's Who*. The human side was more elusive.

And this was the bit he really enjoyed – rooting out the little-known personal details.

Piecing together hints from several sources, Mark found the juicy morsel he needed. Perrin was rumoured to have used his fame to start an affair with the wife of a senior government minister. The story would need more digging, but, if true, might explain why the high-achieving professor had never received a higher honour than the OBE.

He called a retired journo friend who had once been the mainstay of the political pages of the *Herald*. 'Every word is true, Mark. She was the wife of Solly Waterfield, the Home Secretary at the time. Solly would leave his penthouse flat in Chelsea to make a statement in Parliament and Perrin would be waiting outside like a tomcat. Before the minister's car arrived at the House, Perrin and Portia would be at it, banging like the proverbial shithouse door in a gale.'

'Are you certain?'

'The woman who lived underneath listened to Iron Maiden at full volume to drown out the sounds.'

'Did they separate?'

'You mean Solly and Portia? No, they soldiered on. She was twenty years his junior and came into a small fortune. He was no better in bed than he was in government, but the Waterfield millions were her consolation after he died.'

'Plus her toxicologist lover?'

'Perrin wasn't around by then. The affair didn't last that long. I expect she met other men.'

'Was this widely known?'

'Only to a few. Mainly me and the long-suffering neighbour. I could have had an exclusive, but my paper wasn't a scandal sheet in those days.'

'Don't you want to use it now?'

'Not really. This has no news value. No one's interested in what ministers got up to in the eighties.'

'Solly didn't get up to much by the sound of it. All the action came from his wife and Judson Perrin.'

'Couldn't put it better myself.'

Since his retirement, Perrin had lived with his second wife Jane in a flat in the Barbican. His voice sounded lively enough when Mark called him the same day. He took the bait. Yes, he answered over the phone, he wouldn't object to being interviewed for a feature if it was going into one of the quality magazines. He hadn't realised that forty years had passed since Burke-Miller was convicted, but he agreed that the anniversary was a good reason for a look back at how the trial had unfolded. The meeting was arranged for late Friday afternoon. Mark asked if he could bring a photographer with him. 'No problem at all. I have a room set up as a lab here,' Perrin said. 'He can get some pictures of me holding up a test tube or whatever.'

'You've obviously done this before,' Mark said.

'There was a ridiculous amount of interest at the time. I got used to posing behind a flask of fluid with my face distorted. Nobody wants a toxicologist looking normal.'

By Friday, Mark had done his homework. He was feeling confident after a couple of drinks at lunchtime. Dale the photographer would drive them both there, so there was no need to watch his alcohol level.

It was apparent from the moment they met that Dr Perrin would be a good interviewee, delighted to be back in the spotlight. Tall, with watery blue eyes and a florid skin tone, the old man had dressed for the photo session in pinstripes and waistcoat, with a rosebud in his button-hole. It was hard to picture this dignified old guy as the tomcat he'd been described as. He introduced his wife Jane, a sweet-smiling lady in her seventies who offered coffee, but they decided to do the photography first. Just as Perrin had predicted, Dale wanted shots of the toxicologist in his home lab, peering into a microscope and then holding a test tube close to his face so that light was refracted on to his features.

'Is this ghoulish enough for you?' Perrin asked, entering into the spirit of the occasion.

'You terrify me,' Dale said.

'You could try a knowing smile,' Mark suggested, thinking of the revelation to come in the obituary. 'That's nice. Get that, Dale.'

'Anything else?' Perrin asked.

Dale looked around the room. 'Would you have a picture anywhere of the ladybird seeds?'

'I can do better than that. I can show you some of the little beauties. I still have a few in my poisons cabinet.'

'Brilliant. It would be wonderful to get a close-up of them in your open hand.'

Perrin unlocked the wall cabinet and reached for a box at the back. He gave it a shake and it rattled. 'The shells are so hard that they're sometimes used inside maracas.' When he opened the box, the abrin seeds really did look like ladybirds, shiny red, each with a jet-black spot at one end. He gave a mischievous look. 'Hold out your hand.'

Mark was cautious. 'Are they safe to touch? They look innocent enough.'

'They're not alive.' Perrin poured some into his own palm. 'In this state, they can't hurt you. The outer shell is a protection, but I wouldn't advise breaking into one.'

Mark held out his hand and allowed Perrin to pass the seeds over.

'Are they still potent after so long?'

'They will be. Variations in temperature don't affect them. The people who string them together as rosary beads run a risk by drilling into the casing. There are stories of pricked fingers and nasty consequences.'

'You'd better take them back for the picture.'

Dale used a fisheye lens that would exaggerate the size of Perrin's hand. When he'd finished, he asked, 'Are the seeds really so dangerous?'

'Have you heard of ricin? Thirty times more toxic.' Perrin returned them carefully to the box and used a wipe to clean his hands.

'Immediate death, then?'

'I was talking about the degree of toxicity, not the speed. The uptake in the body isn't rapid. Anything from eight hours to three days, and then the symptoms can be confused with a severe stomach upset. Vomiting, diarrhoea, dehydration. That's the beauty of it for a poisoner. For the victim, it's all downhill from there. The effects are unstoppable. There's no antidote.'

'Nasty.'

'It is when your liver, spleen and kidneys stop working. Would you like one of me in profile looking over my shoulder? I'm told that's quite sinister.'

With the photography over, Dale retired to the kitchen to chat with Jane Perrin while Mark invited the toxicologist to share his memories of the Burke-Miller trial.

Perrin's powers of recall were excellent, and the quotes would have fuelled a lead story in any paper. 'The judge is dead now and I haven't got much longer, so I'll say whatever I please. I didn't rate him at all. I wouldn't have let him judge the pumpkin competition at the garden club. As for the rest of the lawyers, they were pig-ignorant, as well as unpleasant. The prosecution chap kept me in the witness box for two days thinking he could trip me up. By the end, he'd chewed his fingernails to the quick. You asked about Burke-Miller. Funnily enough, I felt some pity for him. Fellow doctor and all that. They decided not to put him on the stand. He was a loose cannon, you see. His greed was the finish of him. He should have stopped when he was ahead. No one is going to question one elderly widow dying from multi-organ failure, but five – to misquote Oscar Wilde – sounds like carelessness.'

Mark was making rapid shorthand notes. 'The families must have been grateful to you. Plus any other old ladies who had a lucky escape.'

'Not at all. I had a nasty letter from one old duck who missed the point altogether. She'd arranged to leave him a few thousand. She said he was a lovely man, worth six of me, and she wouldn't be changing her will just because I'd put him in prison. He needed something to look forward to when he came out. People's stupidity never ceases to amaze me.'

'But even if you didn't get much thanks, you had the satisfaction that the law had been upheld and a guilty man got his comeuppance.'

'Didn't get me a wealthy widow, did it?'

Mark laughed. 'Can I quote that?'

'Why not? It's the truth.'

Perrin was so full of himself that Mark decided this was his opportunity. 'I read somewhere that you met plenty of people in high places.' He watched the body language, the puffing up of the chest and the hands meeting across it, fingers touching, making a steeple.

'A few. Who are you thinking of?'

'Wasn't there an invitation to the Home Office?'

'Not exactly. A few drinks at a private address in Chelsea.'

'But you knew the Home Secretary, Solly Waterfield?'

'True.'

'And his wife Portia?'

Perrin's show of swank stalled suddenly. He was frowning. 'They were there, yes. Speaking of drinks, you're a lager man, aren't you? I smelt it on your breath when you came in. Help yourself to a can from the fridge. I won't join you. I'm on medication.' A blatant change of subject.

'Thanks,' Mark said, as he crossed the room to the small fridge under the window. It was stacked with chemicals in glass containers of various sizes, but several cans of a familiar brand of lager were stored behind the door. 'You became good friends with the Waterfields, I heard.'

'Lager is safer than beer,' Perrin went on as if Mark hadn't spoken. 'Did you know beer once contained unhealthy

100

amounts of arsenic? A royal commission was set up in 1903 to investigate a spate of poisonings in Manchester. They used glucose in their brewing, you see. And now you're wondering how glucose can be tainted with arsenic. This glucose was. It was made from contaminated sulphuric acid. And there was arsenic getting into the beer from another source, too. They liked their drink to have a smoky flavour, so they dried the malted barley over a fire. Coke and coal contain appreciable amounts of arsenic.'

To show confidence, Mark removed the ring-pull from the can and drank deeply. 'You were telling me about the Waterfields.'

'No I wasn't.' The mood had changed dramatically. 'You asked me and I confirmed that I met them. There's no more to be said.'

'Aren't you going to tell me about your affair with Portia?'

Perrin's face reddened and his free flow of words changed in a heartbeat to abuse. 'You're a muckraker. That's why you're here. You're not a serious journalist.'

'It's a simple question.'

'And I'm not answering it.'

Mark was stung into saying, 'It can't be ducked, you know. You might as well confirm it for the record. The truth is so much better than innuendo.'

'What do you mean – "for the record"?' Perrin's eyes widened. 'Ha, I see it now. All that stuff about the magazine feature is bollocks. You're writing my obituary and you want to juice it up with scandal, you shit.'

'Your obituary?' Mark said as if it was a foreign word. 'How could I, when you're still alive?' An evasion, if not an outright lie. Mark hoped it carried conviction.

'Barely alive. I've been given three to four weeks. A tumour as big as my fist.'

What could he say to that? Tysoe, damn him, must have known about the tumour. Mark remembered the ugly smile when inside information had been mentioned.

Working for the press toughens anyone. He was there to do a job, but in humanity he couldn't trade insults with a cancer patient.

'Who put you up to this?' Perrin demanded. 'The *Telegraph* or the *Post*?'

'I'm freelance. I didn't know about your tumour or I wouldn't have troubled you. Like I said, I'm here mainly to do a piece to mark the anniversary of the trial.' The truth still sounded insincere and was.

'My private life has fuck all to do with the trial. You mean to smear my reputation – a lifetime of high achievement – by skewing my obituary to make me into some kind of stud.'

'Mr Perrin, we wouldn't have taken all those pictures for an obituary. One mugshot would have been enough.'

'Mugshot. You couldn't put it more clearly. I'm the mug. I've been set up.'

'Okay,' Mark said as the weight of his conscience bore down, 'I'll admit it. I was asked to prepare an obituary, but believe me, Mr Perrin, that's a minor task compared to the magazine feature I want to write.'

'Go to hell, you prick.'

There was a limit to the flak Mark would take from most people, but he simply wanted to extricate himself from this mess. Any chance of more useful quotes had ended.

Perrin was clearly of the same mind. 'You can leave right now. I haven't any more to say to you except if you insist on shaming me after I've gone, my wife will be heartbroken.'

'That's not the point.'

'No? You hacks call it collateral damage.'

'Fine, I'm out of here if that's what you want. But before I go, I'll clean my hands. I noticed when you'd finished with the seeds you wiped your own hands, but you didn't offer a wipe to me.'

'Is this symbolic, washing away your guilt?'

'No, it's being careful.'

Perrin picked up the pack of wipes and pulled out a handful. 'Dry. I'll moisten them.' He reached for a bottle and dampened the wipes before handing them to Mark.

Mark made sure every pore of the hand that had held the abrin seeds was wiped clean.

Perrin changed his tone. 'When do you file your copy? Please don't write anything about the affair. I don't want Jane reading after I'm dead that I was unfaithful.'

'But it happened.'

'I have a son as well.'

'Oh? Who with?' The words were out of Mark's mouth before he sensed their force.

The old man's anger erupted again. 'That's vile. I invite you into my home, pose for your pictures, answer your questions, and all I get in return is trickery and insults. Don't you have any respect at all? Piss off, will you? Get out of my house.'

Mark didn't need telling. He was ready to go. He called out to Dale that they were leaving.

Perrin still had a parting shot. 'Scumbag.'

After driving away, Dale said, 'Got over-excited, did he?'

'Only towards the end when he cottoned on that I was writing his obituary.'

'What does he expect?'

'He thinks I'll skewer him.'

'And will you?'

Mark thought deeply before answering, 'There's a saying of Voltaire I learned when I trained as a journalist: "To the living we owe respect. To the dead we owe only the truth."'

Ten days later, the *Post* contained a news item on an inside page:

SUDDEN DEATH OF JOURNALIST
Freelance journalist Mark Peters, 44, was found dead at his Fulham home on Thursday morning. It is not known how long his body had lain undiscovered. Apparently in good health until recently, he is thought to have succumbed to a severe gastrointestinal disorder leading to multiple organ failure. A post-mortem examination was inconclusive and further tests are being conducted. Mr Peters was an occasional contributor to this newspaper. An obituary will follow in tomorrow's edition.

Judson Perrin read the report with satisfaction. The muck-raking journalist hadn't died from a mystery illness. He'd been poisoned with abrin, but not from contact with the seeds. Abrin is water soluble and can be absorbed through the skin. The moisture sprinkled on the hand wipes had been lethal. And when Perrin himself died a week later, his obituary said nothing about the affair with Portia. It was unchanged from the bland version Tysoe had shown Mark.

Ghosted

This happened the year I won the Gold Heart for *Passionata*, my romantic novel of the blighted love between an Austrian composer and a troubled English girl getting psychotherapy in Vienna. I have never had any difficulty thinking up plots even though my own life has been rather short of romantic experiences. You will understand that the award and the attention it brought me was a high point, because up to then I had written forty-five books in various genres that received no praise at all except a few letters from readers. I hadn't even attended one of the romance writers' lunches at which the awards were presented.

I was a little light-headed by the end. I still believe it wasn't the champagne that got to me and it wasn't the prize or the cheque or shaking the hand of one of the royal family. It was the envy in the eyes of all the other writers. Utterly intoxicating.

Whatever the reason, I can't deny that my brain was in such a whirl when I left the Café Royal that I couldn't think which way to turn for Waterloo station. I believe I broke the rule of a lifetime and took a taxi. Anyway, it was a relief finally to find myself on the train to Guildford, an ordinary middle-aged lady once again – ordinary except for the drop-dead Armani gown under my padded overcoat. That little number cost me more than the value of the prize cheque. Just to be sure my triumph had really happened I took out the presentation box containing the replica Gold Heart, closed my eyes and remembered the moment when everyone had stood and applauded.

'Is that it?' A voice interrupted my reverie.

I opened my eyes. The seat next to me had been taken by a man with cropped silver hair. He was in a pinstripe suit cut rather too sharply for my taste, but smart. He had a black shirt with a silver tie and he wore dark glasses that he probably called 'shades'.

'I beg your pardon,' I said.

'I said, is that it – one day as a star and you shove off home with your gong and are never heard of again?'

I tried not to catch his eye, but I'd seen the glint of gold teeth when he spoke. I've never liked ostentation. Whoever he was, this person had caught me off guard. Quite how he knew so much I had no idea. I didn't care for his forwardness or the presumption behind his question. Besides, it was the coveted Gold Heart, not a gong. I decided to let him know his interest wasn't welcome. 'If you don't mind me saying so, it's none of your business.'

'Don't be like that, Dolly,' he said, giving me even more reason to object to him. My pen-name is Dolores and I insist that my friends call me that and nothing less. The man was bending his head towards me as if he didn't want the other passengers to overhear. It's unnerving at the best of times to be seated next to someone in a train who wants a conversation, but when they almost touch heads with you and call you Dolly, it's enough to make a lady reach for the emergency handle. He must have sensed what I was thinking because he tried to appease me. 'I was being friendly. You're right. It's none of my business.'

I gave a curt nod and looked away, out of the window.

Then he added, 'But it could be yours.'

I ignored him.

'Business I could put your way.'

'I don't wish to buy anything. Please leave me alone,' I said.

'I'm not selling anything. The business I mean is a runaway bestseller. Think about it. What's this book called – *Passion* something?'

'*Passionata.*'

'It will sell a few hundred extra copies on the strength of this award. A thousand, if you're lucky, and how much does the author take? Chickenfeed. I'm talking worldwide sales running into millions.'

'Oh, yes?' I said with an ironic curl of the lip.

'You want to know more? Step into the limo that will be waiting at the end of your street at nine tomorrow morning. It's safe, I promise you, and it will change your life.'

I was about to ask how he knew where I lived, but he stood up, took a black fedora off the rack, held it in a kind of salute, winked, placed it on his head and moved away up the train.

I didn't enjoy the rest of my journey home. My thoughts were in ferment. *Worldwide sales running into millions?* Success on a scale such as that was undreamed of, even for the writer of the best romantic novel of the year. The man was obviously talking nonsense.

Who could he possibly have been? A literary agent? A publisher? A film tycoon? I couldn't imagine he was any of these.

I decided to forget about him and his limousine.

I think it was the anticlimax of returning to my cold suburban semi that made me reconsider. Some more of the paint on the front door had peeled off. There was a rate demand on the doormat along with the usual flyers advertising takeaways. Next door's TV was too loud again. At least it masked the maddening drip-drip of the leaky kitchen tap. I deserved better after writing all those books.

Perhaps the award had really changed my luck.

After a troubled night I woke early, wondering if the man in the train had been a figment of my imagination. If the car materialised, I'd know he had been real. Generally I wear jeans and an old sweater around the house. Today I put on my grey suit and white blouse, just in case. I looked out of the window more than once. All I could see at the end of the street was the greengrocer's dirty white van.

At five to nine, I looked again and saw a gleaming black Daimler. My heart pounded. I put on my shiny black shoes with the heels, tossed my red pashmina round my shoulders and hurried in as dignified a fashion as possible to the end of the street. The chauffeur was a grey-haired man in a grey uniform. He saluted me in a friendly way and opened the car door.

'Where are we going?' I asked.

'I believe it's meant to be a surprise, ma'am.'

'You're not telling, then?'

'That would spoil it. Make yourself comfortable. If you don't want the TV, just press the power switch. There's a selection of magazines and papers.'

'Will it take long?'

'About an hour.'

London, I thought, and this was confirmed when we headed along the A3. I was too interested in where we were going to look at the in-car TV or the magazines. But once we had left the main road I lost track. Before the hour was up, we were into parts of West London I didn't know at all.

Finally we stopped in front of a gate that was raised electronically, the entrance to a private estate called the Cedars with some wonderful old trees to justify the name. Even inside the estate there was a ten-minute drive past some huge redbrick mansions. I was beginning to feel intimidated.

Our destination proved to be a mock-Tudor mansion with a tiled forecourt big enough to take the Trooping of the Colour.

'Will you be driving me home after this?' I asked the chauffeur.

'It's all arranged, ma'am,' he said, touching his cap.

The front door opened before I started up the steps. A strikingly beautiful young woman greeted me by name, my pen-name, in full. She had a mass of red-gold hair in loose curls that looked almost natural. She was wearing a dark green top, low-cut, and white designer jeans. Her face seemed familiar, but I couldn't recall meeting her. She was younger than any of the women I'd met at the awards lunch.

'I'm so chuffed you decided to come,' she said. 'Ash was dead sure he'd reeled you in, but he thinks he's God's gift and not everyone sees it.'

'Ash?' I said, not liking the idea that anyone had reeled me in.

'My old man. The sweet-talking guy in the train.'

'He made it sound like a business proposition,' I said.

'Oh, it is, and we need you on board.'

She showed me through a red-carpeted hallway into a sitting room with several huge white leather sofas. A real log fire was blazing under a copper hood in the centre. A large dog with silky white hair was lying asleep nearby.

'Coffee, Dolores?'

'That would be nice,' I said to her. 'But you have the advantage of me.'

Her pretty face creased in mystification. 'Come again.'

'I don't know your name.'

She laughed. 'Most people do. I'm Raven. Excuse me.' She spoke into a mobile phone. 'It's coffee for three, and hot croissants.'

Even I, with my tendency to ignore the popular press, had heard of Raven. Model, singer, actress, TV celebrity, she made headlines in whatever she'd tried. 'I should have known,' I said, feeling my cheeks grow hot. 'I wasn't prepared. I was expecting someone from the publishing industry.'

'No problem,' she said. 'It's nice not to be recognised. People react to me in the dumbest ways. Did you tell anyone you were making this mystery trip?'

'No. I kept it to myself.'

'Great. You live alone – is that right?'

'Yes.'

'And you've written all those amazing romances?'

I glowed inwardly and responded with a modest, 'Some people seem to like them.'

'I've read every one, from *Love Unspoken* to *Passionata*,' Raven said with genuine admiration in her voice.

This came as a surprise. Her own life was high romance. She didn't need the sort of escapism my books offered. 'I'm flattered.'

'You're a star, a wonderful writer. You deserved that award. You ought to be a best-seller by now.'

I secretly agreed with her, but I'm not used to receiving praise and I found it difficult to take. 'I don't think I could handle fame. I'm rather a coward, actually. I sometimes get asked to give talks and I always turn them down.'

'Who looks after your PR?'

'No one.'

'You must have an agent.'

'I wouldn't want one. They take a slice of your income and I can't afford that.'

'So you do all the business stuff yourself?'

I nodded.

Raven seemed to approve. 'You're smart. If I could get shot of all my hangers-on, I would.'

At this moment a woman arrived with the coffee on a trolley.

'I wasn't talking about you, Annie,' Raven said. 'You're a treasure. We'll pour it ourselves.'

The woman gave a faint smile and left.

'How do you like your coffee, Dolores?'

'Black, please.'

'Same as me. Same as Ash. He's Ashley really, like that footballer.'

I don't follow football and I must have looked bemused, because Raven added, 'Or that guy in *Gone With The Wind*, but no one calls him that. He'll be with us any sec. His timing is always spot on. Ash is smart, or he wouldn't own a pad like this.'

Raven poured three coffees. The croissants were kept warm by a kind of cosy on the lower shelf of the trolley. Mine almost slipped off my plate at the sudden sound of husband Ashley's voice behind me.

'Sensible girl.'

I'm not used to being called a girl, but I was junior to him by at least ten years, so I suppose it was excusable. I got a better look at him than I had when he was seated beside me in the train. He was seventy if he was a day, as wrinkled as a Medjool date. Today he was in a combat jacket and trousers and expensive trainers.

He held out his hand and I felt his coarse skin against mine. The grip was strong. My hand felt numb after he'd squeezed it.

'Can't say I've read any of your stuff,' he said. 'I've never been much of a reader. She tells me you're the best at what you do.'

'She's too generous,' I said.

'How much do you make in an average year?'

This wasn't the kind of question I was used to answering. 'Enough to live on,' I said.

'Yeah, but how much?'

'A writer's income fluctuates,' I said, determined not to give a figure. 'I've earned a living at it for fifteen years.'

'What sort of living?' he asked. 'Don't get me wrong, Dolly, but a semi on the wrong side of Guildford ain't what I call living.'

Raven clicked her tongue. 'Ash, that isn't kind.'

He ignored her. His brown eyes were fixed on me. 'You put in the hours. You do good work. You deserve better. I made my first million before I was twenty-three. It was dirty work nobody wanted, so I did it. Collecting scrap from house to house. Waste management. Landfill. I've covered every angle. Now I have the biggest fleet of refuse lorries in the country. Ash the Trash, they call me. Doesn't bother me. I'm proud of it. I've got houses in London, Bilbao, New York and San Francisco. I did skiing every year until my knees went. And I'm married to the bird half the men in the world are lusting over.'

'That's crude,' Raven said.

'It's a fact.' Now his eyes shifted to his young wife. 'And you're more than just a pretty face and a boob job. I rate you, sweetheart. You've got ideas in your head. Tell Dolly your story.' He turned to me again. 'This'll get you going.'

112

He sat next to her on the sofa opposite mine. 'Come on, my lovely. Spill it out.'

'Well,' she said, 'I don't know what Dolores will think of it. She's a proper author.'

'She has to get ideas,' Ash said, 'and that's where you come in.'

'He never lets up,' Raven said, fluttering her false lashes at me. 'It needs a bit of work, but it goes like this. There's this little girl living in East Sheen.'

'We'll change that,' Ash said. 'Make it Richmond.'

'All right. Richmond. And when she gets to thirteen, she's already got a figure and her mum puts her in for a beauty contest and she wins, but then one of the other girls points out that she's underage. You had to be at least sixteen under the rules, so I was disqualified.'

'She,' Ash corrected her. 'She was disqualified.'

'She.'

'We're calling her Falcon,' Ash said.

'I was coming to that,' Raven said.

Ash turned to me. 'What do you think, Dolly? Is Falcon a good name?'

'Fine,' I said, not wishing to fuel the obvious tension between husband and wife.

'Okay,' Raven said. 'So this girl – Falcon – has to wait until she's older, but she learns all she can about beauty and make-up and fashion and then she enters for another contest even though she's still only fifteen.'

'And she won a modelling contract,' Ash said.

'You're spoiling it,' Raven said.

'That's what happened.'

'Yes, but I'm telling it. I was building up to the modelling. You don't come straight out with the best bit of the story, do you, Dolores?'

'Suspense is a useful device, yes,' I said.

'See?' she said to Ash. 'Now shut it.'

'Before you go on,' I said to Raven, 'I'm not entirely sure why you're telling me all this.' In truth, I had a strong suspicion. 'If it's your life story and you want to get it published, surely you should write it.'

'It's not supposed to be about me. Well, it is really, but it's a romance. I'm leaving out the stuff I don't want people to know.'

'And beefing up the good bits,' Ash said.

'In that case it's autobiography dressed up as fiction. I still think you should write it yourself.'

'She can't write,' Ash said.

'He means I'm not a writer,' Raven said. 'I can spell and stuff.'

'Which is where you come in,' Ash said to me.

'We want you to do the writing,' Raven said, 'give it a makeover, if you know what I mean.'

'We're not daft,' Ash said. 'Her fans will know it's her life story and buy a million copies.'

'But if it isn't in Raven's own style, no one will believe she wrote it.'

'So you rough it up a bit,' Ash said to me. 'Knock out the long words. Give it plenty of passion. You're good at that, I was told. All the celebs hire someone to do the writing. It's called ghosting.'

'I know what it's called,' I said. 'I'm sorry to disappoint you, but I'm not a ghostwriter. I write original fiction. I've never attempted anything like this. I wouldn't know how to start.'

'It's all on tape,' Ash said. 'You write it down, juice it up a bit and with her name on the cover we've got a bestseller.'

'I'm sorry,' I said. 'I can't do it.'

'Hold on. You haven't heard the deal,' Ash said. 'You walk out of here today with ten grand in fifty-pound notes. Another ninety grand on delivery, all in cash. No tax. How does that strike you?'

The figure was huge, far more than I earned usually. But what would a ghosted book do to the reputation I'd built with my forty-six novels?

Ash gave me instant reassurance. 'You won't take any flak for writing it. We're keeping you out of it. As far as Joe Public is concerned, Raven wrote every word herself. That's why it will be a bestseller. She's got fans all over the world and she'll get more when the book hits the shelves. They want the inside story of the nude modelling, the catwalks, the reality shows, the pop concerts, all the stars she's met—'

'And how I met you,' Raven said to him. 'They want to know what I see in a man forty-two years older than me.'

'True love, innit?' Ash said in all seriousness. 'I'm nuts about you. That's why I'm funding this bloody book.'

She kissed his cheek and ruffled his silver hair. 'My hero.'

All this was bizarre. I was actually thinking what I could do with a hundred thousand pounds. The task of writing Raven's life story might not be creatively fulfilling, but it was within my capability, especially if she had recorded it in her own words. 'Just now you said it's on tape.'

'God knows how many cassettes,' Ash said. 'Hours and hours. She's left nothing out.'

This disposed of one concern. Any writer prefers condensing a script to padding it.

'You take them home today, all of them,' Ash said.

'I'm not saying I'll do it.'

'What's the problem, Dolly? You've got the job.'

'But we haven't even talked about a contract.'

'There isn't one,' Ash said. 'There's only one thing you have to promise, apart from doing the book, and that's to keep your mouth shut. Like I said, we're passing this off as Raven's book. If anyone asks, there wasn't no ghost. She done the whole thing herself. I wasn't born yesterday and neither was you. We're paying well over the odds and buying your silence.'

'How soon do you expect this book to be written?'

'How long do you need? Six months?'

This seemed reasonable if it was all on tape already. I wouldn't wish to spend more than six months away from my real writing. Heaven help me, I was almost persuaded. 'And if I needed to meet Raven again to clarify anything, is that allowed for?'

'Sorry. Can't be done,' Raven said. 'I'm doing reality TV in Australia for the next few months and no one can reach me, not even Ash.'

'So you want the book written just from these tapes, without any more consultation?'

'It's the best way,' Ash said. 'Raven is so big that it's sure to leak out if you keep on meeting her. You won't be short of material. There's loads of stuff on the internet.'

'What happens if you aren't happy with my script?'

Raven answered that one. 'It won't happen. That's why I chose you.' She fixed her big blue eyes on me. Her confidence in me was total.

I warmed to her.

'But I'm sure to get some details wrong. Anyone would, working like this.'

'She'll straighten it out when it comes in,' Ash said. 'Let's agree a date.'

*

I must be honest. I'd been persuaded by the money. At home over the next six months I set about my task. The tapes were my source material. Raven had dictated more than enough for a substantial book, but she had a tendency to repeat herself. With skilful editing I could give it some shape. Such incidents as there were had little of the drama I put into my own books. I would have to rely on the reader identifying with 'Falcon' and her steady rise to fame and fortune.

The first objective was to find a narrative voice closer to Raven's than my own. I rewrote Chapter One several times. The process was far more demanding than Ash had predicted. 'Knock out the long words,' he'd said, as if nothing else needed to be done. Eventually, through tuning my ear to Raven's speech rhythms, I found a way of telling it that satisfied me.

The absence of a strong plot was harder to get over. Her story was depressingly predictable. A romantic novel needs conflict, some trials and setbacks, before love triumphs. I had to make the most of every vestige of disappointment, and the disqualification from the beauty contest was about all she had provided. In the end I invented a car crash, a stalker and a death in the family just to 'beef it up', as Ash had suggested.

The biggest problem of all lay waiting like a storm cloud on the horizon while I worked through the early chapters: what to do about Ash. How could I make a romantic ending out of a relationship with an elderly scrap dealer, however rich he was? If I took thirty years off his age he'd probably be insulted. If I changed his job and made him a brain surgeon or a racing driver, he'd want to know why. He was justly proud of becoming a legend in refuse collection, but it wasn't the stuff of romantic fiction.

And I have to admit that he frightened me.

Deliberately I put off writing about him until the last possible opportunity. By then I had shaped and polished the rest of the book into a form I thought acceptable, though far from brilliant. Ash was the last big challenge.

In desperation I researched him on the internet. Being so successful, he was sure to have been interviewed by the press. Perhaps I would find some helpful insights into his personality.

I was in for a shock.

In 1992 Ash had been put on trial for murder and acquitted. His first wife, a young actress, had gone missing after having an affair with the director of a play she was in. Her family suspected Ash had killed her, but her body had never been found. The word 'landfill' was bandied about among her anxious friends. Before she disappeared, she had written letters to her lover telling of mental and physical cruelty. A prosecution had been brought. Ash had walked free thanks to a brilliant defence team.

All of this would have greatly assisted the plot of the book. Of course, I dared not use it. I felt sure Ash didn't want his dirty washing aired in Raven's romantic novel. Nor was I certain how much Raven knew about it.

After reading several interviews online, I concluded that Ash was a dangerous man. He had defended his empire of landfill and dustcarts against a number of well-known barons of the underworld who had threatened to take over. 'You don't mess with Ash,' was one memorable quote.

For the book, I called him Aspen, made him a grieving widower of forty-nine, called his business recycling, gave him green credentials and charitable instincts. He fell in love with Falcon after meeting her at a fund-raising concert and they emigrated to East Africa and started an orphanage there. The book was finished with a week to spare. I was satisfied that it would pass as Raven's unaided work and please her readers.

At nine on the agreed day in March, I walked to the end of my street with a large bag containing the manuscript and Raven's tapes and stepped into the Daimler. Even after so many years of getting published I always feel nervous about submitting a script and this was magnified at least tenfold by the circumstances of this submission.

As before, the front door of the mansion was opened by Raven herself, and she looked tanned and gorgeous after her television show in Australia. 'Is that it?' she asked, pointing to my bag, echoing the words Ash had used when we first met in the train.

I handed over the manuscript.

'I can't tell you how much I've been waiting to read this,' she said, eyes shining.

I warned her that I'd made a number of changes to give it dramatic tension.

'Don't worry, Dolores,' she said. 'You're the professional here. I'm sure whatever you've done is right for the book. Coffee is on its way and so is Ash. I'm going to make sure he reads the book, too. I don't think he's read a novel in the whole of his life.'

'I wouldn't insist, if I were you,' I said quickly. 'It's not written for male readers.'

'But it's my life story and he's the hero.'

'I took some liberties,' I said. 'He may not recognise himself.'

'What's that?' Ash had come into the room behind me, pushing the coffee trolley. 'You talking about me?'

'Good morning,' I said, frantically trying to think how

to put this. 'I was explaining that for the sake of the book I had you two meeting at an earlier point in life.'

'So?'

'So you're a younger man in the story.' Raven put it more plainly than I had dared.

He frowned. 'Are you saying I'm too old?'

'No way,' she said. 'I've always told you I like a man who's been around a bit.'

'So long as he's got something in the bank. Speaking of which,' he said, turning to me, 'we owe you ninety grand.'

'That was what we agreed,' I was bold enough to say.

His eyes slid sideways and then downwards. 'Will tomorrow do? The bloody bank wanted an extra day's notice. They're not used to large cash withdrawals.'

'But you promised to pay me when I delivered the manuscript,' I said.

He poured the coffee. 'I'll make sure it's delivered to you.'

'A cheque would be simpler.'

He shook his head. 'Cheques can be traced back. Like I told you before, this has to be a secret deal.'

I have to say I was suspicious. It had been in my mind that Ash could easily welsh on the agreement. True, I'd been paid ten thousand pounds already, but I wanted my full entitlement.

As if he was reading my mind, Ash said to Raven, 'Is the message from the bank still on the answerphone? I'd like Dolly to hear it, just to show good faith.'

'What message?' she said.

He got up and crossed the room to the phone by the window. 'The message from the bank saying they wouldn't supply the cash today.' He pressed the playback button.

Nothing was played back.

He swore. 'Must have deleted it myself. Well,' he said, turning back, 'you'll have to trust me, won't you?'

'But I don't even have the address of this house, or a phone number, or anything.'

'Better you don't.'

'But you know where I live.'

'Right, and so does my driver. He'll deliver the money tomorrow afternoon.'

At that moment I acted like a feeble female outgunned by an alpha male. I left soon after, without any confidence that I would ever receive the rest of the payment.

Three days later I read in the paper that Ashley Parker, the landfill tycoon and husband of Raven, was dead. He had apparently overdosed on sleeping pills and lapsed into a coma from which he never emerged. He was aged seventy-two.

Raven inherited his forty-million-pound estate and went on record as saying that she would gladly pay twice that amount to get her husband back.

The inquest into Ash's death made interesting reading. There was some gossip in the papers that Raven had over-played the grieving widow to allay suspicion that she had somehow administered the overdose. This was never raised at the inquest. There, she melted the hearts of the coroner and the jury. She said Ashley had always been a poor sleeper and relied on a cocktail of medication that 'would have knocked out most men'. He had been happy to the last, a man with a clear conscience.

A clear conscience indeed. I never did receive the second payment for my work on the book. In fact, I have never heard from Raven since. However, she had enough sense not to publish. I believe she worked out the truth of what happened that morning I visited the house.

You see, when Ash told me I wouldn't get paid that day, I became suspicious. I'd delivered the book and they had no further use for me, but I remained a risk to Ash's scheme. While I was alive I could pop up any time and earn a fat fee from the papers by revealing that I had ghosted the masterpiece supposedly written by Raven. I had become disposable, ready for the landfill. Easier still, I might succumb to an overdose and no one would ever know how it happened, or connect me with Raven and Ash. I'd heard of doctored drinks known as mickey finns, and I could believe that some slow-acting drug might sedate me until I got home and finally kill me. And that was why after the coffee was poured I took the sensible precaution of switching my cup with Ash's. The opportunity came when he acted out his little charade with the answerphone.

What neither of them knew is that as well as romantic novels, I write whodunnits.

The Homicidal Hat

If you want to get ahead, get a hat. Some folk come to the annual conference called Malice Domestic hoping to win Agathas, those coveted teapots. The crowning glory is reserved for later, at the finale of the entire weekend: the hat contest. Such beautiful bonnets, stunning Stetsons, cute cloches and fantastic fedoras. But if you're thinking about making a late entry, forget it.

The likely winners have been months in the making. First the brainstorming session – the quest for some brilliant creation that hasn't been used already; then (after settling for something that *might* just work) the search for the right materials; and finally the construction, making sure your chic chapeau doesn't fall to pieces on the day. Millinery, like all the top pleasures in life, shouldn't be rushed.

Adelina Murphy had tried for seven years to win the 'most beautiful' section. She'd used chiffons and silks and taffeta, vast brims with spectacular drapes, white sea grass and black velour and enormous silk flowers. Each time the judges had looked at her hat with admiration – and then chosen someone else's.

'You'll never win with a face like yours,' her husband Cuthbert told her with his customary cruelty. 'They may say they're judging the hat. They may think they are, but they're not. It's like a rosette on a turnip. It looks all wrong.'

'You're no oil painting yourself,' she told him.

'But I don't go in for beauty shows. I could turn you into a winner, guaranteed.'

'With a face-lift? You're too mean to fork out for that.'

'No. You enter the other section, the most creative.'

'Hah. What do you know about creativity? You couldn't even make a baby.'

All the joy had gone out of their marriage. Adelina wasn't sure why they'd stayed together so long. Her love of mysteries may have had something to do with it. With them, she escaped. Just as Cuthbert did, into his garden workshop filled with mechanical paraphernalia. He was no better than a kid, making his working models of cranes and suspension bridges. He called them automata, as if it was some kind of science. To Adelina they were his toys.

Overnight, she thought about that suggestion of his. Maybe for once he'd talked sense. It could be time to try the creative section. The judging wasn't so dependent on subjective ideas of beauty.

At breakfast she said, 'Before you disappear into your workshop, were you serious about the most creative hat? Do you think I could be a winner?'

'Easy. We're from Texas, remember?'

'It has to have a mystery theme.'

'Okay. What are you reading right now?'

'Lindsey Davis, who is going to be one of the guests, but she doesn't say much about hats. I don't know if the ancient Romans went in for them.'

Cuthbert rolled his eyes. 'You're more ignorant than I thought. Even I remember the first Ellery Queen book was *The Roman Hat Mystery*.'

'A Roman hat on its own wouldn't win the prize. You've got to have a great idea.'

'What's the prize?'

'Free registration for next year's Malice. That's a hundred and fifty bucks.'

'We'll do it,' he said. He was as mean in spending as he was in spirit. 'Who are the other guests this year?'

'Charlaine Harris and Dan Stashower plus some old-timer from England.'

'What are their books about?'

'Charlaine writes about vampires and werewolves.'

'Creatures of the night. Scary.'

'Not to me,' Adelina said. 'I'm married to one.'

'You slay me. What does Stashower write?'

'He's into great writers of the past – Conan Doyle, Edgar Allan Poe. And his Harry Houdini mysteries are a blast.'

'Not easy to picture as a hat. Let's cast it wider. Think of some well-known titles with visual appeal.'

'*Death on the Nile.* I could wear a red fez with a dagger sticking into it.'

'Too obvious.'

'*The Moving Toyshop.*'

'Too difficult. Give me more.' He was starting to sound enthusiastic.

With any luck, Adelina thought, he might get really excited and drop dead. His heart was not the best. He was booked to be fitted with a pacemaker in July. She let the titles roll. '*Murder at the Vicarage, Green for Danger, Murder Must Advertise, The Sign of Four, The Last Camel Died at Noon.*'

'They don't inspire me. Try something else. We might get extra points if we use an Agatha winner. Can you name any?'

'Margaret Maron has won three teapots, at least. *Bootlegger's Daughter, Up Jumps the Devil, Three Day Town.*'

'I might do something with the second one. Keep going.'

'Nancy Pickard is another three-time winner: *Bum Steer*, *IOU* and *The Virgin of Small Plains*.'

Cuthbert clicked his tongue. 'I doubt if she had the hat contest in mind when she chose those.'

'Elizabeth Peters, with *Naked Once More*.'

His eyes lit up.

'Before you say another word, I'm not doing anything risqué,' Adelina said. 'I don't want to offend the judges.'

'Something comical, then?'

'That might be the way to go. Donna Andrews was shortlisted three years running with *Crouching Buzzard, Leaping Loon*, and then *We'll Always Have Parrots*, followed by *Owls Well that Ends Well*.'

'I might use the parrots.'

'I refuse to appear in public with a cockatoo on my head.'

'Where's your sense of humour?'

'In my head, not on it.' She gave the matter more thought. 'We don't actually have to restrict ourselves to a title. Last year L.C. Hayden won with a more general concept, a gorgeous orange hat with crime scene tape for a hatband and various weapons hanging from the brim.'

'And you spent ten times more and came nowhere.'

'You don't have to go on about it. I remember a wonderful hat a couple of years ago that was like an English village scene and there was a train that moved around the brim when the lady cocked her head. That was pretty, too.'

'Did it win?'

'I don't think so. Trains have been used before. There was the *Murder on the Orient Express* hat.'

'We're coming round to titles again. Give me some more of the classics.'

'*The Maltese Falcon, The Nine Tailors, The Lady in the Lake*.'

He snapped his fingers. 'Stop. *The Nine Tailors*. Wasn't that the one about bell-ringing?'

'Yes. Dorothy L. Sayers. Very well known. It must have been done before.'

'Not as I will do it. That's our winner.'

If confirmation were needed of Cuthbert's dedication to the project, it came when he booked a double room in the Crystal Gateway Marriott. Previously he'd always stayed at home in Houston, leaving Adelina to make her way to Arlington. But he declined to register for Malice itself, insisting he wasn't interested in taking part. True to his word, he stayed in the room throughout the weekend. He was perfecting the hat. He refused to show it to Adelina until the afternoon of the all-important tea party.

'I refuse to put that on my head,' she said as soon as she saw it.

The so-called hat was a cardboard model of a church with a tower and steeple. It looked nothing like a hat.

'Don't be such a drag,' he said. 'I've shaped it underneath to fit your head. This is six months' work.'

'They're not going to like it one bit,' she said.

'They'd better. It's a perfect replica of St Mary's, Bluntisham, England, the church where Dorothy L. Sayers' father was rector.'

'They won't know that.'

'I've written it on the card you give them to read out. See the cute little belfry windows with the bells inside?'

She sighed. 'Cuthbert, you don't get credit for the work you put in. I know you've tried hard, but it's not creative.'

'Try it on.'

Reluctantly, just to let him see the catastrophe, she lifted the thing on to her head. He was right in one respect. The fit was snug. She faced the wall mirror.

Grotesque.

'Now take this in your hand.'

'What is it?'

'A remote control. It won't hurt you. Press the button and find out.'

He wasn't going to give up unless she complied. Immediately there was a strong sound above her head that made her start in surprise. Bells were chiming in the church.

Cuthbert clapped his hands. '*The Nine Tailors*! How about that? The best automaton I've ever made. The little bells inside are moving. They've never had anything like it at Malice.'

'It's making my head ring,' she said. 'Those aren't miniature bells.'

'No, it's a recording of real bells chiming. There's a tiny tape recorder hidden in the tower.'

'Turn it off, please.'

'Press the button again. See? Simple.'

She lifted the church off her head. 'Well, it's different, I have to say.'

'The judges will say better than that. It's the sure-fire winner.'

She'd already told several friends she was entering the contest. They'd be expecting her to appear. 'Just this once,' she said, 'but never again.'

'You press the remote at intervals while you're parading round the room. Milk the applause for all you're worth.'

'Will you come down and watch?'

She knew his answer already.

'No, I'm staying in the room.'

*

They judged the most beautiful hats first. Coco Ihle and Monica Ferris, previous winners, looked amazing in their creations, and had stunning outfits to match. It was pure bad luck that their choice of hats was similar, right down to the colour, because a newcomer pipped them both with her rakish Gainsborough look.

Then the contestants in the most creative section were asked to step forward. They were given a near riotous reception. Some earned huge applause for the simplest of ideas. A daughter and mother came in identical white boaters with skeletons mounted on the top and they were announced as *Bones*, by Jan Burke, and *Old Bones*, by Aaron Elkins. Nancy Pickard had a tiny artist's easel attached to her hat and was Nancy Drew. One lady paid her own tribute to the Master (and the late Bill Deeck) with a funereal black wide-brimmed hat from which were suspended several items of red lace underwear. When it was announced as James Corbett's *The Merrivale Mystery* (merry veil, as the announcer translated) there was spontaneous cheering and it looked a runaway winner.

Adelina's moment had arrived. 'In tribute to Dorothy L. Sayers' *The Nine Tailors*, Adelina gives us a perfect replica in miniature of St Mary's, Bluntisham, England, where Dorothy L. grew up. And if anyone is not aware what the nine tailors were, listen up.'

Nervously she took a few steps and then pressed the remote. The bells rang out and the audience stood up and cheered. Cuthbert, give him his due, had judged it right. The hat was getting a rave reception.

As for Adelina, she was almost deafened. He must have turned up the volume. Two chimes, then a gap. Two chimes and another gap. Two chimes more. She pressed the remote to silence the thing.

Toastmaster Dan Stashower had the microphone and happily he'd read *The Nine Tailors*. 'For a man's death, the tenor bell is struck three times, followed by a gap, then three times more and three again.' He stopped. 'Oh, Dan, Dan, what am I saying? We just heard the chimes for a woman's death. Take it off, lady!' With that, he rushed toward Adelina and knocked the cardboard church off her head. There were screams.

The toastmaster had gone berserk. He grabbed Adelina and clawed at her hair. Then he seemed to find something that fell off and hit the floor. He crushed it with his foot. 'Unless I'm mistaken,' he said, crouching to examine the flattened remains, 'that was a brown recluse, the most venomous spider in America.'

Adelina was petrified by all this. 'A spider – in my hair?'

'Do you see the violin shape on its back? They're known as fiddlebacks. You find them in the southern states. Only a half-inch or so, but their bite can be deadly.'

'I know about fiddlebacks,' Adelina said. 'We get them in Texas, but I don't understand what's going on.'

'Someone meant to cause you extreme pain and possibly death,' Dan said. He picked up what was left of the church and examined it underneath. 'Yes, there's a hole in the crown and you can see the small box where the spider was secreted in the tower. When the bell sound was activated, the trap opened as well and the spider fell into your hair. They bite when they feel threatened. Who constructed this evil thing?'

So a real mystery took over at Malice Domestic. The hat contest was suspended and the police were called. The detective in charge looked at the squashed spider and agreed that it had the violin shape on its back. 'I'm from

LA and I know about these critters,' he said to Adelina. 'You don't feel anything when you're bitten. Two to four hours later the venom kicks in and you're in agonising pain.'

'You sure know how to comfort a lady.'

'We should get you checked.'

'First I want a word with my husband.'

'We all want a word with him, ma'am.'

They took the elevator to Adelina's floor. When the doors opened and they stepped out, something was obviously wrong. Other guests were in a huddle in the corridor talking excitedly.

'What happened?' the detective said.

'We heard a shot from 1421.'

'My room,' Adelina said.

'How do you know it was 1421?' the detective asked the man.

'I'm in 1423, the next room.'

'You sure it wasn't the TV?'

'Too loud. I know a gunshot when I hear one.'

The two cops looked at each other. 'Everyone better stand well back,' the senior man said. 'Do you have your plastic key, ma'am?'

Adelina handed it to him and stepped away.

The cop tried knocking on the door, but got no answer. He shouted, 'Armed police. Open up.'

Nothing.

They stood either side of the door with guns drawn. The senior man inserted the plastic and withdrew it and turned the handle. The door swung inwards.

'Grab your hair, brother, and step outside.'

But they were talking to a dead man. They found him on the floor, face up. There was no pulse.

Adelina was called into the room.

'Is this your husband, ma'am?'

Who else could it be but Cuthbert? She made a show of sympathy, even if she didn't feel much. 'He didn't deserve this. Did someone shoot him? How is that possible when he was locked in?'

The cop said, 'I see no sign of a bullet wound.'

'I don't understand. What's going on?'

'Looks like a locked-room mystery, ma'am. Isn't that what you guys read about all the time? But we need to get you checked at the hospital.'

'Yes, I can't stop shaking. I guess it's the shock. Could I fetch my beta blockers from the bathroom?'

'Sure, but don't touch anything else.'

What a relief it was to Adelina when the hospital confirmed she showed no symptoms of a spider bite. She remained in the hotel (in another room) for several days while Cuthbert's death was investigated. The medical-legal autopsy revealed that he'd died of a severe heart attack most likely triggered by his own actions. It was clear that he had put himself under stress through his wicked plot to murder Adelina. He'd transported the spider all the way from Texas and secreted it in the special compartment in the hat. And then waited to find out the result. In the confines of the hotel room under such tension, it was suggested, any small incident such as a sudden loud noise could have caused a massive rush of epinephrine, causing ventricular fibrillation and bringing on the attack in an already diseased heart.

The gunshot remained a mystery to the investigators. Not a trace of ballistic material was found in the room and there was no firearm either.

*

Eventually Adelina was able to bring Cuthbert's body back to Texas for burial and it was understandable that she didn't feel like mourning the passing of the man who had tried to kill her. Back home there was widespread sympathy for her, yet she didn't confide to anyone how she had outwitted her devious spouse. His elaborate scheme had failed through over-confidence. He'd fixed the tape-recording to play six tailors instead of nine, a premature display of triumphalism.

Adelina's method had been simple to the point of perfection. She, too, had used a tape-recorder. Before travelling to Malice Domestic, she'd gone for a farm walk and recorded the sound of a bird-scaring gas gun. One loud report on an otherwise silent tape. She'd left the tape running in the hotel bathroom, timed to trigger Cuthbert's heart attack while she was earning her alibi in the hat contest. When she collected her tablets she removed the little tape recorder.

Husband and wife, each surprising the other, but Adelina's surprise had worked. A winner at last.

With a hatful of gratitude to my informants, Beth Foxwell, Coco Ihle, Judy and Jack Cater.

Oracle of the Dead

'The Oracle of the Dead is not to be missed,' Anton, the tour representative, gushed. 'It doesn't sound like a bunch of laughs, I know, but it makes a fascinating outing with a glorious sea trip as a bonus. I see the honeymooners shaking their heads. Other things on your minds, eh? Speaking for myself, if I'd come all this way, I'd want to visit at least one historical site and that's the one I strongly recommend.'

He picked up a notepad and asked for names.

There were no takers.

'It's fully described in the leaflet with some fabulous photography,' Anton said. 'Maybe you need more time to decide. I'll remind you tomorrow after breakfast.'

Outside the hotel, the warmth and colour of Corfu waited to be experienced. Helen felt David's hand tighten around hers. 'Let's slip away,' he murmured.

She was only too happy to go. She had already put up with as many cheap laughs about newlyweds as she could take. She and David weren't beginners. They were both past thirty-five and each had been married before.

'If I wanted to visit an oracle, which I don't,' David said as they were driven into Corfu town in a carriage drawn by a horse wearing a straw hat, 'I wouldn't want it to be an oracle of the dead. It sounds morbid.'

The scents of jasmine and orange blossom were on the air. Helen leaned back and felt the sun on her forehead and sighed happily.

'Incredible!' David said, a moment later.

Helen was enjoying the blueness of the sky. 'What?'

'A cricket ground.'

'Cricket?' She sat forward and saw that he was right. To their left was a well-watered field with a freshly mown square in the middle. 'Give me strength! Not here!'

'Is true,' Georgios, their driver, turned and informed them. 'Crickets much play in Corfu. Spianada Square is World Heritage Site. More than hundred years since British rule.'

'I wonder which days they play,' David said.

'Today after lunch,' Georgios said.

'That's this afternoon taken care of,' David said.

'You'd better be joking,' Helen said without total confidence that he was. He'd spoken of cricket before, the team he played for and the county he supported in the summer. The cricket season had been over when they had first met last October. She'd assumed marriage would wean him away from the silly game. He would have better things to do now he was married to her.

'Got to give it a try,' he said, as if it was the bounden duty of a true Brit. 'See what the standard is like out here.'

'It's our honeymoon.'

'I know, love. If it's poor stuff, we can find something better to do.'

Like what – enjoying the first day of their honeymoon? And only if the cricket was poor? Stung by his selfishness, Helen turned the other way and found herself looking at the bronze statue of a former high commissioner who had probably introduced the game to Corfu. She felt like spitting at it.

'You play crickets, sir?' she heard Georgios ask David. 'Maybe they need extra man. You want me to find out?'

Helen found herself that afternoon seated in a deckchair behind the boundary line, hurt and humiliated. It made no difference that David waved to her from the middle between overs. It made no difference that other women had been persuaded to watch. This was supposed to be one of the most romantic days of their lives, for pity's sake.

Flannelled fools, they called cricketers. The fools were the women who tagged along in support.

The hurt turned steadily to anger. She'd been through a deeply wounding divorce from her previous husband, whose unrelenting sarcasm had been as cruel as physical abuse. She'd made a terrible mistake marrying Patrick and she didn't want another divorce. The process had been so damaging, so drawn-out, that she had hoped more than once that the scumbag would catch some fatal illness or have a heart attack.

Here she was in her second marriage – but only just – and she seemed to have made another huge mistake. What was it about men, that they changed so much after getting hitched, as they called it, joking about the ball and chain and actually meaning it? Patrick had turned selfish within a few months. David, within a day.

Another divorce would be more than she could face. She would rather murder David and take her chance on getting away with it. Oh, come on, she chided herself, that's way over the top after one hurtful incident. I can't seriously want him dead. I must be a damaged personality to think of such a thing. Well, I *am* damaged from years of mental abuse.

She wasn't certain how long she was tormented by these dark thoughts. She took no interest in the cricket, even when there was clapping. She kept her eyes closed.

'You no see your husband bat?'

She woke from what she supposed had been a nap. She was looking into the grinning, bearded face of Georgios, the carriage driver.

'You want to do something else?'

She shook her head.

'Come, lady,' he coaxed her. 'I take you nice ride.'

She was about to say no, imagining David looking across the turf and spotting the empty chair – and the idea of escape suddenly had some attraction. He'd assumed she would sit dutifully watching all afternoon. She hadn't made him any kind of promise to sit here until the match ended. A shock to his complacency might not come amiss.

She got up.

Georgios helped her into the carriage and drove her up one of the main streets. Feeling conflicted by guilt and vengeance – with vengeance in the ascendancy – she tried to relax and enjoy what she was seeing: glimpses of flag-stoned lanes, tall houses linked by bridges, ornate balconies festooned with washing. Presently, there was the blue-green strip of sea again.

'We come to harbour,' Georgios told her. 'Now you meet my cousin Spyros.'

'I don't want to meet anybody, thank you.'

'Spyros has beautiful speedboat.'

So she had been brought here for a sea trip. To protest was futile. Cousin Spyros, dark-skinned and athletic in build, wearing black jeans and a crisp black polo shirt, was waiting on the quay beside a sleek white boat. He was better-looking than his cousin but didn't smile as much.

'I must get back to the cricket,' Helen said.

'Plenty time,' Georgios said. 'Crickets go on many hours.'

Don't I know it, she thought. For the length of a marriage if you allow it. 'I'm sorry. I can't do this. I don't have enough money with me.'

Spyros shrugged. Georgios said in a shocked tone, 'Is gift. No need for moneys.'

Helen had been told about the tradition of hospitality in Corfu. You gave serious offence if you tried to pay for something that was freely given.

Spyros clearly spoke no English. He helped her into the boat and started the engine. Georgios shouted that he would wait for her and then the boat careered towards the open sea. Helen's long black hair lifted from her back. The boat bucked and bounced at incredible speed and she felt the spray cooling her skin. She would have adored sharing this experience with a man who truly loved her. She felt the tears dampen her eyes gain.

They headed towards a purple land mass that steadily turned green and brown as they approached. For a few minutes they followed the shoreline, then Spyros steered into what appeared to be a river estuary and cut the engine. They glided to a landing stage under a willow.

Spyros gestured to her to climb out. Helen shook her head. He was insistent. He said something forceful in Greek and flapped his hand at her. She obeyed, realising she relied on his goodwill to get back to Corfu.

Some people were walking up a barren, rocky hill towards what looked like a church. Helen glanced back at Spyros. He nodded and pointed, so she joined the others and started to climb. At the top was a man selling admission tickets, but he waved her past as if she had prepaid. She could only assume she was expected here.

Weird.

The church wasn't the attraction. A set of steps led down into a massive pillared structure built into a natural cave.

Ahead of her, a voice said in English, 'So this is where Odysseus came to visit the underworld, the kingdom of Hades. Only the brave came here to consult the oracle, because this is where the dead began their descent into hell.'

The Oracle of the Dead. Helen shivered. She hadn't wanted to visit this place. A hand pressed against her back, pushing her forward, down stone steps worn smooth by millions of feet.

The voice of the guide was behind her saying something about rituals and sacrifices. Helen found herself ushered through an arched entrance into a dimly lit vault. Chill air prickled her flesh.

There was an eerie echo to the commentary. 'So we come to the inner chamber, once guarded by the temple priests. Here, if you got so far, you might put a question to the oracle and you might see the shades of the dead rise up. You were sworn to keep secret whatever you saw and heard. The punishment for breaking this oath was death. Some say the power of the oracle remains. You are welcome to ask your question if you wish.'

Whoever had written the script had a macabre sense of humour. Maybe nothing was meant to be taken seriously.

But it felt serious. Now she was here, Helen had a strong impulse to ask the oracle a question, as if everything about this venture was written in the stars. The words would be mute, in her own head. No one else would be any the wiser. No different really from making a wish when you blew out the candles on a birthday cake.

She squeezed her hands together and asked the oracle, 'How can I get my husband back?'

Surely the dumbest question anyone had ever asked, but it was the thing most on her mind.

Immediately a horrible image flashed into her head. A corpse wrapped in a shroud and lying in an open coffin. There was blood at the top end, where the head was, defining some of the features. She had a strong sense that this was someone she knew.

With a sob, she turned and pushed her way in panic towards the exit.

Spyros was waiting at the jetty. Helen ran down the steep slope, weeping. 'Take me back. Something dreadful has happened. I'm certain it has.'

Although he didn't understand her words, he appreciated that she was in a state of shock. He produced a blanket for her. Then he cast off and started the speedboat racing towards Corfu. All the way, Helen couldn't shift that terrible image from her brain.

Georgios met them at the harbour, grim-faced. Something was said in Greek. He reached out to help Helen ashore. She started to slip the blanket from her shoulders. 'No,' Georgios said. 'You keep.'

'What's happened? Take me to the cricket field.'

'Crickets is finished now,' he said in a voice that was showing strain. He whipped up the horse. They moved off in another direction, skirting the hill that overlooks the town. Some way up a main road, they came to a large entrance with a board outside. The notice was in English as well as Greek.

Corfu Main Hospital.

'No,' Helen moaned. 'Please no.'

But Georgios cracked the whip and drove past on to a more familiar road. A left turn took them to the hotel where she was staying. Some of the tour party were standing outside the gate and when they spotted Helen there were whoops of joy. Anton, their rep, stepped forward to help her down from the carriage. 'Are you okay? It's been panic stations here. Where did you get to?'

She didn't answer. 'Where's my husband? Is he all right?'

'He's in a rare old state, worrying about you. He's gone back to the cricket ground to make another search.'

'He's alive?'

'When I last saw him, he was. You look like you've been crying. What's been going on?'

'I must find David.' She tried to climb back into the carriage.

Anton grabbed her arm and pulled her away. 'Not with this guy, you won't. There are taxis at the front.' He said something angry in Greek to Georgios, who shouted back. The hand gestures from both men left no doubt about their anger.

Helen ran off to find a taxi.

In a small taverna away from the hotel that night, a supper of slow-cooked lamb kleftiko with a bottle of retsina went a long way towards restoring the close relationship Helen had thought was gone for ever. David had been quick to apologise for his thoughtlessness over the cricket and now he promised to give up the game completely. 'This was the shock I needed and deserved,' he told her.

'You don't need to do anything as drastic as that,' she said. 'I might not have minded, but it was the timing, our first day together.'

'I mean it. The game has lost all its charm. I wasn't much good at it anyway.'

'I pictured you being hit in the face by the ball. I was terrified something dreadful had happened.'

'From your visit to the oracle? I'm furious with that Greek guy for taking you there.'

'Don't ask me any more about it. I want to forget if I can.'

'You know what?' David said. 'I'm deeply suspicious there's some kind of arrangement between the two cousins and our rep.'

'Anton?'

'Remember this morning, how hard he pushed the oracle visit? I believe he gets a rake-off for each fare. Georgios and his cousin are bribing him to persuade us tourists to make the trip.'

'They didn't ask me for money.'

'No, that was desperation. There had been no take-up at all, so they had the idea of giving you a free visit so you'd tell the rest of us what a fabulous trip it is.'

'Well, it isn't. The speedboat was wonderful, but I hated being inside the grotto.'

'They must have spent serious money buying the speed-boat, thinking they had something going with Anton, and now they're in danger of getting nothing back.'

'You could be right. There were strong words spoken between Anton and Georgios when I was brought back to the hotel. I'm sure they already knew each other.'

'It was a stupid scam anyway. Who wants to come on holiday and be taken to the gates of hell?'

David's theory was persuasive, and made sense of what had happened, but it wasn't much comfort to Helen. She was traumatised by her experience. Each time she closed her eyes she saw the coffin and the bloodstained shroud. For the rest of the week, she was going to make sure David didn't leave her side. 'I don't think you should say anything to Anton about what we suspect. I get the impression he could turn really nasty if anyone cornered him.'

They missed breakfast next morning. Only late in the day did they meet anyone else in their group. 'Did Anton give you the hard sell again – the Oracle of the Dead?' David asked, wanting to confirm his theory.

'Actually, no,' the woman said. 'He wasn't around this morning.'

David and Helen spent the afternoon pottering around the shops and markets arm in arm, the upset of their first day forgiven and almost forgotten. David bought her a gorgeous dress and she found him a leather belt.

Only when they got back to the hotel did their thoughts return to yesterday. A police car was in front of the entrance.

'Someone in trouble, I expect,' David said and jokingly added, 'Hope it isn't one of our party.'

A uniformed sergeant from the Hellenic police stopped them as they tried to enter and asked to see their passports. He checked with a list he was holding and allowed them in, then told them to remain in the lounge with the other members of their group.

'What's it about?' Helen asked the woman they had spoken to earlier.

'It's awful. There's been a murder in one of the rooms upstairs. They're not saying, but we think it must be Anton.'

'*Anton?*'

'One of the hotel staff said his throat was cut from ear to ear.'

While they were sitting there, two men in forensic suits stepped out of the lift and wheeled out a trolley bearing a corpse in a body bag. It was taken towards a van waiting outside the entrance.

'It's got to be true,' David said.

143

'But who would have wanted to murder him?'

An interpreter arrived and the police questioned everyone from the tour group about their movements in the past twenty-four hours. They were strongly interested in Helen's adventure the previous afternoon.

'Georgios – is he the carriage driver who picks up customers outside the hotel?'

'I think so,' Helen answered. 'He has a beard and his horse wears a straw hat.'

'Did he say who the other guy is – the one with the speedboat?'

'Spyros, his cousin.'

'Describe him, please.'

She did her best.

'Did Spyros tell you he borrowed money from a loan shark to buy the boat?'

'He didn't speak English. I heard nothing about that.'

'He's a dangerous man. Did he demand money from you?'

'I told you already. Georgios said the trip was a gift.' As she spoke, she remembered the old saying about being wary of Greeks bearing gifts.

The interpreter and the policeman exchanged a glance.

Everyone was asked to remain in the hotel that evening for their own safety.

'If we truly want to be safe, we'd be better off booking rooms in another hotel up the road,' David said.

The police didn't agree. They said they had two suspects who had already left Corfu and a nationwide hunt was being conducted.

Next morning a new rep appeared at breakfast, a senior man in a suit. He was full of apologies. 'The two men wanted by the police were arrested on the mainland overnight. They claim they had some sort of arrangement with Anton about a trip they were advertising and invested beyond their limits and stood to lose everything. The company denies this, of course. It has never been our policy to favour one local enterprise over another, as I'm sure you will have discovered. And as a gesture of goodwill, we are offering to underwrite trips of your choice from this new brochure.'

Helen glanced at David. There was one trip she wouldn't be signing up for.

Formidophobia

An ugly word. Formidophobia is a terror of scarecrows and I want to get over it if I can. I came across a magazine article recently that said trying to make sense of a phobia by writing about it is a useful exercise, so here goes.

One of the first films I ever watched on TV was *The Wizard of Oz*. I must have been five or six when my mother decided it was suitable viewing. The Wicked Witch of the West scared me a little and I was disappointed in the Wizard himself, but I loved Dorothy and her three companions on the yellow brick road: the Tinman, the Cowardly Lion and, most of all, the Scarecrow who longs for a brain.

Yes, at that age I felt no fear of the things. We lived in the country and I'd seen them in fields mounted on cross poles and made from old clothes and sacking stuffed with straw. Some moved in the wind, but so what? The idea that such an object could come alive and speak didn't trouble me at all. *The Wizard of Oz* scarecrow didn't have a hay stalk of menace in him.

The seeds of my phobia were sown when my brother Ben, who is six years older than me, was told to take me for a walk. I was eight by then. Our mother, who was divorced, had a friend she told us to call Uncle Serge, but who wasn't a real uncle. He didn't even speak much English.

He was one of those foreigners who arrived in the summer to pick fruit because the farmers couldn't get enough of the locals to do the work. Most of them left when the season ended, but Uncle Serge stayed on. I didn't like him and neither did Ben. He quickly changed from friendly to bossy. He expected Mum to pour him drinks and make a fuss of him and then he would put his arm round her waist as if he owned her. We'd watched him get increasingly possessive. I think he was planning to move in with us. Lately, Mum had started turfing Ben and me out of the house and telling us not to come back for two hours. We knew this meant Uncle Serge would be calling.

Ben was annoyed at having his small brother for company when he could be doing more grown-up things with his friends. At fourteen, he'd done his growth spurt and was as tall as a man. He walked ahead quickly. I always had to jog to keep up with him, but I tagged along hoping he would take me somewhere exciting. One afternoon he started across a freshly ploughed field. I knew it wasn't a place Mum would have wanted us to get into, but she'd shoved us out of the door with orders not to come back before five, so what did she expect? Our shoes sank into mud that reached our ankles in places. We thought it was a laugh.

Ahead I could see a scarecrow and we headed straight towards it. As we got closer, I saw it had a face made of sacking with a mouth and eyes crudely painted on. It was wearing a trilby hat that had gone green from being out in all weathers. Its trousers were frayed at the ends as they should be. It didn't look much like the friendly scarecrow from the film, but I wasn't troubled until I noticed the jacket it was wearing.

'That's Uncle Cyril's.'

'Don't be daft,' Ben said.

'It is. He was wearing it when he called on Boxing Day and did the magic show.'

Uncle Cyril was our *real* uncle, Mum's sister's husband, and his visits were always fun. Each Christmas, he came for dinner with us because he lived only five minutes away and after Aunt Peggy died we were the only relatives he had. This year he had put on this show specially for Ben and me. We didn't know he could do tricks. He made a walking stick dance to music and he produced two white mice out of nowhere and we were allowed to keep them. He made shiny silver coins appear from his empty hands and gave them to us. They were American quarters. I don't know where he got them from. As far as I knew, he'd never been to America.

The sportscoat he had worn that Christmas was dark green with yellow squares. Mum had called it loud. I thought it was just right for a magic show.

The scarecrow was wearing Uncle Cyril's jacket.

Ben said, 'Never.'

I said, 'I bet you.'

Ben said, 'Rubbish.'

I said, 'He was wearing it on Boxing Day. It had slits at the back.'

Ben said, 'They don't call them slits. They're vents.'

I said, 'I don't care what they're called.' I went round the back of the scarecrow. 'See?' I pointed at the slits. I knew I was right, but I wasn't going to touch anything.

Ben was bolder. He lifted the flap and showed the string looped around the waistband instead of a belt. Straw was poking out. 'Double vents. Doesn't prove a thing.' He went round the front again and started feeling in the jacket pockets.

'What are you doing that for?' I asked.

'Something might be left here and show who it really belonged to.' After he finished checking the outside pockets he started on the inside ones. 'I expect it was an old coat the farmer didn't want any more.'

'It's Uncle Cyril's.'

'Why would he give his coat away for a scarecrow to wear? You're talking bollocks.' But he carried on with his search and found something in the tiny inside pocket under the breast pocket. 'There's money here.' He scooped out two silver coins and showed them in his palm.

Shiny American quarters.

'See?' I said.

Ben was frowning. 'I don't get it.'

Uncle Cyril was a legend in the village. Thirty years later, the locals still talk about his triumph over the biggest housing developer in the land, when planning permission had been given for an estate of three hundred new homes on what had once been common ground to the south of us. 'We'll put a stop to that,' he said.

No one knew how. An edict from the government had instructed county councils to make great swathes of land available for building. Morally you couldn't argue. For as long as anyone could remember there had been a national housing shortage. There wasn't even much consultation. It was a done deal. Our community of sixty cottages, a pub, a school, one tiny shop and the church was about to be changed out of all recognition.

Uncle Cyril had no influence with 'County' – as they were known – and no pull with our Member of Parliament. He was living alone in a rented end-terrace cottage opposite the phone box. His wife, our aunt Peggy, had died seven

149

years before. He made his living as an odd-job man. 'Whatever your problem,' he would say, 'leave it to me and I'll fix it.' Cancelling the three hundred homes would be a major fix, even for a man of Uncle Cyril's ability.

Every house in the village was sent a glossy brochure from the developer informing us what a boost to our lives the new estate would be. The houses ranged from five-bedroomed luxury homes to single-occupancy affordable dwellings. A selection of the existing trees would be allowed to grow and 'an avenue of attractive new conifers' would be introduced. There would be a playground with a climbing frame and a balcony fort, swings, springs, seesaws and spinners. The older children would have a 'concrete wave' skatepark. Central to the site was the blue lagoon.

'What's that?' someone asked in our village pub, the Cat and Fiddle.

'Work it out,' Jim the landlord said. 'East of the main road behind the church. It's the village pond.'

'Our pond isn't blue. It was never blue. It's too mucky for that.'

'Don't you worry,' said someone who knew about building projects. 'They give it a bright blue PVC liner. Basically, the lagoon will serve as a retention pond for storm-water runoff. You need to manage the drainage on a big estate.'

'The ducks and moorhens won't like that.'

'The ducks and moorhens can find somewhere else.'

Some of the villagers were thinking they, too, would find somewhere else.

On a Friday afternoon in November, two bright yellow excavators trundled into the village and were parked near the telephone box ready for action. They stayed there all weekend.

On Monday, Uncle Cyril was waiting. 'Don't even think about starting work,' he told the drivers. 'You'll be in breach of international law.'

'Yeah?' said one of them. 'What law is that?'

'The European habitats directive, article 17, regarding areas of special protection.'

'This bit of scrub?' the driver said.

'This bit of scrub, as you put it,' Uncle Cyril said, 'is the habitat of a colony of great crested newts.' He made it sound as if our village had been chosen for the Second Coming.

The driver uttered two short words of disbelief.

The second driver asked where the newts were supposed to be.

'All over,' Uncle Cyril said. 'They spawn in the pond in spring and then come out and spend the rest of the year tucked out of sight among the tussocks and under hedgerows.'

'Show us one, then.'

'Too late. They'll be hibernating by now. We aren't allowed to disturb them, even if we could find one. Next March you'll see them in the pond.'

'That's four months away.'

'Better speak to your governor, hadn't you?'

The heavy machinery remained in place for two weeks and wasn't used. One evening it was driven away and wasn't seen after that. Uncle Cyril became our local hero.

At some expense to the developers, an ecologist carried out a newt survey the following spring. Three great-cresteds were found in the pond. No one asked how they got there. As a result, our village was deemed to be a special protection area. The developers left us alone.

Although the great crested newt is a protected species, they aren't uncommon in Britain. In Europe generally, they have suffered a steep decline in numbers, which is why it is an offence to disturb them.

All of us were cock-a-hoop except Angus White, a land-owner and farmer whose family had lived for generations in a handsome Georgian farmhouse at the edge of the village. He owned several cottages and made a tidy income from the rent. 'In all my years here I've never heard of newts of any sort in the pond,' he said. 'The coots would eat them. We've always had hungry coots.'

'The ecologist found them,' Jim the landlord said.

'A put-up job, in my opinion,' Angus said. 'Cyril must have given him a backhander.'

'Clever old Cyril if he did.'

'It wasn't clever at all,' Angus said. 'The village children are going to suffer. They would have benefited from the playground and the skatepark. They've got nothing now.'

'They've got fields and woods to play in just like we did,' Jim said. 'And a real pond with ducks and moorhens.'

'And newts,' someone added.

'And coots,' Angus said. 'If there's a newt left in that pond, I'm a Dutchman.'

'You're right, Angus,' a voice spoke up. Uncle Cyril had just come into the pub. 'They're not there now.'

'See?' Angus said. 'Do I need to say any more?'

But Uncle Cyril hadn't finished. 'They'll have moved out of the water foraging for food. They won't be far off.'

Everyone laughed except Angus, who made a dramatic exit, slamming the door after him.

'What's he so fussed about?' Uncle Cyril asked.

'Don't you know?' Jim the landlord said. 'He's the managing

director of Swingsnslides, the playground equipment suppliers. They would have had the contract for the play area and the skatepark. You've made an enemy of him, Cyril.'

How big an enemy became clear over the next few months. First, Uncle Cyril's rent was raised. Then a goat mysteriously appeared in his back garden and ate the crop of sweet peas he was growing for the annual flower show. The only goats in the village were Angus White's. Then one night a huge load of slurry was tipped on the street in front of Uncle Cyril's house. When asked, Angus claimed one of his farmhands must have misunderstood an instruction. The heap was removed, but the stink lingered for months.

Swingsnslides had been a failing company before the newts put a stop to the housing development. And now it went into liquidation. Worse, it turned out that the company had been mismanaged and there were big debts. Angus was accused of wrongful trading. His properties in the village had to be sold to pay the company's creditors. He was left with the farm and he had to sell the livestock and lay off all but one of his farmhands. The anger was all too apparent. At sixty, he was forced to do farm jobs he'd not touched in twenty years. Not long after, a FOR SALE board appeared in front of Angus's farmhouse. Nobody had much sympathy. He had never fitted in.

And then Ben and I found Uncle Cyril's jacket on the scarecrow in Angus's main field.

'Shall we tell Mum?' I asked Ben.

'Better not,' he said. 'She wouldn't like to know about us being in that ploughed field.'

'Let's tell Uncle Cyril, then.'

'You can if you want. Leave me out of it.'

I felt brave striding up the main street of the village and knocking on the door of my uncle's cottage.

Only he wasn't in.

That evening I asked Mum if Uncle Cyril had gone on holiday.

'Don't ask me,' she said. 'He's got a life of his own. He doesn't tell me each time he goes away.' She'd never had much time for Uncle Cyril.

I tried again at the end of the week and still got no answer at the door.

On the Wednesday, the estate agent arrived at Angus's farmhouse with a potential buyer. They let themselves in with the spare set of keys and found Angus in the kitchen with his brains blown out and a shotgun beside him.

The potential buyer was a man of strong nerve with a dark sense of humour. He said to the agent, 'I think you're going to have to lower the asking price.'

When the police came, they found a suicide note on Angus's computer. Typically of Angus, it wasn't even nicely worded:

The arsehole who destroyed me is under the scarecrow.

The dig started next morning and they didn't have to go deep. I was told Uncle Cyril was only nine inches below the surface. He had been murdered, shot in the chest at close range with a shotgun, presumably the same one Angus had used on himself. Nobody paid much attention in the village when we heard a gun go off. Most of us kept them for dealing with foxes and squirrels.

Mum, as Uncle Cyril's only living relative, had to go to the mortuary to identify him. Not a nice experience.

Yet I'm the wimp with formidophobia. I get the horrors when I think how I stood in that field with Ben and walked on the ploughed soil that covered my lovely uncle. A few inches of earth. Thirty years on, I still can't look at a scare-crow without feeling ill.

I had enormous respect for Mum, going through an experience like that. She had to attend two inquests, into the deaths of Angus White and Uncle Cyril. Then she had to sort through Uncle Cyril's possessions and sell his collection of antique china. I think she came into some of the money because we moved away from the village that same year and became townies, with a comfortable flat in Cheltenham. I'm glad to say Uncle Serge didn't follow us there. We were a closer family. Mum took driving lessons, got a little car soon after and we started taking holidays abroad. That sounds grander than it really was. They were only short trips across the Channel, renting a holiday home in Brittany. Ben and I enjoyed ourselves because we were both growing up and wanting more freedom. We'd go off for most of each day cycling around the French countryside. Ben did so well with the French language that he got into university and did a degree. He married Marie-Rose, a girl he met in Nantes, moved to France and taught English there.

I wasn't so adventurous. I took holy orders, became a vicar, and lived with Mum.

I think the rest of Mum's life was happy. She joined the Townswomen's Guild and made plenty of friends. She never discussed our tragic last year in the village, not even with me. When she died at home last year, she slipped away peacefully.

I led the funeral service myself and it was well supported by Mum's TG buddies, as she used to call them. Ben and Marie-Rose came over from France. Mum had asked for the simplest of ceremonies, so it took place at the crematorium rather than my church. I invited Ben to give the address and I spoke the words of commendation before the committal.

Ben had given me a copy of his tribute to Mum. He'd even rehearsed with me so that when he came to the front to speak, I wasn't hearing it for the first time. I stood to one side facing the congregation and I could see how moved they were. I must admit that, although I was listening, one part of my brain was taking in the scene. Most of the faces were known to me, but there was one I wasn't prepared for, an elderly man with silver hair and not much of it. He must have been one of the last to arrive because he was right at the back near the door. Like most of the others he was in a dark suit.

Something about his face was familiar, creases at the edges of his eyes that made him appear sympathetic, as you should on such an occasion, but there was more. Those creases were capable of fun in a happier situation. I knew the face could turn mischievous in the nicest way – but how did I know that?

I realised with a jolt that I was gazing at my Uncle Cyril, thirty years older than when I'd seen him last.

A trick of my imagination? A wishful thought that my dead uncle should be there in support? As a man of the cloth, I believe in the life everlasting and the possibility of miracles. Why shouldn't I? I glanced along the rest of that row to see if any others of the departed had joined him – my aunt Peggy perhaps. But all the others were people I used to see every day.

He was real. I was certain.

How was this possible? My thoughts raced when they should have been reflecting on spiritual matters. All those years ago, Mum had identified the body in the field as

Uncle Cyril's. She couldn't have been mistaken. It was Uncle Cyril's coat the scarecrow had been wearing. The police had said Angus White's last act before shooting himself had been to dress the scarecrow in that loud jacket because he had wanted everyone to be in no doubt he blamed Uncle Cyril for his misfortunes and he had taken his revenge.

With a great effort I pulled myself together and spoke the words of the commendation and touched the button that closed the curtains.

The last hymn was 'All Things Bright And Beautiful'. I watched the man I believed was my uncle joining in as lustily as anyone. He was only eight rows back and I could hear his voice. I knew that powerful tone shifting from register to register. He was flesh and blood, no question.

I spoke the words of the Grace and headed down the aisle with unseemly haste to be at the door as everyone left. I wanted to be sure of speaking to him.

But it wasn't the place or the occasion for the questions I wanted to ask, even though he was one of the last to leave. When I thanked him for coming, he gave the smile I remembered from his magic show – that faint twitch of the lips that said he was glad we'd enjoyed the trick, but nothing would persuade him to explain how it was done.

I shook his hand and let him know in the gentlest way that I had recognised him. 'I wasn't expecting you to be here.'

He said something about wanting to pay his respects and then in a trice he was through the door. I couldn't follow. There were other hands to shake.

But you don't rush away from funerals. The floral tributes are displayed outside the crematorium and you spend a few minutes looking at them. That's where more words are spoken. And then the mourners move on to a local hostelry. We'd arranged to have refreshments served in the Cat and Fiddle. I'd already announced that everyone would be welcome to join us. Jim the landlord had long since left us, but one of his daughters had taken over and was a brilliant cook.

I saw him standing well back from all the flowers, looking at his watch. I went over. 'You are my uncle Cyril, aren't you? May I have a word?'

He said, 'No offence, but I'd rather not. I have to be on my way.'

'Aren't you joining us at the pub?'

'Sorry,' he said. 'It would be too emotional for me. I'm glad I came and now I must leave.' With that, he turned and walked away.

My pastoral duties kept me from following him. I needed to be there for the other mourners. I waited until the last of them had moved on before approaching my brother Ben and saying, 'That was our uncle Cyril who came to the service, wasn't it?'

For a moment he was stone-faced. Then he nodded. 'He insisted. He came with us.'

'From France?'

'He's lived there ever since . . . ever since . . .' His words trailed off.

'And you knew he was alive?'

'We all knew except you.'

'All? Who are you speaking about?'

'All the family. That is to say, Marie-Rose and me, and Mum, of course.'

'Mum knew?'

'It was a family secret. We took a decision to spare you from the moral conflict of shielding a . . .'

'Murderer?'

His eyes left mine. 'That's not the word I would use. We

simply thought that you, as a priest, would have been faced with a dilemma too painful to endure. I hope you can forgive us.'

'I'd rather have the truth,' I told him. 'I don't need to be spared, as you put it. I know what goes on in the world.'

'Let it go, Chris,' he said. 'For all our sakes, move on.'

'I can't,' I said. 'It pains me that our own mother knew he was still alive and died without ever sharing it with me.'

'She loved you. She had your best interests at heart.'

'Come on, Ben. You've started to tell me. I'm willing to believe Uncle Cyril pulled off his most spectacular magic trick and got away with murder. I won't turn him over to the police.'

'Don't even think about it,' Ben said.

'Well, it's obvious he fled the country and started a new life abroad. I'm surprised he took the risk of coming over for the funeral. Some of the locals from thirty years ago are still alive. They could easily recognise him. I did.'

'He took the risk because of what Mum did. He felt the least he could do was pay his respects at her passing.'

What Mum did. I understood. I remembered how Mum had been asked to identify the body buried under the scarecrow. She had been to the mortuary and identified it as Uncle Cyril – a blatant untruth. She had committed perjury twice over, at the inquests into the deaths of Angus White and Uncle Cyril. Maybe today of all days it was right to refrain from pushing my fact-finding to a cruel conclusion. I mumbled something to Ben about speaking to him later.

That night I lay awake trying to understand why my mother had acted as she did. Uncle Cyril was her brother-in-law and never close to her. Although he'd lived in the village he'd seldom visited the house except for Christmas. When she spoke of him, it was never with much affection. He was the man who had married her sister and that was how she thought of him. She was sympathetic when he was being victimised by Angus White because of the failure of Swingsnslides, but sympathy was all it ever was.

My troubled brain moved on, trying to see her behaviour from a different perspective. Whose corpse was it? The only individual I could think of who had pushed my uncle to the point of desperation had been Angus, his landlord and tormentor, but Angus had committed suicide. Everyone assumed at the time that he had taken his persecution of Uncle Cyril to its ultimate, murdered him, buried him and then was unable to live with his guilty conscience and shot himself, leaving the message on his computer suggesting that the body was that of the man he blamed for his downfall. The coroner had dealt with both inquests the same day, accepting my mother's identification as reliable. Two deaths, two tragic deaths, but linked and easily resolved.

Whose body had my mother falsely identified if it wasn't Uncle Cyril's? I continued to wrestle with the problem for hours, finally falling asleep towards dawn and no wiser.

My brain must have worked at some level during that sleep, processing the disorganised thoughts that had kept me awake. I've read that during these hours our mental machinery is just as active as when we are awake, performing housekeeping functions, removing unwanted toxins that build up and make it difficult for us to think clearly.

The next morning, I woke later than usual. To my dismay, it was after eleven. But my thoughts were clearer. The explanation came to me while I was showering.

I called Ben on the phone. He said it wasn't convenient. He'd just arrived in France and had a two-hour drive ahead of him. I asked if Uncle Cyril was with him.

Ben said, 'He is.'

'May I speak to him?'

'If this is about what I think it is, you're wasting your time. It's a closed book.'

'One question and I'll be satisfied.'

I heard a muffled consultation going on. I could imagine the three conspirators in the car deciding how much I should be told. 'What's the question, then?'

'The man buried under the scarecrow. Was he Mum's friend Serge?'

After a beat, Ben said in the same terse tone, 'He was. Now will you get off the line and let us continue our journey?'

I'm a man of my word – or try to be. I thanked him and ended the call.

Now I felt free to make sense of those events from long ago. Ben and I had noticed how Serge's friendship with Mum had developed into an unpleasant relationship in which he had become increasingly assertive and she unwilling or unable to escape. We'd noticed bruising on her arms and neck. She had become tense and short-tempered before his visits, at the same time putting on excessive amounts of lipstick and eyeliner and dressing herself in low-cut tops and short skirts that weren't her style at all. Even to us boys there was a sense that she didn't know how to deal with this demanding man. I think she was desperate for help. She must have been, to turn to Uncle Cyril. Either that, or he saw what was going on and offered to take care of the situation. He carried out the murders – yes, murders – of the two most unpleasant people in the village, Serge and Angus. Then he performed the best piece of trickery of his career as a magician. With Mum's help, he vanished. Supposedly he was dead, so no one searched for him.

Other things made sense to me now. I could understand why Mum decided to leave the village as soon as possible. She was guilty of worse than perjury. She had committed conspiracy to murder. She must have discussed the plan with Uncle Cyril.

Clearly our trips to France after we moved to Cheltenham had been an opportunity for Mum to visit Uncle Cyril and take him bits of his property she had cleared from his cottage. Ben and I had gone cycling for hours, leaving her free for the rest of each day. With hindsight, I can hardly believe how dense I had been to miss so much.

But I couldn't stop myself feeling unhappy – if not jealous – that Mum had chosen to share her secret with Ben, but not with me. Was it my priesthood that came between us? Did she think as a man of God I would feel compelled to inform the police? Maybe I should have been thankful that she spared me that choice. I believe I would have kept the knowledge to myself at the cost of a considerable burden on my conscience.

I reconciled myself to having arrived at the truth of the story so late that nothing much could be done to put things right. Even if it all became public knowledge now, Uncle Cyril would deny everything and there would be no evidence left from all those years ago. The police keep items from unsolved cases and still make arrests many years later, but these deaths had been satisfactorily explained at an inquest. There was no reason to have kept DNA, fingerprints, used gunshot cartridges or photos of the scene.

I resumed my uneventful life and immersed myself in pastoral duties until one morning a letter arrived from France. It came from my brother Ben and it was another huge shock.

My dear Chris,

Since we last spoke on the phone, I have been searching my soul because I allowed you to get a wrong impression of what happened when we were boys. I didn't lie to you. I wouldn't, but I didn't tell you everything. I left you to draw your own conclusions and I think they may be mistaken. You are entitled to know the full truth.

It wasn't Uncle Cyril who murdered Serge. It was me. I don't know how much you knew of what was going on. You were only eight at the time and I was fourteen. Mum was lonely after the divorce and formed a friendship with Serge, who worked as a fruit-picker. He was charming at first and they soon became lovers (which was why you and I were told to get out of the house some afternoons) but his behaviour soon changed and became cruel to the point of sadism. I saw what was going on and got angry as only a teenager can. I couldn't bear seeing the changes in Mum's personality. She was quite unable to find the strength to break away from him. Sometimes I could hear her through my bedroom wall, sobbing. It really got into my head.

There was no way I could take him on. I was tall for my age, but he was a grown man, physically strong from years of farm labouring. I decided to shoot him, using the shotgun our dad had left in the loft after he and Mum parted. I knew which days he called and I waited for him one time when you were out all day on a school trip. Mum as usual had asked me to be out of the house. I hid behind the drystone wall in the lane and when Serge came along I stepped out and shot him in the chest. He died immediately. I managed to drag his body to the side and went home and told Mum what I had done. She was horrified, of course, but I wasn't scared. I said I would bury him and no one would know or care. She said it was wrong and it wouldn't work and anyway I'd need help. She was right. Deep down, I knew she was right. While she was still in a panic about what I had done, I walked up the street to Uncle Cyril's. I knew he was a clever bloke from the tricks he had performed at Christmas and, what was more, he was the village handyman, ready to fix any problem.

This was more than just a problem. It was a real emergency, but he agreed straight away to help. Together the same evening, we lashed the body to a sheep hurdle and dragged it out to the centre of a ploughed field, dug a hole and buried it. All we could manage was a shallow grave before it got too dark. I thought that was the end of it, problem solved, but Uncle Cyril was already planning something smarter. He told me one of the key elements in any magic trick is misdirection. I didn't understand at the time. He said I should leave him to manage the next step. I needed to hold my nerve and say nothing to anybody. He would speak to Mum and between them they would make the killing of Serge work to our advantage.

One day the next week I was going along the lane when I looked over the wall at the field where we had buried the body. At first I thought a real person was standing at the same spot and I was terrified our secret had been discovered, but then I saw it was only a scarecrow. I guessed this was something to do with the misdirection Uncle Cyril had spoken about.

I think it was the next day when Mum told you and me to get out of the house for a couple of hours just like she did each time Serge visited. I didn't know at the time, but this was the next part of the plan. I expect you remember coming with me because that was the afternoon we walked across the field to look at the scarecrow. I wanted to see it close up. You spotted straight away that it was wearing Uncle Cyril's jacket. I can tell you I was even more surprised than you were. I couldn't believe he would do anything so obvious as marking the spot and drawing attention to his part in the concealment. Naturally I didn't let on to you that the body was buried there. I held my nerve like Uncle Cyril had said. You insisted on going to his cottage to tell him about the coat, but you didn't get any answer when you knocked.

A few days later, Angus White was found dead at home, shot with his own gun. A suicide note was found on his computer. I like to believe it really was suicide, but I feel sure that the note was written by Uncle Cyril, who must have secretly got into the farmhouse. To this day, I've never had the nerve to ask him the truth of it. He saved me from being charged with murder, so I don't feel I have the right to ask. The note was a classic piece of misdirection, assisted by Mum wrongly identifying Serge's body as Uncle Cyril's.

What I do know for certain is that Cyril was not seen in the village again because he left the country and started a new life here in France. Thanks to him, I avoided being charged with murder and locked up and Mum was spared the double scandal of having her affair made public and her killer son dragged through the courts. We all benefited.

He's an old man now and those dark days are far behind us, but he insisted on joining Marie-Rose and me when we came over for the funeral. He'd seen Mum a few times when we visited Brittany and now he wanted to pay his last respects, as he put it.

I hope this hasn't come as too much of a shock, Chris. Please believe me when I say I feel an even stronger tie to you now that Mum has gone, but it was important that you were told the truth of it all.

Ever your loving brother,

Ben

I have read this letter many times over if only to remind myself how mistaken I was. I use it as a warning against making false assumptions. I wouldn't be human if I didn't sometimes speculate on whether Uncle Cyril shot Angus. He had reason enough to hate him, but by this time Angus was a defeated man and it's not impossible that he took his own life. It would have been a coincidence, I concede, that this happened within a few days of Serge's death, but such things are not unknown.

The Deadliest Tale of All

He wrote 'A Troubled Sleep', stared at it for a time, sighed and struck it out.

'The Unsafe Sleep' didn't last long either.

'In the Death Bed' was stronger, he decided. He left it to be considered later. A good title could make or break a story. He'd tried and rejected scores of them for this, the most ambitious of all his tales. 'Night Horrors'? Possibly not.

Then an inspiration: 'It Comes By Night'. This, he thought, could be right. He barely had time to write it down when there was a knock at the door.

He groaned.

The man from the *Tribune* was creating a bad impression. His manner verged on the offensive. 'Have a care what you say to me. My readers are not to be deceived. I will insist upon the truth.'

The implication was not lost on Edgar Allan Poe.

'Do you take me for a deceiver, then?' he said, scarcely containing his annoyance. He had consented to this interview on the assumption that it would prop up his shaky reputation.

'You will not deny that you are a teller of tall tales, a purveyor of the fantastic.'

'That is my art, sir, not my character, and you had better make the distinction if you wish to detain me any longer. What did you say your name is?'

'Nolz. Rainer Nolz.'

'Ha – it sounds Prussian.'

'Is that objectionable to you?'

'It is if you are unable to temper your questions with courtesy.'

'My family have lived in Virginia for two generations,' Nolz said, as if that absolved him of Prussian tendencies. He seemed bent on establishing superiority. Overweight – fat, to put it bluntly – and dressed in a loud check suit stained with food, he was probably twenty years Poe's senior – too old to be a hack, notebook in hand, interviewing a writer. A competent journalist his age should surely have occupied an editor's chair by now.

He threw in another barbed remark. 'Since you raised the matter of names, yours is an odd one. Poe – what's the origin of that?'

'Irish. The Poes arrived in America about 1750.'

'And the Allans?'

'The family who took me in when I was orphaned. Do you really need to know this?'

'It's not a question of what I need to know, but what my readers will expect to be informed about.'

'My writing,' Poe said, raising his generally quiet voice to fortissimo.

'On the contrary. They can pick up one of your books. Anything from me about your writing would be superfluous. The readers – my readers – are interested in your life. That's my brief, Mr Poe. I've come prepared. I have an adequate knowledge of your *curriculum vitae* – or as much of it as you have put in the public domain. You aren't honest about your age, subtracting years as if you were one of the fair sex.'

'Is that important?'

'To posterity it will be. You were born in 1809, not 1811.'

Poe smiled. 'Now I understand. You've been talking to the unctuous Griswold.'

'And you've been lying to him.'

Rufus Griswold, self-appointed arbiter of national literary merit, had first come into Poe's life probing for personal information for an anthology he was compiling, ambitiously entitled *The Poets and Poetry of America*. At twenty-six, the man had been confident, plausible and sycophantic – a veritable toady. Poe had recognised as much, but failed to see the danger he presented. Writers with a genius for portraying malice do not always recognise it in real life. Griswold was a third-rate writer who fancied himself one of the literati, a parasite by now embedded in Poe's life and repeatedly damaging him. Ultimately the odious creature would take possession of the writing itself. At the time of their first meeting there had seemed no conceivable harm in embellishing the truth.

Nolz was a horse of a different colour, making no pretension to charm. 'But you'll oblige me by answering my questions honestly.'

'Before I do,' Poe said, liking him less by the minute, 'I'm curious to know how much of my work you have read.'

'Not much.'

'The poems?'

'A few.'

'The tales?'

'Fewer. I don't care for the fantastic and horrific. I prefer something of intellectual appeal.'

'You think my work is not for the intellect?'

'Too sensational. At my age, Mr Poe, one has a care for one's health.'

'Are you unwell?'

'My doctor tells me I have a heart murmur. Too much excitement aggravates the condition. But I am here to talk about you, not myself. You are fond of claiming that you could have emulated Byron and swum the Hellespont because as a youth in Richmond you once won a wager by swimming a stretch of the James River.'

Poe was pleased to confirm it. 'Correct. At the mere age of fifteen I swam from Ludlam's Wharf to Warwick against one of the strongest tides ever known.'

Nolz was shaking his head. 'Unfortunately for you, I know Richmond. I have lived there. To have achieved such a feat you must have swum at least six miles.'

'As I did,' Poe answered on an angry rising note. 'I assure you I did. In those conditions there is no question that my swim was the equal of Byron's.'

'And I say it is impossible.'

'Mr Nolz, it happened, and others were there as witnesses. I was an athletic youth. Were I fifteen again and fit, I would not hesitate to duplicate the deed. Sadly, in recent months my health, like yours apparently, has suffered a decline. But I have achieved other things. Shall I tell you about "The Raven"?'

'I would rather you didn't.'

The sauce of this fellow! 'Your readers will expect to be told how it came to be written.'

'I know all that,' Nolz said and smiled in a way that was not friendly. 'I have a copy of your essay, "The Philosophy of Composition", which purports to explain the genesis of the poem.'

'*Purports?*'

'The piece is self-congratulation, a paean to Mr Poe. You omit to mention how much you borrowed from other writers.'

'Name one.'

'Miss Elizabeth Barrett.'

'I am on the best of terms with Miss Barrett.'

'You are on the best of terms with any number of ladies. And I am sure you are on the best of terms with a poem of Miss Barrett's entitled "Lady Geraldine's Courtship" because in "The Raven" you aped the rhythm and rhyme and offered not a word of your debt to her in the essay.'

'She has not complained to me.'

'As a critic you are quick to accuse others of imitation and lifting ideas, but you seem blind to the same tendency in yourself. You are also indebted to Mr Charles Dickens. Allow me to remind you that you were planning to write a poem about a parrot until you read of the raven in *Barnaby Rudge*.'

Poe was silent. The man was right, damn him.

'I suggest to you' – Nolz gave the knife a twist – 'that a parrot saying "Nevermore" would not have impressed the public. It might well have made you a laughing stock.'

Poe said in his defence, 'Whether or not the raven in the Dickens novel put the idea in my head is immaterial. I might as easily have seen one perched on a churchyard wall. The artist cannot choose the source of his inspiration.'

'But he ought to acknowledge it when he claims to be expounding his *modus operandi*. I recall the scene in the novel where Barnaby is imprisoned with Grip the raven for company and the sun through the bars casts the bird's shadow upon the floor while its eyes gleam in the light of the fires set by the rioters outside. Somewhat reminiscent of your unforgettable final stanza, is it not? "And his eyes have all the seeming of a demon's that is dreaming, And the lamp-light o'er him streaming throws his shadow on the floor".'

'Would you tax me with plagiarism?'

'No, sir. Forgetfulness.'

'How charitable! Is there anything else you hold against me?'

Nolz gave a nod, as if tempted to go on. Then he hesitated before saying, 'Mr Poe, you may not appreciate this, but I am your best hope.'

'Best hope! God save us! Best hope of what?'

'Of a lasting reputation.'

'Sir, my written work will ensure my reputation.'

'Without wishing to be offensive, it has not achieved much for you thus far.'

Poe sighed. 'I grant you that. "The Raven" is the most popular poem ever written and I remain in penury.'

Nolz spread his palms. 'You were a fool to yourself, publishing in a newspaper without the protection of copyright. Any cheapjack publisher was free to reprint without redress.'

'And has, a thousand times over.' Poe put his hand to his mouth and yawned. 'Put me out of my suspense. How will you improve my prospects?'

'Materially, not at all,' Nolz said. 'I am a journalist, not a businessman. I spoke just now of your reputation.'

'It doesn't have need of you,' Poe said on the impulse. 'It's second to none.' Yet both knew the statement was untrue. He'd acceded all too eagerly to the request for an interview. He needed shoring up, if it wasn't too late already.

Nolz was looking at him with pity. The man had the power to unnerve, as if he knew things yet to be revealed. The world might be – ought to be – aware that the writer of "The Gold-Bug" and "The Raven" was a genius, but this dislikeable old hack seated across the table was behaving as if he was the recording angel.

'Who are you?' Poe cried out. 'Why should I submit to your churlish questions?'

'I told you who I am,' Nolz said. 'And as to the questions, most of them have come from you.'

'There you go, maligning me, twisting my words. Why should I trust you?'

'Because I have a care for the truth above everything. You have enemies masquerading as friends, Mr Poe. They seek to destroy your reputation. They may succeed.'

Much of what the man was saying was true.

'You keep speaking of this reputation of mine as if it matters. My work is all that matters and it will endure. Poor Edgar Poe the man is a lost cause, a soul beyond hope of redemption.'

'With a well-known flair for self-abasement. Coming from you, this is of no consequence. But when others damn you to kingdom come, as they will, you are going to have need of me.'

'As my protector? You are not a young man, Rainer Nolz.'

'Ray.' He extended his fat hand across the table. 'Address me as Ray. My fellow writers do.'

Poe reached for the hand and felt revulsion at the flabby contact. 'So, Ray . . .'

'Yes?'

'Are there any other failings of mine you wish to address?'

Nolz raised a shaggy eyebrow. 'Are there any, Edgar, that you care to confess?'

'Plenty, I should think! When I drink, I drink to oblivion. One or two glasses are usually enough. I am a fool with women, writing love letters to one whilst pursuing another.

I am hopeless with money. Are you writing this down?'

'It's too well known. Let's address some of the misinformation you have unleashed on the world.'

'Must we?'

Nolz gave a penetrating look with his brown, unsparing eyes. 'If I am to be of service, yes.'

The examination that followed was uncomfortable, depressing, shaming, a ledger of Poe's falsehoods and exaggerations. Why did he endure it? Because Nolz, like the Ancient Mariner, was possessed of a mysterious power to detain. He dissected more of the myths blithely confided to Griswold and given substance in *The Poets and Poetry of America*. The myth that as a young man Poe had run away from home to fight for the liberty of the Greeks in their War of Independence against the Turks. The myth of a trip to St Petersburg where he got into difficulties and was supposedly rescued by Henry Middleton, the American Consul. All this in an attempt to gloss over two years in the ranks, of which Poe was not proud.

Nolz had said he knew the *curriculum vitae*, and so he did, in mortifying detail. He must have gone to infinite trouble to find out so much.

Finally he said, 'Was that good for your soul?'

'Against all expectation, yes,' Poe admitted. 'I am tempted, almost, to ask you to absolve me of my sins.'

Nolz laughed. 'That would be exceeding my duties.'

'I feel shriven, nonetheless, and I thank you for that.'

'No need, Edgar. Instead of absolution I will offer a piece of advice. Beware of Rufus Griswold. He is not your friend.'

'Ha! I don't need telling,' Poe said. 'After all his blandishments, how many of my poems appeared in his book? Three. One Charles Fenno Hoffman had forty-five. I counted them.

Forty-five. A man whose name means little to me or the public.'

'I saw.'

Poe was warming to his theme. 'And who was offered and accepted my job after I was dismissed as editor at *Graham's*? Griswold.'

'And the magazine suffered as a result,' Nolz said, beginning to show some sympathy.

'He even shoulders me aside when I show affection for a lady. There is a certain poetess—'

'Fanny Osgood?'

'You know everything. The first I heard of it was that she had dedicated her collection of poems to him – "a souvenir of admiration for his genius".'

'Why then, Edgar, do you continue to have any truck with a man who treats you with contempt?'

Poe rolled his eyes and eased his finger around his stock. All this was making him sweat. How could he explain without damning himself? 'Griswold has influence. That wretched book of his must have gone through ten editions. Oh, I've tried cutting free of him more than once, but he'll remind me that I have need of him. Since you know so much, you must be aware that he put together another anthology, *The Prose Writers of America*.'

'And invited you to contribute. To which you responded that he was an honourable friend you had lost through your own folly – *your own folly*.'

Now Poe flushed with embarrassment. 'Swallowing my pride. He included several of my tales.'

'He continues to tell his own tales about you to all that will listen, shocking scurrilous stories.'

'I know.'

'Griswold will bring you nothing but discredit.'

He nodded. He knew it, of course. He was destined for the sewers. But surely the work would keep its dignity, whatever was said of its creator?

'And you, Ray? What may I expect from you after this interrogation? Should I be nervous of what you will write in your newspaper?'

'The truth.'

'Exposing the lies?'

'Oh, no. We disposed of them this evening. I needed to make certain. I am now confident that what I write has the force of verified fact. It will not be to your detriment.'

'And when may I look forward to reading it?'

'Never.'

Poe frowned, and played the word over in his brain. 'I don't understand.'

'You will never read it because you will be dead.'

The statement was like a physical blow. His brain reeled. Deep inside himself, he'd feared this from the moment he admitted the stranger to his room. Nolz was not of this world, but an agent of destruction.

'You've turned pale,' Nolz said. 'I must apologise. It was wrong of me to speak of this.'

'Tell me,' Poe whispered, eyes wide. 'Tell me all you know.'

'Edgar, I know only what I have confirmed with you this evening.'

'You spoke of my imminent death.'

'No. I said you will never read what I write because you will be dead. I am a writer of obituaries.'

A shocked silence ensued.

'You are my obituary writer?'

'It's my occupation. I was commissioned to prepare yours.'

'By whom?'

'The editor of the *New York Daily Tribune*. You, as a journalist, will know that obituaries of eminent men are prepared in advance, sometimes years in advance. One cannot write an adequate account of a life on the morning a death is announced.'

'My obituary! I am forty years old!'

'*Ars longa, vita brevis.*'

'I don't want this,' Poe said, panicking. 'I wish I had never spoken to you. How can you compose my death notice when I am still of this earth? It's ghoulish. You've put the mark of death on me.'

Nolz looked shamefaced. 'I have committed an unprofessional act. I should never have told you.'

'I'm still creative. God knows, I still have the talent.'

The journalist cleared his throat. 'With due respect, Edgar, you have not produced much of significance this year.'

'I have not suffered a day to pass without writing.'

'What manner of writing?'

'I revise my earlier work.'

'Previously published work. All this tinkering with things that appeared in print ten years ago is the symptom of an exhausted talent.'

'And poems. I wrote a new poem longer than "The Raven".'

Nolz lifted his eyebrows, leaving the last four words to resonate. 'I doubt if anything you have written in the last six months is worthy of mention in the obituary.'

'Cruel!'

'But true. I told you I must be honest.' Nolz closed his notebook and pushed his chair back from the table. 'I shall take my leave of you now. Take heart, Edgar. Your place in the pantheon is assured. In your short life you have written more masterpieces than Longfellow, Hawthorne and Emerson between them.'

Poe's next words were uttered in a forlorn cry of despair. 'I am not finished.'

'I think my hat is hanging in the passage.'

'Damn you to kingdom come, I am not finished!'

Nolz crossed the room.

Poe got up and followed him, grabbing at his sleeve. 'Wait. There is something you haven't seen, a work of monumental significance. I've been working on it for five years, the best thing I have ever done.'

Nolz paused and turned halfway, his face creased in disbelief. 'Unpublished?'

'You must read it,' Poe said, nodding. 'It's a work of genius.'

'A poem?'

'A tale. It will stand with "The Tell-Tale Heart" and "The Pit and the Pendulum".'

'One of your tales of horror? I told you how I feel about them.'

'Not merely one of my tales of horror, Ray, but the ultimate tale. If you neglect to read it, you will undervalue my reputation, whatever you write in that obituary.'

'What is the title?'

He had to think. '"It Comes By Night".' He rushed to his desk in the corner of the room and started riffling through the sheets of paper spread across it, scattering anything unwanted to the floor. 'Here!' He snatched up a pen and inscribed the title on the top sheet. 'If I die tomorrow, this is my legacy. I beg you, Ray. If you have a shred of pity for a desperate man, give it your attention.' He thrust the manuscript into Nolz's hands. 'Take it with you. I swear it is the best I have ever done, or will do.'

Shaking his head, Nolz pocketed the handwritten sheets, retrieved his hat and left.

Two days later, the script of 'It Comes by Night' was returned to Poe by special messenger. With it was a note:

Dear Sir,
I understand that you are the author and owner of these pages discovered in the rooms of Mr Rainer Nolz, deceased. I regret to inform you that he was found dead in bed yesterday morning. The physician who attended was of the opinion that Mr Nolz suffered some spasm of panic in the night which induced a fatal heart attack. He was known to have an irregular heart rhythm. In these sad circumstances it may be of some consolation to you that your story was the last thing he ever read, for it was found on his deathbed. I return it herewith.
Sincerely,
J.C. Sneddon, Coroner

Poe threw the script into the fire and wept.

Edgar Allan Poe himself died the next month in Washington College Hospital, Baltimore. The mystery surrounding his last days has baffled generations of biographers. He had been found in a drunken stupor in a gutter. Dr John Moran, who attended him in hospital, reported that even when he regained consciousness the writer was confused and incoherent.

When I returned I found him in a violent delirium, resisting the efforts of two nurses to keep him in bed. This state continued until Saturday evening (he was admitted on Wednesday) when he commenced calling for one 'Reynolds' which he did through the night up to three on Sunday morning. At this time a very decided change began to affect him. Having become enfeebled from exertion he became quiet and seemed to rest for a short time, then gently moving his head he said, 'Lord help my poor Soul' and expired.

The identity of 'Reynolds' has never been satisfactorily explained. Poe had no known friend of that name. In *The Tell-Tale Heart, the Life and Works of Edgar Allan Poe*, his biographer, the poet, critic and mystery writer Julian Symons, wrote: '. . . this last cry, like so much else in his life, remains a riddle unsolved.'

Just as the sudden death of Ray Nolz was never explained.

On the day of Poe's funeral, the *New York Daily Tribune* published an obituary announcing the death and stating 'few will be grieved by it' because 'he had no friends'. Poe had been worthless as a critic, always biased, and 'little better than a carping grammarian'. This savage piece was balanced with praise of the stories and the poetry, but the impression of the man was devastating. He was likened to a character in a Bulwer-Lytton novel: 'Irascible, envious, but not the worst, for these salient angles were all varnished over with a cold repellent cynicism while his passions vented themselves in sneers . . . He had, to a morbid excess, that desire to rise which is vulgarly called ambition, but no wish for the esteem or the love of his species.'

The obituary had been prepared by Rufus Griswold.

And the damage didn't end there. The appalling Griswold approached Poe's mother-in-law, Maria Clemm, and by some undisclosed arrangement obtained a power of attorney to collect and edit the writings. The first two volumes were in print within three months of Poe's death, with a preface announcing that they were published as an act of charity to benefit Mrs Clemm. She received no money, just six sets of the books. Griswold's *Memoir of the Author*, published in 1850, became for many years the accepted biography. It contained all the old distortions and lies and added more.

Rainer Nolz and 'It Comes By Night' are inventions. Everything about Rufus Griswold has been checked for the truth.

And The Band Played On

Casey would waltz with a strawberry blonde
And the band played on.
He'd glide 'cross the floor with the girl he adored
And the band played on.
But his brain was so loaded it nearly exploded
The poor girl would shake with alarm.
He'd ne'er leave the girl with the strawberry curls
And the band played on.

Grandpa's thin, reedy voice wasn't loud, but we couldn't shut it out, however hard we tried. He stopped singing and smiled. Some of the family tried to smile back. Our dad sighed and rolled his eyes. Gemma, my youngest sister, who was six and would say anything that came into her head, spoke for all of us. 'Grandpa, I'm tired of that song.'

Our mum shushed her and told her she was only tired because it was past her bedtime. That was enough to send Gemma into the other room where the TV was.

I wouldn't say so in front of my family, but everyone was pissed off by the song. Grandpa didn't know. He was going to carry on singing it until he dropped dead. Mum sometimes said he was getting slow on the trigger, which was putting it gently. He hadn't said anything worth hearing for months. The worst of it was that he remembered every word of the song and it was one of those catchy tunes that stayed in your head.

'Who was Casey, anyway?' I asked Mum. I knew I wouldn't get a sensible answer out of Grandpa.

'I've no idea, Josh,' Mum said, 'and I don't really care.'

'Someone ought to know.'

'It's only a song. Does it matter?'

Sarah, my middle sister, said, 'It's creepy.'

'Why?'

'That line about his brain being so loaded it nearly exploded and the poor girl shaking with alarm. At a dance? I don't get it and I don't like it.'

I did some scrolling. 'Granddad's bit is only the chorus.'

'Don't you dare sing it,' Dad said.

So I simply read them the words. 'Matt Casey formed a social club that beat the town for style and hired for a meeting place a hall. When payday came around each week, they'd grease the floor with wax and dance with noise and vigour at the ball . . .' It's like a story.'

'Crap lyrics,' Becky, my oldest sister, said.

Dad frowned at her and said, 'Language.'

'There's no other word for it.' Becky was seventeen and thought she knew everything.

I carried on reading out what was on my phone. 'Each Saturday, you'd see them dressed up in Sunday clothes—'

'Shh. You'll start him off again,' Mum said.

So I took a quick look at the last part and gave them the gist of it in my own words. 'At midnight they all push off for a late meal except Casey, who tells the band to keep playing so he can carry on waltzing with the strawberry blonde. Finally they get fed up and play "Home, Sweet Home" and he thanks them and now the blonde is his wife.'

'Is that it?' Becky said.

'More or less.'

'Sappy stuff.'

'It's old-fashioned,' Mum said to her. 'A bit sentimental, but people were in the old days.'

'What's a strawberry blonde, anyway?' Sarah, who was sixteen, asked.

'Something between a true blonde and a redhead,' Mum said. 'You can get it with modern hair colouring, but it must have been rare when the song was written.'

'1895,' I told them, thanks to Wikipedia.

'What colour was our grandma's hair?' Sarah asked.

'That's got nothing to do with it.'

'I've never seen a photo of her.'

'That's enough,' Dad said. 'Change the subject.' He never spoke about his parents and he didn't encourage us to ask. We didn't even know we had grandparents until Grandpa turned up at our house one afternoon when I was twelve and off school getting over chickenpox. I was the one who went to the door. This shabby old guy with no teeth was carrying a bag Mum called a holdall and I thought he was selling stuff at the door. He was wearing a thick overcoat on a belting hot day in June. He asked if my parents were in and I shouted for Mum and waited. She came out from the kitchen and he grinned at her and said, 'You must be Hazel. I'm Richard's father.'

Richard is my dad's name. Mum went white. She told me to get upstairs to my room. I sat at the top of the stairs and heard her say in a strange, strained voice, 'You'd better come in.' She took him through to the back. Going by the noise the cups and saucers made, she was making him tea, using the tea service she only ever got out for visitors. Normally she drank from a mug with *Best Mum in the World* written on it. I couldn't hear what was said because she had

184

shut the kitchen door. I was stuck in my room for the rest of the day and when my sisters came home they got sent upstairs as well. Dad got in as usual about six and we all stood on the landing and listened. There was some shouting, but we couldn't work out what was going on.

After about two hours, Mum came upstairs and told Sarah she would have to move out of her room and sleep on the spare bed in Gemma's room. Sarah kicked up a fuss, thinking it was for one night only. She didn't know it was permanent. We were told the old bloke was our grandpa – Dad's father – and he would be using Sarah's room from now on. Luckily for me, it wasn't my room he was given. I'm the boy in the family and not supposed to share with girls.

It was Becky who found out the truth from Mum. Grandpa had been living in a place called Wormwood Scrubs for nearly twenty years.

A prison.

Bit by bit, Becky found out more. She knew she wouldn't get anything out of Grandpa or Dad, but she got to work on Mum. She wasn't supposed to tell us what she found out, but of course she did. What's the point of knowing a secret if you can't have the pleasure of breaking it to your kid sisters and brother? She wanted to see our scared faces and, most of all, mine.

I got the shakes when I first heard.

Our grandpa was a murderer. Our own flesh and blood.

Once you've done a murder, that's it. You can't change who you are by doing time in prison. You're still a murderer when you come out. You stay a murderer for the rest of your life.

He didn't look like a murderer, not to my way of thinking. He was old and ordinary, thin, toothless, a bit pathetic.

He had shot a man, a well-known gangster, and buried the body on Oxshott Common. He'd been sent to prison for life but they'd let him out when they decided he was no danger to anyone else.

How could they know he wasn't dangerous?

Now I knew what he'd done, he didn't seem harmless at all. I tried not to show it, but I was so spooked I wished it was me who was sharing Gemma's room. I didn't like being alone at night any more. I lay awake listening for my bedroom door to open. Sometimes I heard him go to the bathroom humming his song about the strawberry blonde. Like I said, he was confused and he could easily have opened my door and climbed into my bed. As for that song, it was my head that was so loaded it nearly exploded.

Part of me wanted to know more about the murder and part of me didn't. My sisters seemed to lose interest, or else they decided to shut out the horror. I asked Becky if she'd heard anything else and she told me to get a life. I sensed that even if she knew anything she wouldn't tell. She'd had the pleasure of seeing me scared witless and she couldn't top that. I was on my own.

I wasn't going to ask Mum. I could see how uncomfortable she was. She never called Grandpa 'Dad'. She called him Nick, like he wasn't family.

One evening we were watching an old black and white film on TV, Grandpa dozing in the best armchair, the rest of us following the story, which was called *Strangers on a Train*. Dad said it was a Hitchcock and they were always good. The baddie was a character called Bruno. I won't bore you with the story. Quite early, there's a scene in a fairground with a young woman called Miriam enjoying a ride on a merry-go-round with two boyfriends. Suddenly they all start singing the words to the music and you see

Bruno sitting on one of the wooden horses near them joining in.

I heard the tune first and thought it was familiar and when they sang the words I could have kicked myself. Of course I knew what it was.

'And The Band Played On'.

Dad frowned and looked across at Grandpa, who was still asleep. My sister Sarah started giggling and so did the others until Mum put her finger to her lips. Everyone was relieved when Grandpa slept right through the scene.

What none of us realised was that Grandpa's song was a theme that kept coming back when the tension was ramped up. Bruno strangles Miriam, and guess what you hear on the soundtrack? Mum grabbed the remote and turned the sound down because Grandpa was stirring.

'Do we have to watch this?' she asked.

'I want to know what happens,' Becky said. 'I'm enjoying this. It's cool.'

Dad didn't say anything and Grandpa settled down again, so we stayed watching.

And then – would you believe it? – there was another scene on the merry-go-round and the music was playing again. Same tune, Grandpa's song. Guy, the goodie, chases Bruno through the amusement park towards the turning carousel. A cop takes a shot at Bruno but misses and hits the guy in charge of the ride. Guy and Bruno jump on the ride and get into a wrestling match between the moving horses. The suspense gets worse because the mechanism is out of control and the whole thing turns faster and faster. The music gets quicker and louder, too, insanely quick. A kid is almost flung off and Guy breaks off the fist-fight and saves him. On the fairground an old toothless bloke looking awfully like Grandpa says, 'I can handle it,' and squirms under the wildly spinning base, worming his way on his stomach towards the controls in the middle. When he gets there and slams on the brake, the whole merry-go-round comes off its moorings in a screaming, smoking wreck.

We were so caught up in the drama that we'd forgotten about Grandpa. He jerked into life and shouted like he'd been shot.

Mum grabbed the remote and switched to mute. 'It's all right, Nick. You were having a bad dream.'

Dad said, 'I think he's pooed his pants.'

'Ooh, yes,' Gemma said, pinching her nose.

We never saw the end of that film.

Not long after that, I started sleepwalking. One night I woke up standing at the top of the stairs without any memory of how I got there. Another time, my sister Sarah heard the floorboards creak outside her room and screamed. Maybe she thought it was Grandpa coming to murder her. It wasn't. It was me on another sleepwalk. Her screaming woke me up. It woke everyone up except Grandpa.

With all this going on, my schoolwork suffered. I wasn't paying attention and I was getting into fights. Up to that time I'd always had good reports and got on well with the other kids. The Head decided I needed to see a shrink. This Mrs Bailey asked me loads of questions about what was going on in my life and at home. She invited Mum and Dad to meet her later, just the two of them.

I don't know who was more embarrassed when Dad spoke to me the next day. I thought he was going to talk about puberty and stuff which the shrink had brought up. I didn't need telling about sex – least of all from my own father. But he was on a different tack altogether.

'I've never said much to you about my childhood, Josh,' he said. 'It wasn't a good time and I prefer to block it out, but I can tell you're going through some kind of crisis yourself – the sleepwalking and the troubles at school – and Mrs Bailey thinks I should be more open with you than I have. Did you know I was fostered as a child?'

I shook my head.

'This concerns Grandpa as well,' he said. 'He wasn't much older than you when I was born. Fifteen, to be precise. He got a girl of the same age into trouble, as they used to say. Know what I'm talking about?'

I nodded.

'They were only schoolkids, too young to marry. Because of their religion, her parents insisted she had the baby, which was me. So I'm illegitimate.' He paused. 'There's another word for it, an ugly word.'

I knew what it was, but I wasn't going to say so, not to my dad.

He started again. 'My birth mother – I suppose we can call her your grandma – didn't want any more to do with me. She'd done what her parents expected and given birth to me and that was it. Being a baby, I didn't know anything about it until later. I had to be fostered. I was with several different families while I was growing up, some good and some not so good. I didn't know it at the time, but Grandpa felt responsible and took an interest in where I was and who I was fostered with. As I got older, he sent me small amounts of money sometimes and postcards from places overseas, like Aden and Malta. After the scandal of the pregnancy, he'd left school and joined the Air Force as a boy entrant. He did about twenty years in the RAF and got to be a flight sergeant and had several postings abroad.'

Dad had stopped. I was taking it in, understanding so much more now about my father's silences whenever anyone mentioned the past. And his need for a settled family life.

189

But it wasn't helping me much. My head was still overloaded. 'How did he get to be in prison?'

'You know about that?' Dad said, sounding relieved that he didn't have to break it to me.

'Not much,' I said. 'He killed someone, didn't he?'

'An evil man, a well-known gangster called Fred Odell who almost certainly killed several people himself or ordered his gang members to kill them. Nobody shed any tears over Odell's death, but someone had to be brought to justice for it and that was Grandpa.'

'Why?' I said. 'How come he shot this gangster?'

'It was while he was stationed at RAF Uxbridge. This was before you were born, before your older sisters were born. He was in his mid-thirties by then and he'd not been out with a woman since his schooldays. Some of his Air Force mates insisted he went into London with them for an evening out. He had the bad luck to meet Odell's daughter Annie in a dance hall. She was not much over twenty, a natural blonde and pretty. That damned tune was playing, the one he's always singing. They got on well and met a few times more and he was in love with her. He found out too late who her father was. Odell disapproved. He wasn't allowing his daughter to go out with a man fifteen years older than she was, so he warned him off, but your grandfather wasn't having it. He took to carrying a gun for self-defence supposedly, but one evening he went back to Odell's house at Oxshott with Annie, escorting her home, as blokes did in those days, and her father caught them snogging in the front porch. There was a row and threats and Dad took out the gun and fired five shots into Odell's chest. Then he drove out to Oxshott with the body and buried it along with the murder weapon. Unluckily for him, Oxshott Common isn't the quiet spot he thought it was. He was seen by two separate witnesses walking their dogs. One got the number of his car and phoned the police.'

'Was he in uniform?'

'I don't think so, but they found him easily enough. He didn't go into hiding, or anything. He was arrested the next night coming out of a London dance hall, the Hammersmith Palais, with Annie Odell, the girl he loved. The police had tipped off the press and it was front-page news, a picture of him with Annie at his side, eyes wide with fright. That's how I found out. He confessed and pleaded guilty when it came to court. He didn't have much choice. He couldn't pretend it had been accidental or anything. He'd buried the body and the gun. If you murder someone, you get a life sentence, no argument. He did almost twenty years in prison.'

'Did you visit him there?'

'No. I couldn't face it. There was no contact. I scarcely knew him anyway. What could I have said?' Dad stopped speaking for a moment and ran his hand through his hair. 'I suppose I should have manned up and gone there. He'd made efforts to keep in touch with me when I was growing up. I didn't respond, didn't visit him at this low point in his life and now I regret it. What happened after he came out on parole isn't very clear because his mind has gone, as you know. He was sleeping rough on the streets for at least a couple of years before he turned up here out of the blue. There was drinking and drugs, I'm sure. The heroin rots your teeth. Everything he owned in the world was in one bag and most of it was so filthy it had to be binned. None of it was personal except for one small photo he'd kept. You know the rest.'

'What was the photo?'

'It was of Annie Odell, the girl. Has any of this helped?'

I nodded. 'I think so. There is one question: did you ever get in touch with your mother?'

Dad sighed. 'I tried. I managed to trace her. She'd married, divorced and married again to quite a successful man, an architect. I wrote to her. But she refused point blank to meet me. She wrote one sentence back saying that her past was a closed book. The only link I have with my start in life is Grandpa. I'll see that his last years are comfortable.'

'Thanks for telling me, Dad. Appreciate it.'

I wasn't scared of Grandpa any more. I almost respected him. He'd shot a famous gangster and taken his punishment. He'd earned the right to walk free again.

The sleepwalking stopped and my schoolwork improved. I wished I could have talked to him about the experiences he'd had, but he was off his rocker. I bought a small gilt frame for the precious photo of Annie, the gangster's daughter, his strawberry blonde. I think he appreciated that. He watched me fitting it into the frame and it stayed beside his bed for the rest of his life.

He lived two more years and died peacefully.

Dad made the funeral arrangements, just a short service at the crematorium. We didn't expect anyone to be there except our family, but Grandpa sprang one more surprise. Almost every seat was taken. One of the papers had got the story and printed a column headed FRED ODELL'S KILLER PASSES. Three of his old RAF buddies came. Five or six of our neighbours. Two ex-prisoners and their wives. A retired prison officer. A couple who ran a refuge for homeless people. Someone from the Alzheimer's Society.

I found myself sitting next to a silver-haired woman in a dark blue coat with silver frogging and black gloves. She was wearing expensive perfume. Her face was faintly familiar. She said, 'Are you family?'

'His grandson, Josh.'

'And are those your parents at the front?'

'Yes.'

'After the service, there's something I'd like to say to you. Would you mind? I won't be going back to your house for the tea and sandwiches.'

'If you like.'

It wasn't a religious service. There was a humanist guy who took us through the ceremony and admitted he hadn't known Grandpa personally. We had a couple of readings and some taped music, including 'Flying Home', played by the RAF big band Shades of Blue, and the 'RAF March Past'. Dad gave a short address and skilfully managed to say nothing about the two worst episodes of Grandpa's life and finished by inviting everyone back to the house. Then we had the bit called the committal when the curtains closed around the coffin. Do I need to tell you which music was played for his send-off? It was only the tune, but I was thinking the words in my head, imagining that last dance he had with Annie at the Hammersmith Palais before he was arrested. Did they dance to their tune? Was that why he never forgot it? Those troubling words – 'His brain was so loaded it nearly exploded and the poor girl would shake with alarm' – drew tears from my eyes.

There was plenty of handshaking outside the crematorium and we looked at the wreaths people had sent. The whole thing was so much more touching than I expected. All these people cared enough about Grandpa to have come to his funeral ignoring the huge mistakes he'd made.

I'd forgotten the woman who had spoken to me, but she appeared at my side and thanked me for waiting. She drew me aside as if she didn't want anyone overhearing her.

She said, 'Your parents were good to him, taking him in and making his last years peaceful.'

I agreed with her.

But that wasn't all she wanted to say. 'There's something I'd like your father to know, but I won't be speaking to him myself. He doesn't know me. Would you mind telling him that the headline in the paper was cruel and got it wrong? Nick was never a killer.'

'No?' I'd heard what she said and wasn't over-impressed. I thought she meant he wasn't a professional gunman. I guessed she'd been moved by the service, as I had. There were marks under her eyes where the liner had moistened and run.

'He didn't fire the fatal shots, Josh. He wasn't there.'

'What?' I listened up, startled.

'Fred Odell was a monster. He abused his own daughter for years, touched her intimately when she was only a child and forced himself on her before she even reached her teens. When Nick started seeing her, Fred was jealous. He said if she didn't break up with Nick, he'd have him killed. She was shattered. It was the last straw. She shot her own father with one of his guns. Then she phoned Nick in a panic and told him what she'd done. He came to the house and calmed her down and took the body away and buried it. That's how he was caught and mistakenly accused of the murder.'

'You're talking about Annie?' I was so dumbstruck I repeated what she'd just told me in case I hadn't heard right. 'Annie killed her own father?'

'And your grandfather served a life sentence to protect her. Not that she showed much appreciation. She married someone else, stupid woman. There's gratitude!' She rested her black-gloved palm lightly against my chest. 'Promise me you'll tell your father what I said.'

'Yes – but who are you? He's sure to ask.'

'He doesn't need to know.'

Before she turned away, I recognised her. The face was older and more lined than the face in the photo I'd framed and, like I said, her hair was white, but I'm certain she was my grandpa's strawberry blonde.

A Three Pie Problem

Peter Diamond wasn't Scrooge, but Christmas could be a pain. For one thing, he missed Steph more than ever at this time of year. For another, people took pity on him and invited him to stay. His in-laws, Angela and Mervyn, asked him each year to go up to Liverpool for 'a proper family party' and he was forced to think of excuses. He'd tried saying Raffles, his cat, needed looking after, but they didn't regard that as a reason. 'Put him in a basket and bring him with you,' Angela had said. 'We'll fuss him up, same as you.' Raffles, like Diamond, wouldn't relish being fussed up.

This year, Angela had a different strategy. 'You know what I'm going to say,' she told him on the phone in about the second week of December, 'and I know what you're going to say, so forget it. If you won't come to the party, the party is coming to you. It's ages since we visited Bath and we do so enjoy looking round. Don't panic, Peter. I'll do all the cooking and Mervyn will organise the games.'

Games? He almost dropped the phone.

'It's fixed, then. We're arriving the Saturday before and we'll stay until the New Year.'

'I could be on duty,' was all he could think to say.

'Come on, you're the boss, aren't you?'

'A major incident.'

'At Christmas?'

This Christmas, please, he thought.

There was no stopping Angela. They arrived with their hatchback stuffed with suitcases and all the festive para-phernalia, including a plastic tree. Raffles took refuge in the airing cupboard.

For reasons nobody cared to go into, Angela thought the police in general were beneath contempt and her late sister Stephanie – she always used the full name – should never have hitched herself to one of them, let alone an overweight slob like Diamond. His rank did not impress her. His skills as a detective were disregarded. He hadn't papered the walls since they'd bought the house. Hadn't weeded the garden, washed the windows, mended the Hoover, removed the tidemark from the bath. He pampered the cat and cheated at cards. All this was pointed out to him on the first evening.

So the call from Bath Police Station on Christmas Eve came as glad tidings, even great joy, to the beleaguered head of CID.

'Sorry to disturb your Christmas break, sir.'

'No trouble at all. Do you need me there?'

'It could be nothing at all.'

'But on the other hand . . .' he said with a rising note.

'There's an outside chance it was murder.'

'Say no more. Duty calls.'

Angela rolled her eyes upwards and Mervyn looked aghast at the prospect of being alone with his wife. 'Could I come with you, as a sort of observer?'

'No,' Diamond said. 'Too horrible for a man of your good taste. Why don't you redecorate the Christmas tree? Angela thinks my effort was crap.'

He was gone.

*

Bath police had been alerted to the death of one Fletcher Merriman, aged seventy-eight, the senior partner in Merriman & Palmer, a small firm of accountants with an office above a shop in Gay Street. Old Mr Merriman had died two weeks ago in the Royal United Hospital of heart failure.

'There are suspicious elements,' Georgina Dallymore, the Assistant Chief Constable, told Diamond. 'I wouldn't put it any higher than that. He wasn't admitted with a heart condition. They treated him for gastroenteritis following an office party. He was in considerable pain, I gather. The heart attack came later.'

'Poison?'

'The post-mortem was inconclusive. They tested for the known poisons and found nothing of note. He was on medication for a heart problem anyway, so there were traces of various substances in the stomach contents, but nothing lethal.'

'So what's the problem?'

'I hope we're not wasting your time, Peter. It's just that the circumstances could have come straight out of Agatha Christie. He wasn't a nice old man at all. In fact, he was appalling. Everyone at the party had reasons to knock him off.'

'Everyone? How many is that?'

'Three.'

'Small party.'

'All the easier to question them. It could wait until after Christmas, but you left the message saying you wanted to be notified if any serious crimes were reported.'

'Absolutely, ma'am. Maybe if I spend Christmas on this one I can take days off in lieu at a later date.'

'You mean when the in-laws have left?'

He grinned.

*

The surviving partner, Maurice Palmer, had agreed to be in attendance at the office in Gay Street, but it was a woman's voice on the entryphone. Diamond gave his name and entered.

'Sylvie Smith, junior accountant,' she said. She was smart, in her twenties, with dark, intelligent eyes. 'He's expecting you.'

'And did he ask you to come in on Christmas Eve just to show me in?'

'It's a chance to tidy my desk.'

'Don't go away, then. I'd like to speak to you later.'

Palmer appeared from an inner room and introduced himself. Fiftyish, in the obligatory dark suit and striped tie, he looked well capable of tangling with tax inspectors. Or police inspectors.

'Decent of you to see me,' Diamond said. 'I hope this hasn't messed up your holiday plans.'

'Not as yet,' Palmer said, 'but I hope we can clear up any questions now. I'm booked on a flight to Tenerife tonight.'

'Is that a tax haven?'

'If it is, it doesn't come into my plans. I'm going for some winter sunshine, I hope.'

Diamond glanced about him at the filing cabinets and computers. 'So is this the room where the party was held?'

'No, in point of fact. This is the office where the ladies sit,' Palmer said. 'The party was in here.' He swung open the door he'd come through. 'My room.'

Diamond stepped in. 'Nice.'

It was oak-panelled, with a high corniced ceiling and a marble fireplace with gas flames that looked realistic. Leather armchairs, an expensive-looking carpet and a rosewood table with matching chairs testified to the status of the firm. 'Fletcher Merriman used it for many years before he retired from the practice in 2001.' He went to the doorway and said to Sylvie Smith, 'Why don't you finish off what you were doing?' Then he closed the door.

'So old Mr Merriman came in just for the party?'

'His annual visit. It became a tradition. Every December he'd zoom in – you know he used a wheelchair? – with all the seasonal fare, three bottles of sherry, sweet, medium and dry, a dozen mince pies and a huge branch of mistletoe, and tell us it was party time. He loved surprising people.'

'Surprising them? You just said it was a tradition.'

'We had no idea which day he would arrive.'

'From what I hear, he was better at springing surprises than receiving them.'

'His heart condition, you mean? Yes, he had to be careful. He'd had two coronaries since retiring. He withdrew entirely from the business. I've been running it for years.'

'But he remained the senior partner?'

'Sleeping partner is a better description, but "partner" is the operative word.'

'So he still had a slice of the profits?'

'Fifty-fifty. We're still Merriman and Palmer, a respected name in Bath. He deserved some reward for all the years he put in.'

'And will his family get a share of any future profits?'

'There is no family.'

'So it all comes to you now?'

Maurice Palmer turned deep pink above his striped collar. 'Unless I take on another partner.'

Diamond glanced around the room. 'Let's talk about the party. What kind of bash was it?'

'I wouldn't call it that.'

'Did you finish the sherry between you?'

'Not entirely.'

'Three bottles between four of you would have been good going. Were they all freshly bought?'

'Yes, indeed, from the wine merchant in Broad Street.'

'Who opened them?'

'Fletcher – and he did the pouring as well. He liked us to be aware that he was the provider.'

'You didn't keep the bottles, by any chance?'

'The dead men?' He shook his head. 'They went out the same evening with the rest of what was left.'

'And was the mistletoe put to good use?'

Palmer glanced towards the door and lowered his voice. 'You must understand that my esteemed ex-colleague belonged to a generation before PC came in, when a little of what you fancy was no offence.'

'He was an old goat?'

'I wouldn't say that.'

'Would the women?'

'I'm sure they wouldn't be so disrespectful.'

'But you didn't have to be kissed under the mistletoe.'

'Hardly.'

'I'll speak presently to someone who did. Tell me, Mr Palmer, did you try one of the mince pies?'

'I had three. And very good they were. He always bought them from Maisie's, the best baker in town. They were still warm.'

'No ill-effects?'

'None whatsoever.'

'And how did the party end?'

'With Fletcher complaining of stomach pains and saying he needed to get home. We called a taxi. Next morning I heard he was in hospital and some hours later he had a fatal heart attack. Sad, but not unexpected, allowing for his medical history.'

'You didn't shed any tears, then?'

'He was not an easy person to have as a business partner. But that doesn't mean I wished him to suffer.'

Diamond had heard all he needed at this stage, so he asked Palmer to send in Sylvie Smith.

'In here?' Palmer said in surprise.

'The scene of the crime – if, indeed, there was a crime. Where better?'

'You wish to interview her in my presence?'

'No, I suggest you wait outside and see if her double-entries are up to the mark.'

Sylvie Smith looked nervous, and more so when Diamond waved her towards her boss's high-back executive chair. 'Give yourself a treat. One day all this could be yours.'

'I doubt that very much.' She perched uneasily on the edge of the chair.

Diamond preferred to stand. 'So how many of old Mr Merriman's surprise parties have you attended?'

'This was the second. I joined the firm after leaving college, towards the end of last year.'

'The first time it happened you must have wondered what was up when he rolled through in his wheelchair primed with mistletoe and sherry. Did he insist on a kiss?'

Her mouth tightened into a thin line. 'He called it his Christmas cuddle. I'd hardly ever met him.'

'He took it as his right?'

'It makes me sick to think of it.'

'If you'd complained, your job would have been at risk – and there aren't many openings in Bath for freshly qualified accountants.'

She rolled her eyes upwards. 'That's for sure.'

'Did you know this was an annual ordeal?'

'Donna said something about it, but I thought she was winding me up.'

'Donna is the other woman who works here?'

She nodded. 'She's been here six years. She'll be chartered next year if all goes well.'

'But she isn't in today?'

'Decided to take some of her annual leave.'

'Gone away for Christmas?'

'I don't think so. She has a flat in Walcot Street.'

'Lives alone, then?'

'Yes.'

'What age is Donna? All right. Indiscreet question. Is she under forty?'

'I expect so.'

Diamond looked up at the bare ceiling. There was no central light. There were wall-lights representing candles. 'I'm trying to picture this party. Presumably the old boy sat in his wheelchair under some mistletoe. I can't see where it was attached.'

'We had to tie string across the room, from one of the wall-lights to the one opposite. Then the mistletoe was hung over the string just above where you're standing.'

'Got it. When you say "we" . . . ?'

'Me and Donna.'

'I'm getting the picture now. So whoever attached the mistletoe to the string must have stood on this table beside me to do it. Who was that?'

Sylvie rolled her eyes again. 'He insisted it was me. Said I had the longer reach.' She hesitated and turned as red as a Christmas card robin. 'I happened to be wearing a short skirt.'

'The picture is even clearer. Where was Mr Palmer while you were on the table?'

'Mr Palmer? Some way off, by the fireplace, I think. It was Mr Merriman who had the ringside view, almost underneath me in his wheelchair.'

'Did he hand you the mistletoe himself?'

'No. He was far too busy looking up my skirt. It was Donna who helped me.'

'So when he'd got over that excitement, and the mistletoe was in place, the party got under way. Drinks all round, no doubt?'

She nodded. 'I needed one.'

'The sherry was where?'

'On the table.'

'And the glasses?'

'Mr Palmer keeps some in his drawer.'

'As every boss should. Did Mr Palmer pour?'

'Mr Merriman did.'

'Did you notice if the sherry was new, the bottles sealed at the neck?'

'I'm certain of it. He had to borrow scissors.'

'You know why I'm interested? Something upset his stomach and if the sherry was new I'm thinking it must have been the mince pies.'

She shook her head. 'They were fresh, too, fresh as anything, in boxes from Maisie's. Actually they were delicious.'

Diamond felt his stomach juices stirring. 'So you had one?'

'Three, at least. We all did.'

'And could anyone have slipped the old man a mince pie from anywhere else?'

'I don't see how. We were all in here together.'

'Making merry?'

'Making a stab at it.'

'I expect a few glasses of sherry helped.'

She took a sharp breath. 'Not when he grabbed me and forced me onto his lap for the kiss under the mistletoe. That was disgusting. His bony old hands were everywhere.' She shuddered. 'It went on for over a minute. I could have strangled him.'

'But you didn't. Did Donna get the same treatment?'

'Not quite the same. She was wearing trousers.'

'And did you also get a kiss from Mr Palmer?'

'That was no problem. Just a peck on the cheek. He doesn't fancy me, anyway.'

Diamond thanked her and returned to the outer office. 'I'll need the address of your other member of staff,' he told Palmer.

'Donna? There's nothing she can add.'

'How do you know? Maybe she saw something you and Miss Smith missed.'

'You're barking up the wrong tree, superintendent. Nothing untoward happened here. Fletcher died from natural causes.'

'I'll let you know if I agree – after I've heard from Donna.'

First, he returned to the police station and asked his eager-to-please detective sergeant, Ingeborg, to get on the internet. Encouraged by her findings, he called the forensic lab that had analysed the post-mortem samples and suggested a second specific examination of the stomach contents. He was told the chances were not high of finding anything they hadn't already reported and anyway it would have to wait until after the holiday.

'Typical,' he said to Ingeborg. 'We're working. Why can't they?'

The third surviving accountant lived in a classy flat. Donna was a classy lady with a sexy drawl to her voice. Not at all unfazed by Diamond's arrival, she offered him coffee. While she was in the kitchen he used 1471 to check the last call she'd received. It was timed just after he'd left the Merriman and Palmer office – and that had been the source of the call.

It was no crime, of course, to tip her off. Any colleague would do the same.

'Here's my problem,' he told her over the coffee. 'Old Fletcher Merriman was taken home ill at the end of the party. The pains got worse and he ended up in hospital. I've seen the medical notes. Abdominal pain, blurred vision, nausea and low pulse. We're bound to check if he was poisoned, triggering the heart attack that killed him.'

'*Poisoned?*' she said with a disbelieving smile.

He nodded. 'Yet we aren't sure how the poison could have been administered, allowing that he brought his own food and drink to the party and everything was fresh. Poured the drinks himself, in full view of everyone.'

'Did they find poison inside him?' she asked as calmly as if she were enquiring about last night's rain.

'Nothing obvious, but the traditional poisons like arsenic and strychnine are so easy to detect these days that they aren't often used. I've suggested something else and they're testing for it.'

She didn't ask the obvious question. Instead, she said, 'Why would anyone want to kill a retired accountant?'

'This is pure speculation and shouldn't be repeated,' he said. 'Maurice Palmer stood to gain financially. The old man's death leaves him in sole charge of the firm.'

'Surely you don't suspect Maurice.'

Diamond didn't comment. 'And Sylvie Smith told me

she felt like strangling him after the groping she had to endure.

'She's young. She's got a lot to learn about men.'

'His behaviour didn't bother you, then?'

'I've been six years with the firm. I know what to expect from Fletcher the lecher.' She ran her fingertip thoughtfully around the rim of her cup. 'Here's a theory for you, Mr Diamond. Is it possible during a kiss to pass a capsule into someone's mouth?'

'I expect so. Nasty.'

'Something like digitalis that is taken by heart patients but dangerous in an overdose?'

'Ingenious. What gave you this idea?'

She shrugged. 'He insisted on a full mouth-to-mouth kiss. In the absence of any other theory . . .'

'Ah, but I do have another theory. A better one than yours. The mince pies killed him.'

She shook her head. 'We all had mince pies. Rich food, I'll grant you, but the rest of us felt no ill-effects. There was nothing wrong with them.'

'Something was wrong with at least one of the pies Fletcher Merriman ate.'

'I can't see how.'

'It was laced with poison. Bear with me a moment.' He took a notebook from his pocket. 'Tyramine and beta-phenylethylamine.'

'Never heard of them.'

'But you've heard of mistletoe. These are the toxic substances contained in mistletoe berries. The symptoms are similar to enteritis, but with blurred vision and a marked lowering of the pulse. In a tired old body susceptible to heart problems, as Merriman's was, the poison induced a failure of the cardiovascular system. Killed him.'

'But the mistletoe was above our heads.'

'Not when he arrived. You and Sylvie fixed it up.'

'Excuse me. Sylvie tied it to the string.'

'And while she was getting all the men's attention in her short skirt, you were stripping a number of the white berries from the branch before you handed it up to her.'

She frowned. 'Untrue.'

'You waited for the next opportunity, and it came when the old man was kissing Sylvie. You lifted the lid of the mince pie on his plate and tucked the mistletoe berries under it. Lethal and almost undetectable.'

She was as silent as a child waiting for Santa.

He stood up. 'Might I look into your bedroom?'

'Whatever for?'

'To test my theory. This door?'

She was in no position to stop him.

'So you're planning a holiday?' There was a packed suitcase on the bed.

'People do.'

He stepped closer and looked at the label. 'Tenerife. Shame. You're not going any further than Manvers Street nick. I'm arresting you on suspicion of the murder of Fletcher Merriman.'

'So she's singing?' Georgina, the Assistant Chief Constable, said.

'She sang. Better than the Bath Abbey choir.'

'You sound positively festive, Peter.'

'It is Christmas Eve, ma'am.'

'What was her motive?'

'She's a cool lady. Worked hard at her accountancy, filling in the columns, promising herself a promotion when she's chartered next year. She saw the young woman, Sylvie, bright and ambitious, and decided she wasn't willing to wait and be overtaken. Cosied up to Maurice Palmer and promised to spend Christmas in Tenerife with him. She reckoned she could persuade him to take her on as his new partner, but first old Fletcher Merriman had to be sent to the great audit in the sky. She knew his annual ritual, so she could plan how to do it. A mince pie contains a rich mix. After digestion is anyone likely to detect some mistletoe berries in it?'

'Did they?'

'Not yet, but she thinks it's a done deal, and she's confessed.'

'Murder by mince pie. Who would have thought of it?'

'An ambitious woman with time running out.'

'You don't think Palmer had a hand in it?'

'No, ma'am. He's not that brave, or bright.'

'Case solved, then, and all in one day. You can get back to your family and enjoy the rest of Christmas.'

Diamond took a sharp, audible breath. 'Not for some time. There's all the paperwork.'

'Leave it for later.'

'No, I don't trust my memory. I'll be here for a while yet. I know where to put my hands on a beer or two. And the odd mince pie.'

'Not too odd, Peter. We need you.'

Remaindered

Agatha Christie did it. The evidence was plain to see, but no one *did* see for more than a day. Robert Ripple's corpse was cold on the bookshop floor. It must have been there right through Monday, the day Precious Finds was always closed. Poor guy, he was discovered early Tuesday in the section he called his office, in a position no bookseller would choose for his last transaction, face down, feet down and butt up, jack-knifed over a carton of books. The side of the carton had burst and some of the books had slipped out and fanned across the carpet, every one a Christie.

Late Sunday, Robert had taken delivery of the Christie novels. They came from a house on Park Avenue, one of the best streets in Poketown, Pennsylvania, and they had a curious history. They were brought over from England before World War II by an immigrant whose first job had been as a London publisher's rep. He'd kept the books as a souvenir of those tough times trying to interest bookshop-owners in whodunnits when the only novels most British people wanted to read were by Jeffery Farnol and Ethel M. Dell. After his arrival in America, he'd switched to selling Model T Fords instead and made a sizeable fortune. The Christies had been forgotten about, stored in the attic of the fine old weatherboard house he'd bought after making his first million. And now his playboy grandson planned to demolish the building and replace it with a space-age dwelling of glass and concrete. He'd cleared the attic and wanted to dispose of the books. Robert had taken one look and offered five hundred dollars for the lot. The grandson had pocketed the cheque and gone away pleased with the deal.

Hardly believing his luck, Robert must have waited until the shop closed and then stooped to lift the carton on to his desk and check the contents more carefully.

Mistake.

Hardback books are heavy. He had spent years humping books around, but he was sixty-eight, with a heart condition, and this was one box too many.

Against all the odds, Robert had stayed in business for twenty-six years, dealing in used books of all kinds. But Precious Finds had become more than a bookshop. It was a haven of civilised life in Poketown, a centre for all manner of small-town activities – readers' groups, a writers' circle, coffee mornings and musical evenings. Some of the locals came and went without even glancing at the bookshelves. A few bought books or donated them out of loyalty, but it was difficult to understand how Robert had kept going so long. It was said he did most of his business at the beginning through postal sales and later on the internet.

Robert's sudden death created problems all round. Tanya Tripp, the bookshop assistant, who had been in the job only a few months, had the nasty shock of discovering the body and found herself burdened with dealing with the emergency, first calling a doctor, then an undertaker and then attempting to contact Robert's family. Without success. Not a Ripple remained. He had never married. It became obvious that his loyal customers would have to arrange the funeral. Someone had to take charge, and this was Tanya.

Fortunately she was a capable young woman, as sturdy in character as she was in figure. She didn't complain about the extra workload, even to herself.

Although all agreed that the effort of lifting the Agatha Christies had been the cause of death, an autopsy was inescapable. The medical examiner found severe bruising to the head and this was attributed to the fall. A coronary had killed Robert.

Simple.

The complications came after. Tanya was unable to find a will. She searched the office where Robert had died, as well as his apartment upstairs, where she had never ventured before. Being the first to enter a dead man's rooms would have spooked the average person. Tanya was above average in confidence and determination. She wasn't spooked. She found Robert's passport, birth certificate and tax returns, but nothing resembling a will. She checked with his bank and they didn't have it.

Meanwhile, one of the richest customers offered to pay for the funeral and the regulars clubbed together to arrange a wake at Precious Finds. The feeling was that Robert would have wished for a spirited send-off.

The back room had long been the venue for meetings. The books in there were not considered valuable. Every second-hand bookshop has to cope with items that are never likely to sell: thrillers that no longer thrill, sci-fi that has been overtaken by real science and romance too coy for modern tastes. The obvious solution is to refuse such books, but sometimes they come in a job lot with things of more potential, such as nineteenth-century magazines containing engravings that can be cut out, mounted and sold as prints. Robert's remedy had been to keep the dross in the back room. The heaviest volumes were at floor level, outdated encyclopaedias, dictionaries and art books. Higher up were the condensed novels and book-club editions of long-forgotten authors. Above them, privately published fiction and poetry. On the top, fat paperbacks turning brown and curling at the edges, whole sets of Michener, Hailey and Clavell.

The saving grace of the back room was that the shelves in the centre were mounted on wheels and could be rolled aside to create a useful space for meetings. A stack of chairs stood in one corner. Robert made no charge, pleased to have people coming right through the shop and possibly pausing to look at the desirable items shelved in the front rooms. So on Tuesdays the bookshop hosted the Poketown history society, Wednesdays the art club, Thursdays the chess players. Something each afternoon and every night except Sundays and Mondays.

And now the back room was to be used for the wake.

The music-appreciation group knew of an Irish fiddler who brought along four friends, and they set about restoring everyone's spirits after the funeral. The place was crowded out. The event spilled over into the other parts of the shop.

It was a bitter-sweet occasion. The music was lively and there was plenty of cheap wine, but there was still anxiety about what would happen after. For the time being the shop had stayed open under Tanya's management. There was no confidence that this could continue.

'It has to be sold,' Tanya said in a break between jigs. 'There's no heir.'

'Who's going to buy a bookstore in these difficult times?' George Digby-Smith asked. He was one of the Friends of England, who met here on occasional Friday nights, allegedly to talk about cricket and cream teas and other English indulgences. Actually, George was more than just a friend of England. He'd been born there sixty years ago. 'Someone will want to throw out all the books and turn the building into apartments.'

'Over my dead body,' Myrtle Rafferty, another of the Friends of England, piped up.

'We don't need another fatality, thank you,' George said.

'We can't sit back and do nothing. We all depend on this place.'

'Get real, people,' one of the Wednesday-morning coffee group said. 'None of us could take the business on, even if we had the funds.'

'Tanya knows about books,' George said at once. 'She'll be out of a job if the store closes. What do you say, Tanya?'

The young woman looked startled. It was only a few months since she had walked in one morning and asked if Robert would take her on as his assistant. In truth, he'd badly needed some help and she'd earned every cent he paid. Softly spoken, almost certainly under thirty, she had been a quiet presence in the shop, putting more order into the displays, but leaving Robert to deal with the customers.

'I couldn't possibly buy it.'

'I'm not suggesting you do. But you could manage it. In fact, you'd do a far better job than old Robert ever did.'

'That's unkind,' Myrtle said.

George turned redder than usual. 'Yes, it was.'

'We are all in debt to Robert,' Myrtle said.

'Rest his soul,' George agreed, raising his glass. 'To Robert, a bookman to the end, gone but not forgotten. In the best sense of the word, remaindered.'

'What's that meant to mean?'

'Passed on, but still out there somewhere.'

'More like boxed and posted,' the man from the coffee club murmured. 'Or pulped.'

Myrtle hadn't heard. She was thinking positively. 'Tanya didn't altogether turn down George's suggestion. She'd want to continue, given the opportunity.'

Tanya was silent.

'When someone dies without leaving a will, what happens?' George asked.

Ivor Ciplinsky, who knew a bit about law and led the history society, said, 'An administrator will have to be appointed and they'll make extensive efforts to trace a relative, however distant.'

'I already tried,' Tanya said. 'There isn't anyone.'

'Cousins, second cousins, second cousins once removed.'

'Nobody.'

Myrtle asked Ivor, 'And if no relative is found?'

'Then the property escheats to the state's coffers.'

'It what?'

'Escheats. A legal term, meaning it reverts to the state by default.'

'What a ghastly sounding word,' George said.

'Ghastly to think about,' Myrtle said. 'Our beloved book-shop grabbed by the bureaucrats.'

'It goes back to feudal law,' Ivor said.

'It should have stayed there,' Myrtle said. 'Escheating. Cheating comes into it, for sure. Cheating decent people out of their innocent pleasures. We can't allow that. Precious Finds is the focus of our community.'

'If you're about to suggest we club together and buy it, don't,' Ivor said. 'Paying for a wake is one thing. You won't get a bunch of customers, however friendly, taking on a business as precarious as this. You can count me out straight away.'

'So speaks the history society,' Myrtle said with a sniff. 'Caving in before the battle even begins. Well, the Friends of England are made of sterner stuff. The English stood firm at Agincourt, a famous battle six hundred years ago, in case you haven't covered it on Tuesday evenings, Ivor. Remember who faced off the Spanish Armada.'

'Not to mention Wellington at Waterloo and Nelson at Trafalgar,' George added.

'Michael Caine,' Edward said. He was the third member of the Friends of England.

There were some puzzled frowns. Then George said, '*Zulu* – the movie. You're thinking of the Battle of Rorke's Drift.'

'The Battle of Britain,' Myrtle finished on a high, triumphant note.

'Who *are* these people?' the coffee club man asked.

It was a good question. Myrtle, George and Edward had been meeting in the back room on occasional Friday nights for longer than anyone could recall. They must have approached Robert at some point and asked if they could have their meetings there. An Anglophile himself, at least as far as books were concerned, Robert wouldn't have turned them away. But nobody else had ever joined the three in their little club. This was because they didn't announce their meetings in advance. If you weren't told which Fridays they met, you couldn't be there, even if you adored England, drank warm beer and ate nothing but roast beef and Yorkshire pudding.

George was the only one of the three with a genuine English connection. You wouldn't have known it from his appearance. He'd come over as a youth in the late sixties, a hippy with flowers in his hair and weed in his backpack, living proof of that song about San Francisco. In middle age he'd given up the flowers, but not the weed. However, he still had the long hair, now silver and worn in a ponytail, and his faded T-shirts and torn jeans remained faintly psychedelic.

Edward, by contrast, dressed the part of the English gent, in blue blazer, white shirt and cravat and nicely ironed trousers. He had a David Niven pencil moustache and dark-tinted crinkly hair with a parting. Only when he spoke would you have guessed he'd been born and raised in the Bronx.

Myrtle, too, was New York born and bred. She coloured her hair and it was currently orange and a mass of loose curls. She had a face and figure she was proud of. Back in the nineties, her good looks had reeled in her second husband, Butch Rafferty, a one-time gangster, who had treated her to diamond necklaces and dinners at the best New York restaurants. Tragically, Butch had been gunned down in 2003 by Gritty Bologna, a rival hood he had made the mistake of linking up with. The widowed Myrtle had quit gangland and moved out here to Pennsylvania. She wasn't destitute. She still lived in some style in a large colonial house at the better end of town. No one could fathom her affiliation to the old country except there was not much doubt that she slept (separately) with George and Edward. She had travelled to England a number of times with each of them. Either they were not jealous of each other or she controlled the relationship with amazing skill.

Little was known of what went on at the Friends of England meetings in the bookshop. Comfortable and cosy as the back room was, it was not furnished for middle-aged sex. Tanya, understandably curious, had questioned Robert closely about how the Friends passed their evenings. He'd said he assumed they spent their time looking at travel brochures and planning their next trip. The meetings did seem to be followed quite soon after by visits to England, always involving Myrtle, usually in combination with one or other of her fellow Friends.

The three were now in a huddle at the far end of the back room, where they always gathered for their meetings and where – appropriately – three out-of-date sets of the *Encyclopaedia Britannica* took up the entire bottom shelf.

'If the shop is . . . what was that word?' Edward said when the music once more calmed down enough for conversation.

'Escheated.'

'If that happens, they'll want a quick sale and we're in deep shit.'

'But there's a precious window of opportunity before it gets to that stage,' George said. 'They have to make completely sure no one has a claim on the estate and that can't be done overnight. We need to get organised. Myrtle was talking about a trip to the Cotswolds before the end of the month. Sorry, my friends, but I think we must cancel.'

'Shucks,' Myrtle said. 'I was counting the days to that trip. You figure we should stay here and do something?'

'We can't do nothing.'

'Do what?' Edward said, and it was clear from his disenchanted tone that it had been his turn to partner Myrtle to England.

George glanced right and left and then lowered his voice. 'I have an idea, a rather bold idea, but this is not the time or the place.'

'Shall we call a meeting?' Myrtle said, eager to hear more. 'How about this Friday? We don't need Robert's permission any more.'

'In courtesy, we ought to mention it to Tanya,' George said.

'Tell her your idea?'

'Heavens, no. Just say we need a meeting, so she can book us in.'

On Friday they had the back room to themselves. Tanya was in the office at the front end of the shop and there were no browsers. The footfall in Precious Finds had decreased markedly after Robert's death had been written up in the *Poketown Observer*.

Even Edward, still sore that his trip to the Cotswolds with Myrtle had been cancelled, had to agree that George's plan was smart.

'It's not just smart, it's genius,' Myrtle said. 'We can save the shop and carry on as before.' She leaned back in her chair and caressed the spines of the *Encyclopaedia Britannica*. 'The Friends of England can go on indefinitely.'

'For as long as the funds hold up, at any rate,' George said. 'We've been sensible up to now. Let's keep it like that.'

George had to be respected. His wise, restraining advice had allowed the three of them to enjoy a comfortable retirement that might yet continue. If the truth were told, the Friends of England Society was a mutual benefit club. George and Edward had once been members of Butch Rafferty's gang and they were still living off the spoils of a security-van heist.

'My dear old Butch would love this plan,' Myrtle said with a faraway look. 'I can hear him saying, "Simple ain't always obvious".'

'If Butch hadn't messed up, we wouldn't be here,' Edward said, still moody. 'We'd be back in New York City, living in style.'

'Don't kid yourself,' Myrtle said. 'You'd have gambled away your share inside six months. New York maybe, but by now you'd be sleeping rough in Central Park. I know you better than you know yourself, Edward.'

'There are worse places than Central Park,' he said. 'I've had it up to here with Poketown, Pennsylvania. We should have got outta here years ago.'

'Oh, come on.'

'It's only because we live in Pennsylvania that my plan will work,' George said.

Edward's lip curled. 'It had better work.'

'And I'm thinking we should bring Tanya in at an early stage,' George said.

'No way,' Edward said. 'What is it with Tanya? You got something going with her?'

'How ridiculous. You're the one who can't keep his eyes off her.'

Myrtle said, 'Leave it, George. Act your age, both of you. I'm with Edward here. Keep it to ourselves.'

Edward almost purred. 'Something else Butch once said: "The more snouts in the trough, the less you get."'

'As you wish,' George said. 'We won't say anything to Tanya. She'll get a beautiful surprise.'

'So how do we divide the work?' Myrtle said.

'Unless you think otherwise, I volunteer to do the paper-work,' George said. 'I'm comfortable with the English language.'

'Keep it short and simple. Nothing fancy.'

'Is that agreed, then?'

Edward concurred with a shrug.

'But we should all join in,' Myrtle said. 'Another thing Butch said, "Everyone must get their hands dirty."'

'Suits me – but what else is there to do?' Edward said.

'I need one of Robert's credit cards,' George said.

Edward shook his head. 'The hell you do. We're not

going down that route. That's a sure way to get found out.'

George took a sharp, impatient breath. 'We won't be using it to buy stuff.'

'So what do we want it for?' Edward said, and immediately knew the answer. 'The signature on the back.'

'Right,' Myrtle said. 'Can you take care of that?'

'Tricky,' Edward said.

'Not at all. Robert must have used plastic. Everyone does.'

'How do we get hold of one?'

'How do *you* get hold of one,' Myrtle said. 'That's how you get your hands dirty. My guess is they're still lying around the office somewhere.'

'Tanya's always in there.'

Myrtle rolled her eyes. 'God help us, Edward, if you can't find a way to do this simple thing you don't deserve to be one of us.'

George, becoming the diplomat, said, 'Come on, old friend, it's no hardship chatting up Tanya. You can't keep your eyes off her ample backside.'

Myrtle said at once. 'Cut that out, George.' She turned to Edward. 'Get her out of the office on some pretext and have a nose around.'

'It's not as if you're robbing the Bank of England,' George said.

'Okay, I'll see what I can do,' Edward said without much grace, and then turned to Myrtle. 'And how will you get your hands dirty?'

'Me? I'm going to choose the perfect place to plant the thing.'

Almost overnight, Tanya had been transformed from bookshop assistant to manager of Robert's estate as well as his shop. It wasn't her choice, but there was no one else to step into the breach. At least she continued to be employed. She decided she would carry on until someone in authority instructed her to stop. She would allow the shop to remain open and operate on a cash-only basis, buying no new stock and keeping accurate accounts. She couldn't touch the bank account, but there was money left in the till and there were occasional sales.

Meanwhile, she did her best to get some order out of the chaos that had been Robert's office. He had given up on the filing system years ago. She spent days sorting through papers, getting up to date with correspondence and informing clients what had happened. Someone at some point would have to make an inventory of the stock. What a task *that* would be. Nothing was on computer, not even the accounts. He had still been using tear-out receipt books with carbon sheets.

She glanced across the room at the carton of Agatha Christies that had been the death of poor Robert. After his body had been taken away she had repaired the carton with sticky tape, replaced the loose books and slid the heavy load alongside the filing cabinet. She really ought to shelve them in the mystery section in the next room. But then she wasn't certain how to price them. Robert had paid five hundred for them, so they weren't cheap editions. The copy of the invoice was in one of the boxes. The titles weren't listed there. It simply read: *Agatha Christie novels as agreed.*

She went over and picked up *The Mysterious Affair at Styles*, the author's first novel, obviously in good condition and still in its dust jacket. A first edition would be worth a lot, but she told herself this must be a second printing or a facsimile. It was easy to be fooled into thinking you'd found a gem. According to the spine the publisher was the Bodley Head, so this copy had been published in England.

Yet when she looked inside at the publication details and the 1921 date, she couldn't see any evidence that the book was anything except a genuine first edition. It had the smell of an old book, yet it was as clean as if it had not been handled much.

Was it possible?

She was still learning the business, but her heart beat a little faster. Robert himself had once told her that early Agatha Christies in jackets were notoriously rare because booksellers in the past were in the habit of stripping the books of their paper coverings at the point of sale to display the cloth bindings.

Among the reference works lining the office back wall were some that listed auction prices. She took one down, thumbed through to the right page, and saw that a 1921 Bodley Head first edition *without* its original dust jacket had sold last year for just over ten thousand dollars. No one seemed to have auctioned a copy in its jacket in the past fifty years.

She handled the book with more respect and looked again at the page with the date. This had to be a genuine first edition.

'Oh, my God!' she said aloud.

No wonder Robert had snapped up the collection. This volume alone was worth many times the price he had paid for them all. He was sharp enough to spot a bargain, which was why the Christie collection had so excited him. It was easy to imagine his emotional state here in the office that Sunday evening. His unhealthy heart must have been under intolerable strain.

The find of a lifetime had triggered the end of a lifetime.

And now Tanya wondered about her own heart. She had a rock band playing in her chest.

If a copy without its jacket fetched ten grand, how much was this little beauty worth? Surely enough to cover her every need for months, if not years, to come.

So tempting.

Robert had never trusted the computer. He'd used it as a glorified typewriter and little else. His contact details for his main customers were kept in a card index that Tanya now flicked through, looking for people interested in what Robert had called 'British Golden Age mysteries'. She picked out five names. On each card were noted the deals he had done and the prices paid for early editions of Agatha Christie, Dorothy L. Sayers and Anthony Berkeley. They weren't five-figure sums, but the books almost certainly hadn't been such fine copies as these.

It wouldn't hurt to phone some of these customers and ask if they would be interested in making an offer for a 1921 Bodley Head edition of *The Mysterious Affair at Styles* – with jacket.

'I'd need to see it,' the first voice said, plainly trying to sound laid back. Then gave himself away by adding, 'You haven't even told me who you are. Where are you calling from? I don't mind getting on a plane.'

Tanya was cautious. 'In fairness, I need to speak to some other potential buyers.'

'How much do you have in mind?' he said. 'I can arrange a transfer into any account you care to name and no questions asked. Tell me the price you want.'

Collecting can be addictive.

'It's not decided yet,' she said. 'This is just an enquiry to find out who is interested. As I said, I have other calls to make.'

'Are you planning to auction it, or what?'

'I'm not going through an auctioneer. It would be a

private sale, but at some point I may ask for your best offer.'

'You say it has the original jacket? Is it complete? Sometimes they come with a panel detached or missing.'

'Believe me, it's complete.'

There was a pause at the end of the line. Then: 'I'd be willing to offer a six-figure sum. If I can examine it for staining and so on and you tell me the provenance, I could run to more than that.'

A six-figure sum? Did he really mean that?

'Thank you,' Tanya succeeded in saying in a small, shocked voice. 'I must make some more calls now.'

'Screw it, a hundred and twenty grand.'

She swallowed hard. 'I'm not yet accepting offers, but I may come back to you.'

'One forty.' He was terrified to put the phone down.

'I'll bear that in mind,' Tanya said, and closed the call.

She tried a second collector of Golden Age mysteries and this one wasn't interested in staining or provenance. He couldn't contain his excitement. 'Lady, name your price,' he said. 'I'd kill for that book.' Without any prompting, he offered a hundred and fifty thousand, 'In used banknotes, if you want.'

She didn't bother to call the others. She needed to collect her thoughts. Robert's sudden death had come as such a shock that no one else had given a thought to the value of the Agatha Christies. She was the only person in Poketown with the faintest idea and she could scarcely believe what she'd been offered. Could the existence of a dust jacket – a sheet of paper printed on one side – really mean a mark-up of more than a hundred grand?

She lifted more books out, first editions all. *The Murder on the Links*, *The Secret of Chimneys* and *The Murder of Roger*

Ackroyd. The beauty of this was that there was no written evidence of how many were in the carton. The invoice had lumped them all together. *Agatha Christie novels as agreed.* She could take a dozen home and no one would be any the wiser. But she would be richer. Unbelievably richer.

Her time as stand-in manager would soon end. There was already talk of an administrator being appointed.

The phone on the desk buzzed. She jerked in surprise. Guiltily, as if someone was in the room with her, she turned the books face down and covered them with her arm.

'Miss Tripp?'

'Speaking.'

'Al Johnson here, from the bank, about the late Mr Ripple's estate.'

She repeated automatically, 'Mr Ripple's estate.'

'You were planning a further search for his will when we last spoke. I guess you'd have called me if you'd been successful.'

'I guess.'

'Are you okay, Miss Tripp? You sound a little distracted.'

'There's a lot going on,' she said. 'Sorry. You asked about the will. It didn't turn up. I looked everywhere I could think of.'

'How long has it been now – five weeks? I think we're fast approaching the point of assuming he died intestate.'

'I'm afraid so.'

'Neglecting to provide for one's death is not as unusual as you might suppose, even among the elderly. The law is quite straightforward here in Pennsylvania. We get an administrator appointed and he or she will calculate the total assets and make a search for relatives who may inherit.'

She made a huge effort not to think about the Agatha Christies. 'I tried to contact the family before the funeral, but there doesn't seem to be anyone left. He was unmarried, as you know, and had no brothers or sisters. I couldn't even trace any cousins.'

'If that's really so, then the Commonwealth of Pennsylvania will collect. Robert's main asset was the bookshop and his apartment upstairs, of course. Do you have other plans yet?'

'Plans?' Sure, she had plans, but this wasn't the moment to speak about them.

'To move on, get another job.'

'Not really. How long have I got?'

'In the shop? About a week, I'd say. It's up to me to ask for the administrator to take over and there's usually no delay over that. Everything is then put on hold.'

'We have to close?'

'Between you and me, you should have closed already, but I turned a blind eye, knowing what a blow this will be for our community.'

After the call, Tanya reached for a Precious Finds tote bag and filled it with Agatha Christie firsts. She couldn't help the community, but she'd be crazy if she didn't help herself.

Edward, the David Niven lookalike from the Friends of England, was waiting outside the office door immaculate as always, a carnation in his lapel, when Tanya unlocked next morning. He held a coffee cup in each hand.

'Howya doin?' The charm suffered when he opened his mouth.

'Pretty good,' she said, and meant it. 'But it's looking bad for the shop. I think we'll be in administration by the end of the week.' She was trying to sound concerned.

'Soon as that? Too bad.' Strangely, Edward didn't sound over-worried either. 'I picked up a coffee for you, Tanya.

Skinny latte without syrup, in a tall cup, right?' He handed it over.

'How did you know?'

'I was behind you in Starbucks the other morning.'

'And you remembered? What a kind man you are. Why don't you come in?' She could offer no less.

He looked around for a chair but there wasn't a spare one, so he stood his coffee on the filing cabinet Tanya had been trying to get back into some kind of order. He appeared to stand it there. In fact the cup tipped over, the lid shot off and his black Americano streamed down the side of the metal cabinet.

Tanya screamed, 'Ferchrissake!' She grabbed some Kleenex from the box on her desk and moved fast.

'No sweat,' Edward said after rapidly checking his clothes. 'Missed me.'

She was on her knees, dragging the remaining Agatha Christies away from the still dripping coffee, her voice shrill in panic. 'It's all over the books.'

He stepped around the cabinet for a closer look. 'Aw, shit.' He pulled the pristine white handkerchief from his top pocket and sacrificed it to mop the surface of the filing cabinet. Then, seeing Tanya's frantic efforts to dry the books in the box, he stooped and began dabbing at them.

'Don't – you'll make it worse,' she said.

'Are they special?'

'"Special"?' She felt like strangling him, the idiot. Words poured from her before she realised how much she was giving away. 'They're first-edition Agatha Christies, worth a fucking fortune. Help me lift them out. The coffee has ruined most of them.'

He started picking out soggy books and carrying them

to her desk. 'Agatha Christies, huh? And you say they're valuable?'

'They were until you—' She stopped in mid-sentence, realising she'd said too much. She tried to roll back some of what she had revealed. 'Okay, it was an accident, I know, but Robert paid five hundred dollars for these.'

He whistled. 'Five hundred bucks for used books? I thought people gave them away.'

'Not these. Most of them are more than seventy years old and with hardly a stain on them . . . until now.'

'You can still read them when they're dry.'

Tanya sighed. The blundering fool didn't get it. He had no conception of the damage he'd done – but maybe this was a good thing. After the initial shock she was trying to calm down. They had finished emptying the carton. She told herself this could have been a far worse disaster. Fortunately the real plums of the collection were safe in her apartment. The ones she'd left were there for show, in case anyone asked about Robert's last book deal.

Edward gave another rub to the filing cabinet, as if that was the problem. 'You tidied this place good.'

'Sorting it out,' she said, still shaking. 'Robert wasn't the best-organised person in the world.'

'And you never found the will?'

'The will?' She forced herself to think about it. 'Let's face it. There isn't one – which is why we don't have any future.'

'Where did he keep his personal stuff?'

'All over. Birth certificate upstairs. Tax forms and credit-card statements down here in the desk drawers. His bank documents were at the back of the filing cabinet.'

'Driving licence?'

'In the car outside on the street. I even looked there for the will.'

'Credit cards?'

'A bunch of them were in a card case in his back pocket. They came back from the morgue last week. I shredded them after making a note of the numbers.'

'Good thinking,' Edward said, but his facial muscles went into spasm.

'So it's the end of an era here in Poketown,' Tanya said and she was beginning to get a grip on herself. 'What will happen to your Friends of England group? Will you be able to go somewhere else?'

Edward shook his head. 'Wouldn't be the same.'

'The end of the line for you, then?'

'Seems so.' But he still didn't appear depressed at the prospect. He glanced at the line of sad, damp books. 'I wanna find some way of saying sorry. How about lunch?'

'It's not necessary.'

'After what I just did, it's the least I can do. Someone I knew used to say, "You shoot yourself in the foot, you gotta learn to hop."'

She managed a smile. 'Okay. What time?'

They lunched at Jimmy's, the best restaurant on Main Street. By then Tanya had recovered most of her poise. After all, she had enough undamaged Agatha Christies at home to make her rich. And this tête-à-tête with Edward was as good a chance as she would get to discover the main thing she had come to Poketown to find out.

She waited until she had finished her angel-hair pasta with Thai-spiced prawns – by which time Edward had gone through three glasses of Chablis.

'Now that Precious Finds is coming to an end, do you mind if I ask something?'

'Sure. Go ahead.'

'What exactly went on at the meetings?'

'Meetings?' he said as if he didn't understand the word. She hoped he hadn't drunk too much to make sense.

'Of the Friends. I asked Robert once, but I don't think he knew. He was pretty vague about it, in that way he had of telling you nothing.'

Edward gave a guarded answer. 'We don't do much except talk.'

'In that case, you could talk in some other place. It's not a total disaster if the shop closes, as it will.'

He seemed to be avoiding eye contact. 'It's not so simple. We can't just shift camp.'

'I don't understand why not.'

'You don't need to.'

She should have waited for him to sink a fourth glass of the wine. 'But you can tell me how you three got together.'

'We know each other from way back, when we all lived in New York City.'

'And Myrtle was married to that man who was murdered?'

He nodded. 'Butch Rafferty.'

'Mr Rafferty had a hard reputation as a gang leader, didn't he? I can understand a woman being attracted to that kind of guy.' She noted his eyes widen and his chest fill out. 'Did you know him?'

'Did I know Butch!' Out to impress, he jutted his jaw a fraction higher.

'Closely, then?'

Edward put down his glass, made a link with his pinkies and pulled them until they turned red. 'We were like that.'

'Wow! They must have been dangerous times for any friend of Butch Rafferty. Is that why you moved away?'

'We didn't run,' he said.

'When you say "we", do you mean yourself, Myrtle and George?'

'Sure. It suited us to come here.'

'I heard there was a big robbery of a security van that in some way caused the falling-out between Butch and Gritty Bologna.'

His mouth tightened. 'You seem to know a lot about it.'

She felt herself colour a little. 'It was in the papers at the time. I looked it up later after I heard who Myrtle's husband had been. I was curious.'

'Curiosity killed the cat,' Edward said and ended that line of conversation. It wasn't one of Butch's sayings.

'Well, thanks for the meal. I really enjoyed it,' Tanya said a few minutes later.

'Let's do it again tomorrow,' Edward said, and it was music to her ears.

'Why not? And I'll pay.' She could afford to, now she was dealing in first-edition Agatha Christies. She'd get him talking again after a few drinks, no problem.

Her mention of the robbery hadn't put him off entirely, she was pleased to discover. And now Edward played the assertive male. 'This afternoon I'm gonna check the filing cabinet.'

'There's no need. It was locked,' she said.

'Some of my coffee could have seeped inside. I'll take a look.'

'What in the name of sanity is Edward up to?' George asked Myrtle later that week. 'I saw them leaving Jimmy's at lunch today. It's become a regular date.'

'He's keeping her sweet, I figure,' Myrtle said. 'We encouraged him, if you remember.'

'That was when we needed the credit card with Robert's signature. He found an old receipt book full of Robert's signatures in the filing cabinet, but that was three days ago. He handed it to me and it's all I want. His work is done. He has no reason to be lunching with Tanya every day.'

'Silly old fool,' Myrtle said. 'He stands no chance with her. Smart clothes can only do so much for a guy. God help him when he takes them off.'

'Is that one of Butch's sayings?'

'No. I said it.'

'I'm worried, Myrtle.' George showed the stress he was under by pulling the end of his silver ponytail across his throat. 'We don't want him telling her anything.'

'About this?'

'No – about the heist of the van.'

'She isn't interested in that. She has too much on her mind, and soon she'll have a whole lot more. How's the project going?'

'My part is complete,' George said, reaching into his pocket. 'It's over to you now.'

'Fine,' Myrtle said. 'I'll plant the little beauty tomorrow lunchtime, while Edward is working his charm on her in Jimmy's.'

'I was thinking,' Tanya said, at the next lunch date.

'Yeah?' Edward had already finished the bottle of Chablis and was on Bourbon. His glazed eyes looked ready for a cataract operation.

'About Robert,' she went on, 'and how you three linked up with him. Was he ever in New York?'

'Sure,' he said, with a flap of the hand, 'but way back, when we were all much younger.'

'In Butch Rafferty's gang?'

'I wouldn't say Robert was in the gang,' he said, starting to slur the words, 'but we all knew him. He was a bartender then, some place in the Bowery where we used to meet.'

'Someone you trusted?'

'Right on. Like one of the family.'

'Butch's family?'

'Yeah. Butch liked the guy and so did the rest of us. Robert knew how to keep his mouth shut. Jobs were discussed. It didn't matter.'

'A bartender in New York? That's a far cry from owning a bookshop.'

'He had a dream to get out of town and open a bookstore and that's what he did when he had the money.'

'Just from his work in the bar?' she said, disbelieving.

'Butch helped him. Butch was like that. And it wasn't wasted. Butch knew if he ever needed a bolt-hole he could lay up for a while here in Poketown, Pennsylvania.' He shook his head slowly. 'Too bad he was shot before he had the chance.'

Tanya knew all this, but there was more she didn't know. 'So after Butch was killed, some of you left town and came here?'

He nodded. 'Myrtle's idea. She knew where Robert had set up shop.'

'Was she an active member of the gang?'

'She didn't go on jobs, but she has a good brain and she's cool. She helped Butch with the planning.' He blinked and looked sober for a second. 'You're not an undercover cop, by any chance?'

She laughed. 'No way. I'm starstruck by how you guys operate.'

Reassured, he reached for the Bourbon and topped up his glass. 'Sexy, huh?'

'It's a turn-on. I'll say that.'

'You're a turn-on without saying a word.'

'Flatterer.' She was still on her first glass of wine, picking her questions judiciously. The process required care, even with a half-cut would-be seducer like this one. The query about the undercover cop was a warning. Edward couldn't have been more wrong, but it would be a mistake to underestimate him. 'What is it with the Friends of England? Is that the only way you can meet in private?'

'We could meet anywhere. It's a free country.'

'Be mysterious, then,' she said, smiling.

He grinned back. 'You bet I will. There's gotta be mystery in a relationship.'

'Who said anything about . . .' She didn't get any further. His hand was on her thigh.

She'd got him just as she wanted.

He needed support as he tottered back to Precious Finds and Tanya supplied it, allowing him to put his arm around her shoulder.

'Why don't we close the shop for the afternoon?' he said.

'What a good idea,' she said. 'I was thinking the same thing.' She'd already closed for lunch and didn't have to reopen. She let them inside, fastened the bolts and left the *Closed* notice hanging on the door.

Inside, she said, 'After all that wine, some coffee might be a good plan.'

'I can think of a better one,' Edward said, reaching for her breasts.

She swayed out of range. 'Coffee first. I only have instant, but I'm not sending you to Starbucks again. Tell you what. I'll make it here and we'll carry it through to the back room, so we can both have a chair.'

'And if I spill it, I can't do so much damage,' he said with a grin.

She carried both mugs through the shop after the coffee was made, insisting he went ahead. She didn't want him behind her.

Edward managed to lift two chairs from the stack and sank into one of them. 'Never thought I'd get to be alone with you.'

And so drunk you can't do anything about it, Tanya thought, but she said, 'Yes, it's great to relax. And in the company of a famous New York mobster.'

He looked stupidly flattered.

'I'd love to hear about the last big job you did – the security van,' she said. 'I thought they were so well protected no robber would even think about a hold-up.'

'Takes brains,' he said.

'Was it your idea, then?'

'The part that worked, yeah.' He ogled her. 'You wanna hear about it? I'll tell you. In a job like this you go for the weak spot. You know what that is?'

'The tyres?'

'The people. You surprise the guard in his own home before he reports for work. You tell him his mother has been kidnapped and he has to cooperate. You tape dummy explosives to his chest and tell him you can detonate them by remote whenever you want.'

'Brilliant,' Tanya said. 'Was that you doing all that?'

'Most of it. From there on he's so scared he'll do anything. He drives you to where the vans are kept. You're wearing a uniform just like his. He drives the security van to the depot where the bank stores the money. He does the talking and you help load the van.'

'How much? Squillions?' She was wide-eyed, playing the innocent.

'They don't deal in peanuts,' Edward said. 'And when you're outta there and on the street, your buddies follow in the transit van.'

'George?'

'He was one of the bunch, yeah. Some were Butch's people and some worked for Gritty Bologna. Gritty had a line into the security outfit, which was how we got the uniform and the guard's address. You drive to the warehouse where you transfer the loot and that's it.'

'What about the guard?'

'Tied up and locked in his van. No violence.'

'How much did you get?'

'Just under a million pounds.'

'*Pounds*?'

Edward looked sheepish. 'Yeah. We screwed up. We thought this van was delivering to the major banks like all the others. Too bad we picked the one supplying British money to currency exchanges at all the major airports in New York.'

'You had a vanload of useless money.'

'Uhuh. Crisp, new banknotes for tourists to take on their vacations.'

'What a let-down.'

'Tell me about it. Gritty went bananas. He blamed Butch. There was a shoot-out and Butch was the loser. Some of us figured Gritty wouldn't stop at one killing, so we left town.'

'You and George and Myrtle?' She'd been incredibly patient waiting for the pay-off.

'Myrtle remembered Robert here in Poketown, and this is where we came.'

'With the pounds?'

'With the pounds. I figured we might think of a way to use them. It took a while, but with Robert's help we worked it.'

'All those trips to England? That's neat.'

'Twenty, thirty grand at a time. Some notes we exchange and bring dollars back. Some we spent over there. It's small scale. Has to be, with new, numbered banknotes.'

'And this is why you call it the Friends of England? I love it!' She clapped her hands. 'Edward, you're a genius. Is there any left, or is it all spent?'

'More than half is left.'

'Who's got it?'

'This is the whole point. We call ourselves friends, but we're professionals. Stealing is our trade. We can't trust each other, right? Never trust another crook. So the money is kept on neutral ground, where each of us see how much is still there.'

'Neutral ground? Where?'

'Right here in the safe. That's why we can't let the place close.'

He'd lost her now.

'I haven't found the safe,' she said, as casually as if she was talking about the one copy of Jane Austen the shop didn't stock. 'I don't know what you're talking about.'

He just smiled.

'When you say "right here", do you mean the back room?'

He wagged his finger like a parent with a fractious infant. 'Secret.'

Infuriating. To her best knowledge there wasn't a safe on the premises. Robert had always left the takings in the till. There wasn't enough to justify using a safe. She teased Edward with a frigid stare. 'If that's how you want to play this, I won't be showing you my secret either.'

'Whassat?' he asked, gripping the chair-arms.

'Wouldn't you like to know, naughty boy.'

She watched the struggle going on in front of her, rampant desire taking over from reality. 'You gotta do better than that,' he said.

'Okay. To show you my secret we have to go upstairs, to the bedroom.'

'Hell,' he said, shifting in the chair as if he was suddenly uncomfortable. 'Is that an offer?'

She hesitated, then gave a nod.

He groomed his moustache with finger and thumb and took a deep, tremulous breath. 'The safe is right where you are. You could touch it with your knee.'

She looked down. 'Get away.'

'*Encyclopaedia Brit . . . Brit . . .*' To his credit he'd got the first word out.

'*Britannica?*'

'Middle five volumes. False front.'

She stooped and studied the spines of the large books that took up the whole of the bottom shelf. With their faded lettering and scuffed cloth bindings they looked no different from the others.

'1911 edition,' Edward said. 'Green. Press the showy gold bit on volume twelve and see what happens.'

She pushed her thumb against the royal coat of arms and felt it respond. Just as Edward had said, the five spines were only a façade attached to a small, hinged door that sprang open and revealed the grey metal front of a safe with a circular combination lock.

Eureka.

'That's amazing.'

'If I could see straight, I'd open it for you,' he said, 'but there's only stacks of notes in there.'

'You have to know the combination.'

'Zero-four-two-three-one-nine-six-four, but I didn't tell you that, okay?'

'Smart. How do you remember?'

'It's Myrtle's birthday. April twenty-three, sixty-four. Shut it now and we'll go upstairs.'

In his inebriated state, he couldn't have stopped her if she'd walked out and left him there. But, hell, she wanted the satisfaction of showing him her secret, as she'd put it.

'Will you make it?'

He chuckled. 'You bet I will, baby.' And he did, even though he took the last few stairs on all fours. 'So which one is the bedroom?' he asked between deep breaths.

'That's another adventure, lover boy. Next floor.'

'Stuff that. There must be a sofa right here.'

Tanya shook her head and pointed her finger at the ceiling.

After some hesitation Edward seemed to accept that this had to be on Tanya's terms. 'Which way, then?'

'The spiral staircase at the end of the corridor.'

Gamely, he stepped towards it and hauled himself to the top. 'Makes you kinda dizzy.'

'That's not the fault of the staircase.' She pushed open a door. 'In here, buster.'

Robert's bedroom matched the size of the back room downstairs. The king-size bed was constructed of oak, with headboard and footboard graciously curved and upholstered in a French empire style. All the furniture matched and there was plenty of it, dressing table, wardrobes, chests of drawers and easy chairs, but no sense of crowding. More books lined the facing wall and there was a 50-inch plasma TV as well as a sound system with chest-high speakers. There was an open door to an en-suite shower room. A second door connected to a fire escape.

'This'll do,' Edward said, stepping towards Tanya.

She moved aside. 'Not so fast.'

'C'mon, I showed you my secret.' He patted the bed.

'Fair enough. Here's mine.' She crossed to the dressing table, swung the mirror right over and revealed a manila envelope fastened to the back. 'It's ridiculous. I checked the mirror a week ago and nothing was there. This morning I found this. Robert's will.'

'Yeah?' he said, his thoughts elsewhere.

'You'd better listen up, because it names you.' She slipped the document from the envelope and started to read. '"This is the last will and testament of Robert Ripple, of Precious Finds Bookshop, Main Street, Poketown, Pennsylvania, being of sound mind and revoking all other wills and codicils. I wish to appoint as co-executors my good friends George Digby-Smith and Edward Myers." That's you. And you and George divide his money between you after all expenses are paid, but I doubt whether any will be left.'

'No problem,' Edward said. 'Now why don't you put that down so we can give this bed a workout?'

'Listen to this part: "I leave my house and shop in trust to become the sole property of my devoted assistant manager, Tanya Tripp, on condition that she continues to trade as a bookseller on the premises for ten years from the date of my decease." Nice try.'

'Don't ya like it?' Edward said, frowning.

'It stinks. This wasn't drafted by Robert. It's a fake. I know why you wanted his credit cards the other day and why in the end you walked off with that old receipt book.

241

So you could fake his signature. Well, it's a passable signature, I'll give you that, but you forgot something. A will needs to be witnessed. There are no witnesses here.'

'No witnesses, huh?' He raised his right hand in a semi-official pose and intoned in a more-or-less coherent manner, 'The state of Pennsylvania doesn't require witnesses to a will. You're in the clear, sweetheart. It's all yours, the house and the shop. Just be grateful someone thought of you.'

'Thought of *me*? You were only thinking of yourselves, keeping up the old arrangement, taking your stolen pounds from the safe and spending them in England. I'm supposed to give up ten years of my life to keep this smelly old heap of wood and plaster going just to make life dandy for you guys. Well, forget it. I don't buy it.' She held the will high and ripped it apart.

The force of the action somehow penetrated the alcohol in Edward's brain. Suddenly he seemed to realise that there was much more at stake than getting this young woman into bed. 'I've got your number. You figure you can do better for yourself with those Agatha Christies you have in the office. Worth a fucking fortune, you said. Few spots of coffee didn't harm them much. You're aiming to take them with you when the shop closes down and cash in big time.'

Tanya felt the blood drain from her face. She'd been hoping her agitated words the other day had passed unnoticed. This was dangerous, desperately dangerous. It wasn't quite true because the best books weren't stained. They were safe in her apartment. Even so, this stupid, drink-crazed man could put a stop to everything.

She still had ammunition and her reaction was to use it. 'You don't know who I am. I can bring down you and your thieving friends. I'm Gritty Bologna's daughter, Teresa. That money in the safe isn't yours to spend. We spent years

242

tracking you to this place. I took the job with Robert to find out where the banknotes are and now I know.'

'You're Teresa Bologna?' he said in amazement. 'You were in school at the time of the heist.'

'I'm family, and family doesn't give up.'

He moved fast for a drunk. Fear and rage mingled in his face. He came at her like a bull.

He was blocking her route to the door and the en suite would be a trap. Her only option was to use the fire escape. She turned and hit the panic bar and the door swung open. She grabbed the rail and swung left just as Edward charged through.

No one's movements are reliable after heavy drinking. Edward pitched forward, failed to stop, hit the rail hard with his hips and couldn't stop his torso from tipping him over. He may have screamed. Tanya (or Teresa) didn't remember. But the sickening thud of the body hitting the concrete forty feet below would stay in her memory for ever.

The autopsy revealed substantial alcohol in Edward's blood. No one could say what he had been doing above the bookshop in the dead owner's bedroom. Those who might have thrown some light had all left Poketown overnight and were not heard of again. An open verdict was returned at the inquest.

In the absence of a will from Robert Ripple, Precious Finds was duly put under the control of an administrator and escheated to the state of Pennsylvania. It ceased trading as a bookshop and was converted into apartments.

About a year later, a married couple set up home on a remote Scottish island. He was thought to be an ex-hippy, she an American. They called themselves Mr and Mrs English and they helped the home tourist industry by forever taking holidays in different towns.

Copies of several extremely rare Agatha Christie first editions in dust jackets enlivened the book market in the years that followed, changing hands for huge sums. Their provenance was described as uncertain, but they were certainly genuine.

Agony Column

Dear Dr Wisefellow,

My husband Hamish is behaving very strangely. He has started going for long walks on his own. At least, I *suppose* he is alone. Sometimes he is gone for more than two hours, and when he comes back really late in the evening he is not much company when the lights go out – if you know what I mean. Should I be concerned?

    Yours truly,

    Neglected of Littlehampton

    PS We do not own a dog.

Dear Neglected,

There is not much to worry about, so far as I can see. It's not unusual for a man to go for an evening walk, even without a dog, and if Hamish is gone for two hours, it's understandable that he's tired when he gets back. Have you suggested joining him? He may be glad to have you along.

Dear Dr Wisefellow,

Thanks you for your advice. I suggested what you said and Hamish replied in very strong terms. He told me he didn't *something* want me on his *something* walks. So now I'm getting suspicious. He has always

245

had a roving eye, but I've never caught him out. Do you think I should follow him one evening?

PS He is *still* not much company when the lights go out – if you know what I mean.

Dear Neglected,
It may not be such a good idea to follow your husband on his walks. Why not try breaking him of the habit by cooking a very special meal and getting in a bottle of his favourite wine? Be sure to light some candles and put on your most attractive dress and I think you will not be disappointed when the lights go out.

Dear Dr Wisefellow,
I did everything you suggested. Hamish ate the meal and drank the wine and *still* went for a walk. The only difference was that it was even later when he got home. And there is worse. He opened a book and insisted on reading in bed until he fell asleep. This is a new development – I mean the reading, not the falling asleep.

Dear Neglected,
It might give me an insight into your husband's behaviour if you tell me the title of the book he is reading.

Dear Dr Wisefellow,
I wish you hadn't asked me about the book. I have just checked the title. It is *Poisonous Plants and Fungi.* Whatever is Hamish up to now? I was awake all night worrying. And he was talking in his sleep, saying some extremely peculiar things. Please advise me what to do.

Dear Neglected,

I was pleased to hear that Hamish has started talking in his sleep because this can be very indicative. Next time you go to bed I want you to smuggle in a small battery-operated tape-recorder. You can get them at Currys for £9.99. Then each time you hear Hamish say something, get it on tape. Make a transcript next day and send it to me, even if it sounds peculiar.

   PS In the meantime, if he offers to do any cooking, thank him nicely and say no.

Dear Dr Wisefellow,

I followed your instructions and now I'm more desperate than ever. These are some of the strange things Hamish said in his sleep last night:

   At 1 a.m.: Maybe a blunt instrument would work better.

   At 1.15: Careful, there may be fingerprints.

   At 2.15: Damn and blast! I forgot to renew my passport.

   At 2.25: Oh, no, not another one!

   And at 2.45: Some of you may be wondering why I asked you to assemble in the library.

   Soon after this I must have fallen asleep because I woke up at 4.30 in a state of terror with a metal object pressing into my back. I was lying on the tape-recorder. Doctor, I'm out of my mind with worry. Should I go to the police before it is too late?

Dear Neglected,

There is no need to go to the police. I can now set your fears at rest. Your husband Hamish is undergoing a change that happens occasionally to certain men – and women as well.

The symptoms you describe are unmistakable. Hamish is becoming a crime writer. A peculiar condition, but not usually dangerous. Soon you will find that he gives up those long walks and starts shutting himself away in a place of isolation, like the garden shed or an attic. If you pass anywhere near, you may hear a tapping sound, or, more likely, shouts of 'Blast!' as paper is screwed up and thrown across the room. If you have a cat, keep it out of his way at these times. Keep out of his way yourself unless he asks for help. He may wish to see if you will fit into a trunk or a piano. He may even creep up on you when you are taking a shower. If so, be sure to cooperate. Situations such as these, sensitively handled, will present opportunities for that resumption of relations you have found lacking of late. It isn't easy being married to a crime writer, but it can have exciting moments.

Dear Dr Wisefellow,

How can I thank you enough? Your diagnosis was absolutely right. Hamish finished his book and got it published and sold the film rights and here we are six months later beside the pool at our villa in the south of France. The publisher told Hamish the best way to remain a best-seller is to write a strong plot spiced with plenty of passion. I help by giving him ideas and trying them out, just as you suggested. One of my best ideas is the hero catching the blonde lying beside the pool just as nature intended, and I must end this letter because Hamish wants to try it out again.

PS In case you were wondering, Hamish is much better company now that it's all out in the open – if you know what I mean.

The Bathroom

'Sorry, darling! I mean to have my bath and that's the end of it!' With a giggle and a swift movement of her right hand, Melanie Lloyd closed the sliding door of her bathroom. The catch fastened automatically with a reassuring click. Her husband William, frustrated on the other side, had installed the gadget himself. 'None of your old-fashioned bolts or keys for us,' he had announced, demonstrating it a week before the wedding. 'The door secures itself when you slide it across from the inside. You can move it with one finger, you see, but once closed, it's as safe as your money in the bank.'

She felt between her shoulders for the tab of her zip. William could wait for her. Sit in bed and wait while she had a leisurely bath. What was the purpose of a luxurious modern bathroom if not to enjoy a bath at one's leisure? William, after all, had spent weeks before the wedding modernising it. 'Everything but asses' milk,' he had joked. 'Mixer taps, spray attachment, separate shower, bidet, heated towel-rails and built-in cupboards. You shall bathe like a queen, my love. Like a queen.'

Queenly she had felt when she first stepped through the sliding door and saw what he had prepared for her. It was all there exactly as he had promised, in white and gold. All that he had promised, and more. Ceramic mosaic tiles.

Concealed lighting. Steam-proof mirrors. And the floor – wantonly impractical! – carpeted in white, with a white fur rug beside the bath. There was also a chair, an elegant antique chair, over which he had draped a full-length lace negligee. 'Shameless Victoriana,' he had whispered. 'Quite out of keeping with contemporary design, but I'm incurably sentimental.' Then he had kissed her.

In that meeting of lips she had shed her last doubts about William, those small nagging uncertainties that would probably never have troubled her if Daddy had not kept on so. 'I'm old-fashioned, I know, Melanie, but it seems to me an extraordinarily short engagement. You feel that you know him, I've no doubt, but he's met your mother and me only once – and that was by accident. The fellow seemed downright evasive when I questioned him about his background. It's an awkward thing to do, asking a man things like that when he's damned near as old as you are, but, hang it, it's a father's right to know the circumstances of the man who proposes marrying his daughter, even if he is past fifty. Oh, I've nothing against his age; there are plenty of successful marriages on record between young women and older men. Nothing we could do to stop you, or would. You're over twenty-one and old enough to decide such things for yourself. The point is that he knew why I was making my enquiries. I wasn't probing his affairs from idle curiosity. I had your interests at heart, damn it. If the fellow hasn't much behind him, I'd be obliged if he'd say so, so that I can make a decent contribution. Set you both up properly. I would, you know. I've never kept you short, have I? Wouldn't see you come upon hard times for anything in the world. If only the fellow would make an honest statement . . .'

One didn't argue with Daddy. It was no use trying to talk to him about self-respect. Every argument was always swept aside by that familiar outpouring of middle-class propriety. God, if anything drove her into William Lloyd's arms, Daddy did!

She stepped out of the dress and hung it on one of the hooks provided on the wall of the shower compartment. Before removing her slip, she closed the venetian blind; not that she was excessively modest, nor, for that matter, that she imagined her new neighbours in Bismarck Road were the sort who looked up at bathroom windows. The plain fact was that she was used to frosted glass. When she and William had first looked over the house – it seemed years ago, but it could only have been last April – the windows, more than anything else, had given her that feeling of unease. There were several in the house – they had been common enough in Victorian times when the house was built – small oblong frames of glass with frostwork designs and narrow stained-glass borders in deep red and blue. They would have to come out, she had decided at once, if William insisted on living there. They seemed so out of keeping, vaguely ecclesiastical, splendid in a chapel or an undertaker's office, but not in her new home. William agreed at once to take them out – he seemed so determined to buy that one house. 'You won't recognise the place when I've done it up. I'll put a picture window in the bathroom. The old frames need to come out anyway. The wood's half rotten outside.' So the old windows went and the picture window, a large single sheet of glass, replaced them. 'Don't worry about ventilation,' William assured her. 'There's an extractor fan built in above the cabinet there.' He had thought of everything.

Except frosted glass. She *would* have felt more comfortable behind frosted glass. But it wasn't *contemporary*, she supposed. William hadn't consulted her, anyway. He seemed to know about these things. And there were the venetian blinds, pretty plastic things, so much more attractive than the old brown pelmet they replaced.

She fitted the plug and ran the water. Hot and cold came together from a lion's-head tap; you blended the water by operating a lever. Once you were in the bath you could control the intake of water with your foot, using a push-button mechanism. What would the first occupants of 14, Bismarck Road, eighty years ago, have thought of that?

Melanie reviewed the array of ornamental bottles on the shelf above the taps. Salts, oils, crystals and foam baths were prodigally provided. She selected an expensive bath oil and upended the bottle, watching the green liquid dispersed by the cascading water. Its musky fragrance was borne up on spirals of steam. How odd that William should provide all this and seem unwilling for her to use it! Each evening since Monday, when they had returned from the honeymoon, she had suggested she might take a bath and he had found some pretext for discouraging her. It didn't matter *that* much, of course. At the hotel in Herne Bay she had taken a daily bath, so she didn't feel desperately in need of one immediately they got back. It was altogether too trivial to make an issue of, she was quite sure. If William and she had to have words some time it wasn't going to be about bath nights, at any rate. So she had played the part of the complaisant wife and fallen in with whatever distractions he provided.

Tonight, though, she had deliberately taken him by surprise. She had hidden nightie and book in the towel chest earlier in the day, so when she hesitated at the head of the stairs as they came to bed he was quite unprepared. You don't go for a late-night bath empty-handed, even when your bathroom has every convenience known to the modern home designer. She was sliding the bathroom door across before he realised what had happened. 'Sorry, darling! I mean to have my bath and that's the end of it!'

The door slid gently across on its runners and clicked, the whole movement perfectly timed, without a suspicion of haste, as neatly executed as a pass in the bullring. That was the way to handle an obstructive husband. Never mind persuasion and pleading; intelligent action was much more dignified, and infinitely more satisfying. Besides, she *had* waited until Friday.

She tested the water with her hand, removed her slip, took her book and plastic shower-cap from the towel chest, shook her mass of flaxen hair and then imprisoned it in the cap. She turned, saw herself unexpectedly in a mirror, and pulled a comical face. If she had remembered, she would have brought in a face pack – the one thing William had overlooked when he stocked the cosmetics shelf. She wasn't going into the bedroom to collect one now, anyway. She took off the last of her underclothes and stepped into the bath.

It was longer than the bath at home or the one in the hotel. Silly really: neither William nor she was tall, but they had installed a six-foot, six-inch bath – 'Two metres, you see,' the salesman had pointed out, as though that had some bearing on their requirements. Over the years it would probably use gallons more hot water, but it was a beautiful shape, made for luxuriating in, with the back at the angle of a deckchair on the lowest notch, quite unlike the utility five-footer at home with its chipped sides and overhanging geyser that allowed you enough hot water to cover your knees and no more. William had even insisted on a sunken bath. 'It will sink to four inches below floor level, but that's the limit, I'm afraid, or we'll see the bottom of it through the kitchen ceiling.'

Accustomed to the temperature now, she pressed the button with her toe for more hot water. There was no hurry to rise from this bath. It wouldn't do Mr William Lloyd any harm to wait. Not simply from pique, of course; she felt no malice towards him at all. No, there was just a certain deliciousness – a man wouldn't understand it even if you tried to explain – in taking one's time. Besides, it was a change, a relief, if she was honest, to enjoy an hour of solitude, a break from the new experience of being someone's partner, accountable for every action in the day from cooking the dinner to clipping one's toenails.

She reached for the book, one she had found on William's bookshelf with an intriguing title, *Murder is Methodical*. Where better to read a thriller than in a warm bath behind locked doors? There hadn't been much opportunity for reading in the last three weeks. Or before, for that matter, with curtains to make and bridesmaids to dress.

She turned to the first page. Disappointing. It was not detective fiction at all. Just a dreary old manual on criminology. 'William Palmer, the Rugeley Poisoner' was the first chapter. She thumbed the pages absently. 'Dr Crippen: a Crime in Camden Town'. How was it that these monsters continued to exert such a fascination over people, years after their trials and executions? The pages fell open at a more whimsical title – from her present position, anyway – 'George Joseph Smith: the Brides in the Bath'. Melanie smiled. That chapter ought to have a certain piquancy, particularly as one of the first place-names to catch her eye was Herne Bay. Strange how often one comes across a reference to a place soon after visiting there. With some slight stirring of interest, she propped the book in the chromium soap-holder that bridged the sides of the bath, dipped her arms under the water, leaned back and began to read.

George Joseph Smith had stayed in Herne Bay, but not at the New Excelsior. Wise man! If the food in 1912 was anything like the apologies for cuisine they dished up these days, he and his wife were far better off in the house they took in the High Street. But it wasn't really a honeymoon the Smiths – or the Williamses, as they called themselves – spent at Herne Bay, because they had been married two years before and he had deserted her soon after, only to meet her again in 1912 on the prom at Weston-super-Mare. In May they had come to Herne Bay and on 8 July they made mutual wills. On 9 July, Smith purchased a new five-foot bath. Bessie, it seemed, decided to take a bath on the twelfth, a Friday. At 8 a.m. next morning a local doctor received a note: *Can you come at once? I am afraid my wife is dead.* On the sixteenth she was buried in a common grave and Smith returned the bath to the supplier, saying he did not require it after all. He inherited £2,500.

£2,500. That must have been worth a lot in 1912. More, almost certainly, than the £5,000 policy William had taken out on her own life. Really, when she considered it, the value of money declined so steadily that she doubted whether £5,000 would seem very much when they got it in 1995, or whenever it was. They might do better to spend the premiums now on decorating some of the rooms downstairs. Super, to have a luxury bathroom, but they would have to spend a lot to bring the other rooms up to standard. 'Insurance policies are security,' William had said. 'You never know when we might need it.' Well, security seemed important to him, and she could understand why. When you'd spent your childhood in an orphanage, with not a member of your family the least interested in you, security was not such a remarkable thing to strive for. So he should have his insurance – it was rather flattering, anyway, to be worth £5,000 – and the rest of the house would get decorated in due course.

There was another reason for insurance which she did not much like to think about. For all his energy and good looks, William was fifty-six. When the policy matured, he would be over eighty, she fifty-two. No good trying to insure him; the premiums would be exorbitant.

For distraction, she returned to the book, and read of the death of Alice Burnham in Blackpool in 1913. Miss Burnham's personal fortune had amounted to £140, but the resourceful George Smith had insured her life for a further £500. She had drowned in her bath a month after her wedding, on a Friday night in December. Strange, that Friday night again! Really it was exquisitely spine-chilling to be sitting in one's bath on a Friday night reading such things, even if they had happened half a century ago. The Friday-night bath, in fact, she learned as she read on, was an important part of Smith's infamous system. Inquest and funeral were arranged before there was time to contact the relatives, even when he wrote to them on the Saturday. Alice Burnham, like Bessie Mundy, was buried in a common grave early the following week. 'When they're dead, they're dead,' Smith had explained to his landlord.

Melanie shuddered slightly and looked up from the book. The appalling callousness of the murderer was conveyed with extraordinary vividness in that remark of his. For nearly twenty years he had exploited impressionable girls for profit, using a variety of names, marrying them, if necessary, as unconcernedly as he seduced them, and disappearing with their savings. In the early encounters, those who escaped being burdened with a child could consider themselves fortunate; his later brides were lucky if they escaped with their lives.

It was reassuring for a moment to set her eyes on the modern bathroom, its white carpet and ceramic tiles. Modern, luxurious and *civilised*. Smith and his pathetic brides inhabited a different world. What kind of bathroom had those poor creatures met their fates in? She had a vision of a cheap tin bath set on cold linoleum and filled from water jugs, illuminated by windows with coloured-glass panels. Not so different, she mused, from the shabby room William had converted – transformed, rather – for her into this dream of a modern bathroom. Lying back in the water, she caught sight of the cornice William had repainted, highlighting the moulding with gold paint. So like him to preserve what he admired from the past and reconcile it with the strictly contemporary.

Friday night! She cupped some water in her hands and wetted her face. George Joseph Smith and his crimes had already receded enough for her to amuse herself with the thought that his system would probably work just as well today as it did in 1914. The postal service hadn't improved much in all those years. If, like Daddy, you insisted on living without a telephone, you couldn't get a letter in Bristol before Monday to say that your daughter had drowned in London on Friday evening.

How dreadfully morbid! More hot water with the right toe and back to the murders, quite remote now. When had Smith been tried and executed? 1915 – well, her own William had been alive then, if only a baby. Perhaps it wasn't so long. Poor William, patiently waiting for her to come to bed. It wouldn't be fair to delay much longer. How many pages to go?

She turned to the end to see, and her eye was drawn at once to a paragraph describing the medical evidence at Smith's trial.

The great pathologist Sir Bernard Spilsbury stated unequivocally that a person who fainted whilst taking a bath sitting in the ordinary position would fall against the sloping back of the bath. If water were then taken in through the mouth or nose it would have a marked stimulating effect and probably recover the person. There was no position, he contended, in which a person could easily become submerged in fainting. A person standing or kneeling might fall forward on the face and then might easily be drowned. Then, however, the body would be lying face downwards in the water. The jury already knew that all three women had been found lying on their backs, for Smith's claim that Miss Lofty was lying on her side was nonsense in view of the size of bath in Bismarck Road.

Bismarck Road. Melanie jerked up in the water and read the words again. Extraordinary. God, how horrible! It couldn't possibly be. She snatched up the book and turned back the pages, careless of her wet hands. There it was again!

Margaret made her will and bequeathed everything, nineteen pounds (but he had insured her life for £700), to her husband. Back at Bismarck Road, Highgate, a bath was installed that Friday night. Soon after 7.30 the landlady, who was ironing in her kitchen, heard splashes from upstairs and a sound which might have been wet hands being drawn down the side of the bath. Then there was a sigh. Shortly after, she was jolted by the sound of her own harmonium in the sitting room. Mr John Lloyd, alias George Joseph Smith, was playing 'Nearer, my God, to Thee'.

Mr John Lloyd. Mr John *Lloyd*. That name. Was it possible? William had said he knew nothing of his parents. He had grown up in the orphanage. A foundling, he said, with nothing but a scrap of paper bearing his name; abandoned, apparently, by his mother in the summer of 1915. The summer, Melanie now realised, of the trial of George Joseph Smith, alias John Lloyd, the deceiver and murderer of women. It was too fantastic to contemplate. Too awful . . . An unhappy coincidence. She refused to believe it.

But William – what if he believed it? Rightly or wrongly believed himself the son of a murderer? Might that belief have affected his mind, become a fixation, a dreadful, morbid urge to relive George Joseph Smith's crimes? It would explain all those coincidences: the honeymoon in Herne Bay; the insurance policy; the house in Bismarck Road; the new bath. Yet he had tried to keep her from having a bath, barred the way, as if unable to face the last stage of the ritual. And tonight she had tricked him and she was there, a bride in the bath. And it was Friday.

Melanie's book fell in the water and she sank against the back of the bath and fainted. An hour later, her husband, having repeatedly called her name from outside the bathroom, broke through the sliding door and found her. That, at any rate, was the account William Lloyd gave of it at the inquest. She had fainted. Accidental death. A pity Sir Bernard Spilsbury could not have been in court to demonstrate that it was impossible. Even in a two-metre bath.

The Tale of Three Tubs

The author on George Joseph Smith
and the Brides in the Bath

I first read about 'The Brides in the Bath' in a book called *The Life of Sir Edward Marshall Hall*. Odd reading for a ten-year-old whose friends were working their way through Enid Blyton and Richmal Crompton, but my house had recently been destroyed by a VI flying bomb and we had almost nothing left. This was a damaged copy belonging to my father that must have been salvaged from the bombsite. At an age when my inner world had been transformed by reading, I picked up the book and was enthralled. Marshall Hall was the renowned defence lawyer involved in many of the sensational trials of the past fifty years. And what evocative titles they had: the Green Bicycle Murder; the Camden Town Murder; Seddon the Poisoner; the Yarmouth Beach Case, and Madame Fahmy at the Savoy. Then I came to the Brides in the Bath. For some mysterious reason the bath was in the singular as if the same tub had been used over and over. But the book soon put me right. Three 'brides' were murdered in baths as far removed from each other as Herne Bay, Blackpool and Highgate.

This was a complex case involving scores of locations. The serial bigamist, George Joseph Smith, could not risk staying in one place for long. He is known to have made at least six illegal marriages. A hundred and twelve witnesses gave evidence at his trial. That he was guilty of wilful murder was agreed by the jury in just over twenty minutes, despite Marshall Hall's best efforts. Smith did himself no favours by several times interrupting the judge during the summing-up. He was described by the author of his entry in the *Notable British Trials* series as 'the most atrocious English criminal since Palmer'. On the other hand, his first victim wrote, 'He is a thoroughly good husband, and I am as happy as any woman breathing, in fact, everybody seems to take to him.'

More than anything, it was Smith's formula for making money – his 'system', as it was termed at the trial – that made the case exceptional. Three women were destroyed by it. Shortly before their deaths each was persuaded to make a will in Smith's favour. Two took out life insurance policies and the other had a substantial trust fund that passed to Smith after her death. All three were induced to visit a doctor complaining of headaches and the same doctor was called in soon after to confirm that they were dead. Each woman took a bath in an unlocked room. On each occasion, Smith drowned her, went out briefly to buy food, returned and made sure someone else in the house was with him shortly after he 'discovered' the body. Used once, the system was artful and efficient. Twice, and it was risky. Three times, ruinous.

So much has been written about the personalities in the case – Smith, Marshall Hall, the expert witness, Bernard Spilsbury, and the victims – that I thought it might be different to approach it obliquely by focusing on the baths and their part in the case and after. They have an intriguing history.

Let us start in an ironmonger's shop in the seaside town of Herne Bay in July 1912. This is a time when poorer houses weren't equipped with bathrooms. A customer is examining a bath, not a hip bath, but a cast-iron, five-foot bath with a plug. The shop-owner, Adolphus Michael Hill, 41, recognises him as Henry Williams, a slim, handsome man about his own age who has leased a house in the High Street for at least a couple of months. We know him as George Joseph Smith. The bath is second-hand, Hill explains. 'How much do you want for it?' the customer asks. 'Two pounds,' Hill says. The customer says he will think about it – which any shopkeeper knows is often a get-out – and leaves.

Two days afterwards, Mrs Bessie Williams comes into the shop and says she is interested in buying the bath, but not for as much as two pounds. She is willing to offer half-a-crown less. Hill ponders the matter and notices that the lady is pitifully agitated and excited. 'Mr Williams told me to say you must let us have it,' she says. Hill is sympathetic and agrees to the reduction. He promises to deliver it to the house in the High Street the next day. No money changes hands. These are people he has met and trusts.

It slightly undermines the 'brides in the bath' tag to reveal that Bessie was not a recent bride. Smith had met and married her eighteen months before, in 1910. She was one of the string of hapless women he cheated out of their savings in bigamous marriages before disappearing from their lives. She had inherited £2,500 from her father, a bank manager. Her uncles, as trustees, had placed this considerable sum (worth more than a quarter of a million pounds in modern money) into a trust fund for Bessie, enabling her to draw £8 a month in interest. Within a week of their register office wedding in 1910, Smith realised he stood no chance of getting his hands on the capital sum. Instead, he demanded £138 that he said was legally due to Bessie in excess interest. When the trustees' cheque arrived at Bessie's solicitors he insisted on having it cashed. He then deserted her. Devastated, Bessie sent a telegram to her uncle Herbert: 'Husband left me today. Taken money. Please send me some. Writing. Bessie.'

As if being abandoned was not cruel enough, Bessie received a letter next day from Smith that began, 'Dearest, I fear you have blasted all my bright hopes of a happy future. I have caught from you a disease which is called the bad disorder, for you to be in such a state proves you could not have kept yourself morally clean.' He added that this would cost him a great deal of money to be cured and might take years.

She called the police and wrote to her uncle, 'I do hope my husband will be caught . . . I quite see now what I have fallen into, and I feel I have disgraced myself for life.' There her ordeal might have ended were it not for a twist of fate, a coincidence you would not expect to find outside a Thomas Hardy novel.

In March 1912, eighteen months after Smith deserted her, Bessie took a short holiday in Weston-super-Mare. While walking on the promenade she chanced to meet her errant husband. But instead of calling the police, she allowed herself to be persuaded that he still loved her and had been looking for her and that he had been mistaken about the sexually transmitted disease. The £2,500 was still being held in trust and Smith had thought of a new way of getting his hands on it. The couple were reconciled. Fast forward to Herne Bay in July 1912.

When he arrives to deliver the bath, Adolphus Hill, the ironmonger, is surprised to be told he and his assistant must carry it upstairs to the back bedroom. This is strange for a bath that won't be plumbed in. The only water supply is downstairs. Bucketfuls of heated water will have to be carried up two flights of stairs, and later the process will go into reverse when the bath needs to be emptied. The room where the bath is to go is about as far away from the copper downstairs as it is possible to be. Unusually, the couple have their bed downstairs in the dining room. On the first floor there's a vacant bedroom with a lock, but Hill and his assistant are told to pass that and go up more stairs to this small room that doesn't have a lock. Later it is calculated that when Mrs Williams half filled her bath the trips up and downstairs with the bucket must have taken forty-two minutes.

Four days after, Smith returns to the shop and asks Mr Hill to collect the bath from the house, as he wishes to return it. He says he will be leaving Herne Bay shortly. The bath has still not been paid for, so the shopkeeper retrieves his property. He only hears later that Mrs Williams died in it, apparently of an epileptic fit.

The sequence of events over that week in July 1912 became the blueprint for George Joseph Smith's 'system'. On 8 July, the couple had attended a solicitor's and completed the process of making wills, leaving all their worldly goods to each other. On the tenth they had visited a doctor and reported that Bessie had a fit the previous day. On the twelfth the doctor was called to the house at 1.30 a.m. because, the husband said, Bessie had had another fit. The doctor prescribed more medicine, deciding she might be epileptic. On the thirteenth, Smith called the doctor out again because Bessie was dead in the bath. This was early Saturday morning. An inquest was held on the Monday and the coroner concluded she drowned accidentally while suffering another fit. The funeral was Tuesday.

All remarkably quick. And because there was no post on Sunday, there wasn't time to invite Bessie's family to the funeral. They lived in Wiltshire, almost two hundred miles away. Smith disliked them anyway, and the feeling was mutual. The Mundys had been suspicious from the start that he married Bessie for her money.

The inquest on Bessie was at best perfunctory. It was held in the Herne Bay council chamber at 4.30 in the afternoon and was concluded the same day. The coroner, Rutley Mowll, when questioned at Smith's trial, couldn't remember many of the details. He couldn't be sure whether the jury, who visited the house, had been shown the bath. He thought the body was seen in a coffin upstairs. No post-mortem had been ordered. No measurements had been taken of the body or the bath. The coroner's officer, PC Kitchingham, was better informed. He had been called to the house on the day of the death and seen the body upstairs lying naked on the floor and the bath three parts full of soapy water. When the inquest jury had visited, the body was in a coffin in the dining room downstairs. They hadn't gone upstairs to see the bath and hadn't asked to see it. The only other witness at the inquest, apart from Smith, was Dr French, who had been called to the house on the morning of the death.

Under questioning in 1915 at Smith's trial for murder, Dr French explained why he had concluded that the cause of Bessie's death was asphyxia caused by drowning in the course of an epileptic fit. He had been told at the first consultation that she had suffered a fit and he had been called out in the night to see her because of another. 'The following day I am called in and I find her drowned in a bath. Again I have no suspicion; I have no reason for suspicion that there is any foul play.' She was a tall woman, at five feet nine inches, and she was lying on her back in the five-foot bath with her face submerged and her feet out of the water resting against the sloping end. The bath was about two-thirds full. He had removed the body from the bath and tried artificial respiration. There were no marks of violence. Her right hand was still clutching a bar of Castile soap.

If Smith had settled for one profitable murder, the crime was unlikely ever to have been detected. However, the system had worked so efficiently that when an opportunity arose he couldn't resist using it again.

So the Herne Bay bath was returned to the ironmonger's. Whether it was bought by anyone else in the two and a half years before the law caught up with Smith, I cannot say with any certainty. It seems unlikely that a cheap, used bath would have been allowed to take up room in the shop all that time. In 1915 its whereabouts were traced and it was transported to London, to Kentish Town police station, where a murder enquiry was under way. Two more baths had been brought there, one from Blackpool, the other Highgate. The sensational story of the 'Brides in the Bath' was about to break.

The Blackpool victim was Alice Burnham, a nurse. She had met Smith in mid-September, 1913 (two months after Bessie's death), in the Congregationalist chapel in Southsea, near Portsmouth. He liked to portray himself as a devout man. His letters – of which many survived – are peppered with sanctimonious sentiment. He was also a past master at charming the ladies. He must have felt confident with Alice because he used his own name when he introduced himself. Within two months she married him, on 4 November 1913. But they didn't have a chapel wedding. He preferred the local register office.

The system powered into action again: demands and threats to the family for money. Alice wasn't an heiress like Bessie, so the best way to capitalise on her coming death was to take out life insurance. A honeymoon by the sea in Blackpool. This time, the house where they lodged was furnished with a plumbed-in bath. A visit to a local doctor, to get something for Alice's headaches. On the third evening, 12 December, Alice announces she would like to take a bath and the landlady's daughter runs the taps for her. Smith goes out briefly, returns, shouts for assistance and asks the family to fetch the doctor – who discovers Alice dead in a bath filled to the top with soapy water. Smith is supporting her. Between them, they lift her out and try artificial respiration, but it is too late. The police are called and a sergeant inspects the body downstairs, but doesn't look into the bathroom. The inquest, next day, is got through in half an hour. This time the doctor has already carried out a post-mortem and found the symptoms of drowning. He describes Alice as 'well nourished, very fat' and observes that the heart was enlarged and the valves diseased. This, he feels, probably contributed to her collapse. The verdict of the jury – who listen to statements, but don't visit the house – is that she 'was probably seized with a fit or a faint'. Another accidental death.

Smith profited by £140 of Alice's money, plus life assurance of £500. It wasn't enough to fund him for long, so he fitted in another bigamous marriage – his fifth – before resorting to murder again. He met another Alice in Woolwich and deprived her of her savings of £78, her piano, furniture and spare clothes, and then deserted her while out walking in a park. Alice Reavil lived to tell the tale.

The next bride did not. In December, 1914, Smith decided to use the system again. He married a Bristol woman, Margaret Lofty, in – of all places – Bath. She was less well off than either of the previous brides, but she was an easy catch, having recently been badly let down by a fiancé who had turned out to be married already. Smith, now masquerading as John Lloyd, persuaded Margaret to take out an endowment insurance policy for £700. The system required that the murder must take place a long way from Bristol, so he travelled to London in advance and found lodgings in Orchard Road, Highgate. He was seen by one of the lodgers there, a Mrs Heiss, who sometimes handled arrangements for the landlady, Mrs Lokker. When shown the vacant room, he asked if there was also a bathroom. The bath was rather small for his purpose. He studied it with calculation and finally commented, 'I daresay it is large enough for someone to lie in.' He paid six shillings as a deposit, but when asked for a reference said the ready money ought to be reference enough. He would return with his wife on the following Thursday.

Everything was in place once more, the insurance, the register office wedding, the trip to London for the honeymoon and the lodgings furnished with a bathroom. But there was a hitch. When the couple arrived at the house about three in the afternoon, the room wasn't ready. They were asked to come back about six. Smith was annoyed and made his feelings clear. They left their luggage in the hall and returned a little after five-thirty and knocked several times, but no one came to the door. They had to wait until six. Mrs Lokker was cautious about who she took on as lodgers, and Smith sounded troublesome. She had arranged for a male friend, who happened to be a detective sergeant, to stand in for her and tell this unpleasant man that as he hadn't provided a reference he was not a desirable lodger. 'Mr Lloyd' said, 'This is a funny kind of house. I want my deposit back.' The couple were forced to walk the gas-lit streets of Highgate looking for another place to spend their wedding night.

Smith wasn't deterred from his plan. They parked their bags – a holdall and a Gladstone bag – at Highgate tube station and started the search. On the way, they passed a doctor's surgery in Archway Road, duly noted. Eventually they found rooms to let at 14, Bismarck Road. Miss Blatch, the landlady, carrying a lighted candle, took them up to the attic on the second floor and showed them the furnished room. On the way downstairs, Mrs Lloyd asked if there was a bathroom and Miss Blatch pointed to a first-floor room with a bath and wc. The bath was slightly longer, at five foot six, plumbed in and cased in wood. Smith agreed to take the room at seven shillings per week and paid in advance. Then he went off to collect the luggage while Miss Blatch made tea for Mrs Lloyd. Later, the couple went out again to visit the doctor and get something for a headache Margaret had developed.

The murder next day went according to plan. During the afternoon Mrs Lloyd enquired whether she could have a bath later. Miss Blatch got it ready for her about seven-thirty, heating some water in the kitchen and providing towels and soap. The Lloyds had been for a walk and were in the sitting room downstairs. Soon after, Miss Blatch was ironing in the kitchen below the bathroom when she heard someone go upstairs. 'A few minutes after that I heard a sound from the bathroom. It was a sound of splashing. Then there was a noise as of someone putting wet hands or arms on the side of the bath, and then a sigh. The splashing and the hands on the bath occurred at the same time. The sigh was the last I heard. The next sound I heard was someone playing the organ in the sitting room.'

Mr Lloyd was playing 'Nearer My God to Thee'. Quite a musician in his way, he filled the house with music for ten minutes, and then Miss Blatch heard the front door slam. Presently the doorbell rang and she opened it to find Lloyd there with a paper bag in his hand. He told her he'd been out to buy tomatoes for Mrs Lloyd's supper and forgotten he had a latchkey. He asked if his wife was down yet. He went upstairs and called her name.

The process followed the usual pattern. A shout from Lloyd: 'She is in the bath. Come and help me.' After finding him in the gas-lit bathroom holding his wife's upper body above the water, Miss Blatch said she would go for help. It was pretty obvious to her that the woman was dead. Lloyd said, 'Fetch Dr Bates. I took her to him last night.' By chance, Miss Blatch met a police officer on patrol duty only fifty yards away. PC Heath ran to the house and discovered Lloyd kneeling beside the body on the floor. The constable tried artificial respiration until Dr Bates arrived. The doctor decided the woman must have died from asphyxiation caused by drowning. Later he would say at the inquest that she might have fainted in the hot bath. He had thought she may have had a mild form of influenza, which was rife at the time.

The inquest and funeral followed, although not so rapidly as after the previous deaths. Smith was obliged to remain at 14, Bismarck Road longer than he had planned. The inquest was four days after the death, on 22 December, and then adjourned until 1 January because Miss Blatch had injured her knee and was unable to get there. However, the coroner allowed the funeral to take place on 23 December. The only mourners were Smith and one of the Lofty family, a cousin. Like the other dead wives, Margaret was buried in a common grave. Rather than remaining at

Bismarck Road over Christmas, Smith left for what he said was a cycling tour. He returned for the resumed inquest and it went according to plan. Mrs Lloyd, the jury decided, had died accidentally, from suffocation by drowning.

All done. It remained only to cash in. On 4 January 1915, Smith visited a solicitor and produced the marriage certificate, the life policy and the will, and instructed him to obtain probate. The system appeared to have worked for a third time in three years. But there was something he had not factored in: the power of the press.

The story of a bride found dead in her bath was perfect material for the *News of the World* with its reputation for scandalous and suggestive human interest stories. FOUND DEAD IN BATH: *Bride's Tragic Fate on Day after Wedding*, ran the headline on 3 January. The paper would be seen by more than two million readers, and one of them was Charles Burnham, the father of Smith's second victim. Burnham's dislike of Smith was absolute. He had fought to prevent him getting his hands on Alice's modest savings. This, of course, had incensed Smith. When Burnham had requested information about his background, Smith had replied on a postcard, 'Sir, In answer to your application regarding my parentage etc. My mother was a Buss horse, my father a cabdriver, my sister a rough rider over the Arctic Regions. My Brothers were all gallant sailors on a Steam roller. This is the only information I can give to those who are not entitled to ask such questions contained in the letter I received on the 24th inst. Your despised son-in-law, G. Smith.'

Charles Burnham read the account of the Highgate incident in the *News of the World* and couldn't fail to notice the similarities to Alice's drowning, even though the names of the husbands were different. He took out a cutting about his daughter's tragedy he had kept from a local paper: BRIDE'S SUDDEN DEATH: *Drowned after Seizure in a Hot Bath.* He showed both to his solicitor, who sent them to the police. Meanwhile, Joseph Crossley, the son-in-law of the Blackpool landlady, was also a *News of the World* reader and he, too, wrote to the police.

The true horror of what had been committed was about to be exposed. The newspaper clippings were attached to a memo headed SUSPICIOUS DEATHS and forwarded to Detective Inspector Arthur Neil, who was based at Kentish Town police station and actually lived in a flat in Archway, the Highgate street 'Mr Lloyd' had walked along on his way to Bismarck Road. Neil spoke to PC Heath, the officer Miss Blatch had called to the house the night Margaret Lloyd had died. Heath had discovered the lifeless woman lying naked on the floor in the bathroom doorway. He had tried unsuccessfully to resuscitate her. He had formed a bad impression of the husband – having to tell him 'in pity's name' to fetch something to cover her modesty.

Inspector Neil decided to see the Bismarck Road bathroom for himself. He swiftly decided it was 'a physical impossibility' for someone to drown accidentally or through fainting in a bath of this size. Its entire length was five feet six and the inside length, where someone taking a bath would recline at the base of the sloping end with their feet against the vertical end, was four feet two. Moreover it was encased in wood that overhung the bath by five inches at the head end and two and a half inches at the foot end.

Intensive enquiries were set in motion. As well as interviewing Miss Blatch – who thought it impossible for Mr Lloyd to be in any way responsible – the inspector spoke to Dr Bates and the cousin who had been at the funeral. None of them appeared to have any doubts that it had been an accidental death. But no one seemed to know where Mr Lloyd was living now.

At this stage, there were suspicions of two murders. The motive: financial gain. The Blackpool police had discovered that Smith had insisted he needed a number of extra copies of Alice's death certificate, which was likely to mean he had claims with several insurance companies. Inspector Neil traced the Bristol insurance company Mr Lloyd had used in connection with Margaret's death and, through them, a Mr Davies, the solicitor who was acting on Lloyd's behalf and had obtained probate. Lloyd had given Davies an address that was no longer current, but he had recently called at the solicitor's to enquire about his legacy. It hadn't been ready. More documents were required before the money could be released. Smith had been annoyed at the delay. This was quite a breakthrough, because it gave the police a chance – in modern parlance – to stake out the solicitor's office on the Uxbridge Road in confidence that Lloyd would be back.

Days passed while the police kept surveillance, first from the street and later from a room over the pub opposite. Finally, on 1 February 1915, a man answering Lloyd's description was seen entering the solicitor's office and was arrested as he came out.

'Are you John Lloyd?' Inspector Neil asked.

'Yes.'

'Your wife died in a bath at Bismarck Road, Upper Holloway, on the eighteenth December last – the day after she was married to you.'

'Quite right.'

'You are also said to be identical with George Smith, whose wife died under similar circumstances on the thirteenth December 1913 at Blackpool, and to whom you were only married a few weeks.'

This was too much. 'Smith? I'm not Smith. I don't know what you're talking about.'

When pressed – informed that Alice's father was prepared to come down and identify him – the prisoner owned up to the double identity, insisting that the deaths of his two wives were 'a phenomenal coincidence'.

With Smith in custody, held on the lesser charge of causing a false entry to be inserted in the marriage registry, a spate of police activity got under way. Tracing the bigamous marriages and stashes of money in banks and post offices was a huge challenge, involving forces all over the country. And within a week came the astonishing news from Kent of a case two years earlier involving the sudden death of another young woman in a bath – Bessie Williams, in Herne Bay. The picture of the husband, known as Henry Williams, bore a striking resemblance to George Joseph Smith.

The notion of coincidence had stretched beyond breaking point. For Inspector Neil, the investigation moved to a new, more challenging phase. If Smith had murdered the women, how had he done it? A quick-acting poison? Brute force? There had been no attempt at concealment except for the changes of name. Two of the murders had been carried out in guest houses where other people were present. In all three cases a doctor had been called. There had been no sounds of violence, no screams. There were almost no marks on the bodies, just some slight bruising of the third victim's arm.

The victims were exhumed for post-mortem examination by Dr Bernard Spilsbury, a rising forensic pathologist who had been an expert witness at the trials of two notorious murderers, Dr Crippen and Frederick Seddon. Both had been poisoners, but in Smith's case, no traces of poison were found in any of the victims. They had drowned, but how?

While Spilsbury was giving his attention to the post-mortem results, Inspector Neil arranged to have a closer look at the three bathtubs. He had them all brought to his police station at Kentish Town. The ones in Blackpool and Highgate were disconnected and removed from the respective boarding houses and the bath from Herne Bay was also traced and transported there.

To Neil's eye, it was difficult to imagine anyone drowning naturally in any of these baths. The largest, the Highgate one, was only four feet two inches along the bottom. He was unable to work out how the women could have been held underwater without grabbing the sides and struggling – in which case their bodies would surely have taken some bruising. He decided to experiment. Another drama was about to be enacted. He sought the help of a young woman swimmer, 'used to diving, plunging and swimming from early girlhood'. All three baths were filled and 'in each one demonstrations were given by this young lady in a swimming costume in many positions'.

The volunteer must have been courageous to agree to climb into each bath in turn, knowing that a woman had died there, and was probably murdered. After a series of experiments to see whether there was a risk of accidental drowning as the woman lowered herself into the water and then leaned forward as if to wash her hair, she was asked to lie back and allow Neil to put pressure on her forehead and force her head under the water. It wasn't the answer. She grabbed the sides to save herself.

The next experiment almost resulted in another drowning. Neil wanted to test sudden immersion, so without warning he grasped the young woman's legs and lifted them. She slid below the water and showed no resistance.

To his horror, Neil realised she had lost consciousness. He raised one of her arms and it was lifeless. He and his colleagues lifted her limp body from the bath. 'For nearly half an hour my detectives and I worked away at her with artificial respiration and restoratives.' That must have been one of the worst half hours of Neil's life. Eventually, the life-saving efforts worked. Some colour returned to the subject's face. When able to speak, she said the water had rushed into her mouth and up her nostrils and she remembered nothing else until her consciousness returned.

The experiments ceased at once. Bernard Spilsbury's biography makes clear that he had not witnessed what went on and had disapproved of it. However, he certainly profited from Neil's discovery. He was able to make a convincing case in court that Smith's *modus operandi* was to reach into the water and raise the legs high.

When the trial opened in June 1915, the only victim named in the charge was Bessie Mundy, the Herne Bay victim. Even so, all three bathtubs had been brought to the Old Bailey and stored under the courtroom. They would all be exhibits in the case, for early in the trial the judge, Mr Justice Scrutton, ruled that evidence of Smith's alleged system of murder would be allowed. This enabled the prosecution to point to similarities between all three drownings and it effectively sealed Smith's fate. The trial was one of the longest on record, with one of the swiftest of verdicts.

So the baths had their day in court. On Day Three, when Adolphus Hill, the ironmonger, gave evidence, the Herne Bay bath was brought in and set on the end of the solicitors' table in front of the jury, the first time such a bizarre exhibit had ever been seen in the Central Criminal Court. At one stage, the foreman of the all-male jury asked that someone should be put in the bath 'for ocular demonstration'. The judge was having none of it. 'I can only suggest to you that when you examine these baths in your private room you should put one of yourselves in. Get some one of you to try who is about the height of five feet nine.'

Imagine the thoughts of the jury at this minute, eyeing each other to see who was the nearest in height. Marshall Hall, appearing for the defence, suggested that the prosecution should provide someone in open court, but the judge dismissed the suggestion. 'It is much better the jury should try for themselves, Mr Hall. There are disadvantages in the French system of reconstructing a crime.'

On Days Four and Five the court's attention turned to the drowning of Alice Burnham. The Blackpool bath and its wooden casing were brought into court. George Billing, the doctor Smith had called to the house, was given a red pencil and asked to mark the place where he thought the dead woman's buttocks had been positioned. Unusually, she had been lying with her head – supported by Smith – towards the taps when he was called to the house.

The Highgate bath appeared on Day Six, when Miss Blatch, the landlady at Bismarck Road, gave evidence and recalled hearing noises from upstairs when she was ironing in the kitchen. 'It was a sound of splashing. Then there was a noise as of someone putting wet hands or arms on the side of the bath, and then a sigh . . . The next sound I heard was someone playing the organ in the sitting room.'

The evidence of the pathologists, Spilsbury and Dr William Willcox, took up most of the next day. After explaining at length why he did not believe Bessie Mundy had died from some form of fainting or fit (she would have recovered consciousness at the moment of submersion), Spilsbury asked for the Herne Bay bath to be brought in again (by which time the court functionaries who did the heavy work must have been silently cursing) to demonstrate how a person might be drowned in only nine inches of water when the feet were pulled up and the head pressed down. The inrush of water through mouth and nostrils would cause a shock, resulting in immediate loss of consciousness. Willcox endorsed the theory. Nothing Marshall Hall extracted in hours of cross-examination undermined the expert witnesses.

When the judge summed up on the ninth day, he was compelled to point out that there was no direct evidence that Smith murdered Bessie. If they arrived at a guilty verdict, it would be based on circumstantial evidence. But as the circumstances were gone over in minute detail, including all the financial manoeuvrings and the so-similar deaths of the other brides, the case against Smith became so overwhelming that the prisoner himself started interrupting the judge. Wisely, Marshall Hall had kept him silent up to then, but he shouted repeatedly: 'You may as well hang me at once the way you are going on'; and 'Go on, hang me at once, and done with it'; and 'What about it? That does not say I done a murder. It is a disgrace to a Christian country, this is. I am not a murderer, though I may be a bit peculiar.'

The jury agreed that he was a bit peculiar. But they also decided he was a murderer. They retired at 2.48 p.m. and returned their verdict at 3.10.

An appeal was heard and dismissed on 29 July and on 13 August Smith was hanged at Maidstone. His last words were, 'I am innocent.'

Curiously, while under sentence of death, he succeeded in convincing the chaplain at Maidstone Prison that indeed he had been wrongly convicted. The chaplain asked the Bishop of Croydon to come and meet Smith, and he, too, became convinced that although the man had 'been steeped in every villainy' for over twenty years, he was not a murderer. Marshall Hall, who corresponded with the bishop, wrote back: 'That he did not drown them in any of the ways suggested by the evidence, or the *ex parte* suggestions of the judge, I am convinced; but I am equally convinced that it was brought about by hypnotic suggestion. I had a long interview with Smith, under very favourable circumstances, and I am convinced that he was a hypnotist.' Hall didn't go on to suggest that the chaplain and the bishop had been hypnotised, but instead surmised that Smith had satisfied his own conscience that the act of drowning was induced by his will and was, 'to all intents a voluntary act on the part of the woman'.

Edith Pegler, one of the bigamously married 'wives' who survived, told the *Weekly Dispatch* shortly after the execution, 'He had an extraordinary power over women. The power lay in his eyes. When he looked at you for a minute or two you had the feeling that you were being magnetised. They were little eyes that seemed to rob you of your will.'

Professional hypnotists insist that nobody in a trance can be induced to do anything harmful to themselves. Drowning oneself in a bath while hypnotised would surely be impossible. Smith was a controlling man who demonstrated time and again that he could persuade women to trust him absolutely, and this must surely have facilitated his 'system'. All three of his victims went with him to a doctor complaining of headaches just when it suited him, and each decided to take a bath within forty-eight hours of the consultation – events remarkable enough to suggest that his willpower had been impossible to resist.

Whatever were the secrets of his persuasiveness, Smith had paid with his life and few, if any, would miss him. But his notoriety held an enduring fascination, particularly for writers. The best-selling novelist Edgar Wallace reported on the trial for *Tit-Bits*. The playwright George R. Sims, who also attended at the Old Bailey, was inspired to write *The Bluebeard of the Bath*. William Bolitho produced a small masterpiece of irony, an essay headed *The Self-Help of G.J. Smith*. And in due course the case was written up by Eric R. Watson for the *Notable British Trials* series. Among crime writers who referred to Smith in their books were Dorothy L. Sayers, Agatha Christie, Margery Allingham, John Dickson Carr, Graham Greene and Patricia Highsmith. George Orwell wrote nostalgically about the harmonium-playing in *Decline of the English Murder*. Eric Ambler went in search of the boarding houses where the murders took place. William Trevor's short story 'The Child of Dynmouth' reworked the plot. As recently as 2010, a new account of the case by Jane Robins, *The Magnificent Spilsbury and the Case of the Brides in the Bath*, was published to critical acclaim.

After their court appearances, the three baths could no longer remain in the bowels of the Old Bailey and they would not have been welcomed back to Kentish Town police station or the guest houses that had housed them originally. However, there was interest from Madame Tussaud's for their Chamber of Horrors, a section of the waxwork show intended to chill visitors' spines. The macabre extra element was that some of the exhibits were relics of notorious crimes. For many years the wax figures were dressed in the actual clothes of murderers, acquired after execution from the public hangmen, who considered this one of their perks.

Tussaud's did a deal for the bath from Bismarck Road, Highgate. Soon after Smith's execution, it was exhibited at Marylebone Road and became a feature of the show for many years, labelled as the bath in which Smith's final victim,

Margaret Lofty, had been murdered. If I may become personal again, I recall being impressed by it – and by Smith's figure beside it – on a visit there in the nineteen-forties.

Another of the baths was retained by Scotland Yard for what was then known as the Black Museum and now the Crime Museum. Many years later, on a privileged visit with members of the Crime Writers' Association, I saw the dusty old bath stored in a small room along with a fine collection of macabre items such as death masks, hangmen's nooses, Jack the Ripper's letters and Charlie Peace's burglary instruments. One of our party sat on the edge of the bath while we were being given a lengthy explanation about some other gruesome exhibit. When told its story, the lady shot up as if it was red-hot.

With the passage of time and the arrival of new items for both exhibitions, the two baths were put into storage. The third, the Herne Bay bath, had long ago been turned into scrap. You might think this was the end of the story, but it isn't. There is another twist.

Newspaper accounts of the Black Museum from the nineteen-thirties onwards suggested that *their* bath was the one from Bismarck Road. This seems to have gone unchallenged until a family historian, Gordon Lonsdale, decided to investigate a story that his great-grandfather, William Ashforth Drabble, a Blackpool detective inspector, assembled evidence for the trial, including the bath Alice Burnham had died in, and travelled with it by train to London. The family legend was that he had scratched his initials, WAD, on the bath. Gordon Lonsdale emailed the Crime Museum in June 2013 to see if there was any way the story could be checked. Paul Bickley, the curator, and formerly a detective inspector in the Flying Squad, had no reason to doubt the provenance of the bath in the Yard's possession, but he decided to investigate. For at least a quarter of a century the bath had been stored in a warehouse at Charlton, but it was no longer there. Paul Bickley eventually traced it to a disused room at Hendon Police Training College. And when he examined it, he found Drabble's initials scratched quite small on the inside. The family story was confirmed and Scotland Yard concluded that their bath was, after all, the Blackpool one. As extra confirmation, a second set of initials, JC, was found. They are assumed to have been put there by Joseph Crossley, the son-in-law of the Blackpool landlady. Crossley was one of the people who had seen the *News of the World* item and written to the police. The whole story was written up in the Blackpool *Gazette* of 10 December 2013 and appeared on the internet.

For the latest thinking on the tale of the tubs, I consulted the historical researcher and actor Keith Skinner, who is a part-time volunteer at the Crime Museum. He told me that the discovery had prompted a fresh inspection of the files. They showed that when Inspector Neil decided to bring the three baths to Maida Vale early in 1915, two of them (from Herne Bay and Blackpool) were bought from the owners and became the property of the police. The third (from Highgate) was acquired on loan and the astute owners waited until it was returned to them and then sold it to Tussaud's along with a few extra items relevant to the case. This bath was removed from the Chamber of Horrors some years ago and is now apparently in storage.

After Smith's trial and execution the former owner of the Blackpool bath contacted Scotland Yard and offered to buy it back, but this was seen as a possible attempt to exploit the crimes and rejected. The Black Museum didn't have the space for two baths, so the one from Herne Bay was destroyed. The Blackpool bath was retained for the museum

– which wasn't open to the public – and somehow in the years between the two world wars it was mistakenly assumed to have been the one from Bismarck Road, Highgate.

In 2013, the surviving (Blackpool) bath made another journey, on extended loan to the Galleries of Justice museum in Nottingham. And there, in September 2014, it went on display as part of a World War I: Heroes and Villains exhibition. No need to ask which category Smith represented. The perversity that so many hours were spent in 1915 deliberating over his fate while thousands of innocent soldiers were losing their lives had not been lost on the court – and was commented on by both the judge and Marshall Hall, who called it 'a tribute to our national system of jurisprudence'.

So the Blackpool bath was exhibited along with Sir Bernard Spilsbury's forensic evidence cards as well as the actual dock from Bow Street Magistrates' Court where the accused man stood when he was committed for trial. With nice timing, the exhibition came to an end in August 2015, exactly a century after George Joseph Smith's notorious life was brought to a close.

Sources

Trial of George Joseph Smith (Notable British Trials series), Eric R. Watson (Ed), 1922

Murder for Profit, William Bolitho, 1926

The Life of Sir Edward Marshall Hall, Edward Marjoribanks, 1929

Forty Years of Man-Hunting, Arthur Fowler Neil, 1932

Famous Trials II, Harry Hodge (Ed), 1940

Bernard Spilsbury, His Life and Cases, Douglas G. Browne and E.V. Tullett, 1951

The Official Encyclopedia of Scotland Yard, Martin Fido and
  Keith Skinner, 1999
The Magnificent Spilsbury and the case of the Brides in the Bath,
  Jane Robins, 2010

With thanks to Bev Baker, Joan Lock and Keith Skinner.

A Monologue
For Mystery Lovers

This little old lady is in the pub and her voice is extra
    loud.
She's had a few of the local brew and is playing to the
    crowd.
Her speech is slurred and her cheeks are pink and her
    eyes are shining bright,
As she explains to a bunch of the lads what brought her
    here this night.

Fill 'em up, she says to the landlord Les. The drinks are
    all on me.
Sixty years ago in this very bar I met my destiny.
He was tall and dark and handsome, too – as handsome
    as handsome goes,
With piercing eyes and a cultured voice and a very
    distinguished nose.
And above all that a deerstalker hat perched atop his
    six-foot frame.
I'm not going to spoil my story, but you'll probably guess
    his name.
Truth to tell, I was under his spell before the night began.
Oh, his silver hair was beyond compare – I adore an
    older man.

Now I need to make clear to all of you here that I was
    just nineteen
And my rosebud face had won first place in the Tatler
    magazine.
But I acted coy with the average boy, keeping a low
    profile.
In the pub I'd sit at the back and knit, and hardly ever
    smile.
As I recall, I was knitting a shawl in a pretty pink
    three-ply
Upon the night the distracting sight of this stranger met
    my eye.
Without dropping a stitch, I made my pitch to this
    dream with the gorgeous nose.
Men are easy to pull with a ball of wool, as every woman
    knows.
With a nonchalant toss I bowled it across to where my
    hero stood.
A line so true that it found his shoe like the nudge of a
    bowler's wood.
There was deathly quiet inside the bar when he eyed this
    ball of pink.
Nothing was said. He just turned his head and requested
    another drink.
But a man called Bruce said, Can you deduce the source
    of this woolly sphere?
There were laughs all round, an ugly sound made more
    ugly by the beer.
It chilled my skin and I wished I'd been outside the
    bar-room door.
The wool, you see, was linked to me, by a thread across
    the floor.

Then my heart-throb spoke, a brilliant stroke, or where is
 genius from?

He said, I deduce, if my thoughts are of use, that this
 ball is an anarchist bomb.

The laughter died and they rushed outside – ah, you
 should have seen them flee.

Scared out of their shoes, they quit their booze, all
 except him and me.

After quite some while, he gave me a smile that flashed
 like a carving knife,

Prompting me to say, in my modest way, Sir, I lead a
 sheltered life.

He replied, My dear, that's abundantly clear to a man of
 my profession.

The clothes, the hair, the tonic you drink, the mild-as-
 milk expression.

Your name is Jane, you're a first-class brain, and as pure
 as the driven snow.

I can also see you're attracted to me, and that's very
 good to know.

Don't ask how I tell, it bores me to hell to answer this
 type of question.

But now we're alone, the birds having flown, may I make
 a bold suggestion?

Next time you feel like an intimate meal, why not travel
 to London town?

Baker Street for high tea, 221B, is an offer one shouldn't
 turn down.

Reaching up to a shelf, he then helped himself to a very
 fine champagne.

Without more talk, he popped the cork and it flew like
 an aeroplane.

Now the lads out back heard the cork go crack and knew
where it was from.

A controlled detonation was their explanation: we had
dealt with the anarchist bomb.

Feeling rather more bold, they came in from the cold to
find the pub forsaken.

Not wanting trouble, we had left on the double, with
only the bubbly taken.

The place is hushed. We all feel crushed, not knowing if
it's ended,

This gripping tale from the lady frail: it seems to be
suspended.

Then she smiles, the old dear, and asks for a beer, and
we offer a glass of champagne,

If she will reveal: did she go for that meal, high tea in
his rooms with her swain?

She says, What's one glass to a lady of class? It's a
magnum or nothing for me.

So we have a whip-round, and raise fifty pound, for a
magnum of Mumm '83.

She sinks one or two of this premier cru, then gives a
peculiar smile.

Yes, I went for the tea at 221B, and the visit was very
worthwhile,

For apart from the food, which was frightfully good, what
followed was out of this world:

The violin strain, the shot of cocaine, the pipe smoke
that twisted and curled.

I have to confess that my memory is less than exact as to
what happened then,

But I wish to point out, in case there is doubt, that I had
    little knowledge of men.
You have to believe I was rather naïve; I didn't quite
    understand
When a question was posed by my glamorous host: had I
    heard of his Speckled Band?
I thought, Janey, my dear, you must get out of here if
    you value your reputation.
But he said with a smile, It's a case in my file, a famous
    investigation.
In you I detect a fine intellect that could be as sharp as
    my own.
I tell you in truth, you will make a good sleuth if I teach
    you the things I have known.
Well, he told me the history of many a mystery including
    his Speckled Band,
The Lion's Mane, and the Second Stain and the thumb
    from the engineer's hand.
The Five Orange Pips came hot from his lips along with
    his Sign of Four.
Crime after crime, I lost count of time, and still he
    detained me with more.
When a pause came at last, I was really aghast, for
    midnight was just coming round.
I cried out, I must go! But he said, No, no, no. There's
    the tale of the gigantic hound.
Now who would pass up the Baskerville pup from the lips
    of the Baker Street master?
My option was plain: I had to remain, just hoping he'd
    go a bit faster.
It was dark and profound, his account of the hound, with
    effects he had not used before.

I was really afraid, when he actually bayed, just like that
thing on the moor.
I said, Please would you stop. This is over the top. It's
making me queasy with fright.
So he kissed me instead and took me to bed – and the
dog didn't bark in the night.
You may think I was lax to run off the tracks, staying late
in 221B.
Yet I claim in defence that in more than one sense that
night was the making of me.
Sixty years later I'm an investigator unashamedly
shedding a tear,
Recalling the night that Miss Marple was launched – on
the start of her brilliant career.

A Peter Lovesey Checklist

Novels

Wobble to Death, Macmillan 1970; Dodd, Mead 1970 (Sergeant Cribb)

The Detective Wore Silk Drawers, Macmillan 1971; Dodd, Mead 1971 (Sergeant Cribb)

Abracadaver, Macmillan 1972; Dodd, Mead 1972 (Sergeant Cribb)

Mad Hatter's Holiday, Macmillan 1973; Dodd, Mead 1973 (Sergeant Cribb)

Invitation to a Dynamite Party, Macmillan 1974; as *The Tick of Death*, Dodd, Mead 1974 (Sergeant Cribb)

A Case of Spirits, Macmillan 1975; Dodd, Mead 1975 (Sergeant Cribb)

Swing, Swing Together, Macmillan 1976; Dodd, Mead 1976 (Sergeant Cribb)

Waxwork, Macmillan 1978; Pantheon 1978 (Sergeant Cribb)

The False Inspector Dew, Macmillan 1982; Pantheon 1982

Keystone, Macmillan 1983; Pantheon 1983

Rough Cider, Macmillan 1986; Mysterious Press 1987

Bertie and the Tinman, Bodley Head 1987; Mysterious Press 1988 (Bertie)

On the Edge, Century Hutchinson 1989; Mysterious Press 1989

Bertie and the Seven Bodies, Century Hutchinson 1990; Mysterious Press 1990 (Bertie)

The Last Detective, Scribners 1991; Doubleday 1991 (Peter Diamond)

Diamond Solitaire, Little, Brown 1993; Mysterious Press 1993 (Peter Diamond)

Bertie and the Crime of Passion, Little, Brown 1993; Mysterious Press 1993 (Bertie)

The Summons, Little, Brown 1995; Mysterious Press 1995 (Peter Diamond)

Bloodhounds, Little, Brown 1996; Mysterious Press 1996 (Peter Diamond)

Upon a Dark Night, Little, Brown 1997; Mysterious Press 1998 (Peter Diamond)

The Vault, Little, Brown 1999; Soho Press 2000 (Peter Diamond)

The Reaper, Little, Brown 2000; Soho Press 2000 (Peter Diamond)

The House Sitter, Little, Brown 2003; Soho Press 2003 (Peter Diamond)

The Circle, Time Warner 2005; Soho Press 2005 (Hen Mallin)

The Secret Hangman, Sphere 2007; Soho Press 2007 (Peter Diamond)

The Headhunters, Sphere 2008; Soho Press 2008 (Hen Mallin)

Skeleton Hill, Sphere 2009; Soho Press 2009 (Peter Diamond)

Stagestruck, Sphere 2011; Soho Press 2011 (Peter Diamond)

Cop to Corpse, Sphere 2012; Soho Press 2012 (Peter Diamond)

The Tooth Tattoo, Sphere 2013; Soho Press 2013 (Peter Diamond)

The Stone Wife, Sphere 2014; Soho Press 2014 (Peter Diamond)

Down Among the Dead Men, Sphere 2015; Soho Press 2016 (Peter Diamond)

Another One Goes Tonight, Sphere 2016; Soho Press 2016 (Peter Diamond)

Beau Death, Sphere 2017; Soho Press 2017 (Peter Diamond)

Killing With Confetti, Sphere 2019; Soho Press 2019 (Peter Diamond)

The Finisher, Sphere 2020; Soho Press 2020 (Peter Diamond)

Diamond and the Eye, Sphere, 2021; Soho Press, 2021 (Peter Diamond)

Short Stories

I: Collections

Butchers and Other Stories of Crime, Macmillan 1985; Mysterious Press 1987

The Staring Man and Other Stories, a signed limited edition containing four stories from *Butchers and Other Stories of Crime*, Eurographica, Helsinki 1989

The Crime of Miss Oyster Brown and Other Stories, Little, Brown 1994; Crippen & Landru 2019

Do Not Exceed the Stated Dose, Crippen & Landru 1998; Little, Brown 1998

The Sedgemoor Strangler and Other Stories of Crime, Crippen & Landru 2001; Allison & Busby 2002

Murder on the Short List, Crippen & Landru 2008; Severn House 2009

Reader, I Buried Them and Other Stories, Soho Press 2022; Sphere 2022

II: Collaborations

'Plotting the Perfect Murder', Sarah Caudwell, Tony Hillerman, Peter Lovesey, Nancy Pickard and Donald E. Westlake, edited by Jack Hitt, *Harper's Magazine*, September 1988

The Rigby File, edited by Tim Heald, Hodder & Stoughton 1989

The Perfect Murder, Lawrence Block, Sarah Caudwell, Tony Hillerman, Peter Lovesey, Donald E. Westlake, with Jack Hitt, edited by Jack Hitt, HarperCollins 1991

The Ideas Experiment, Liza Cody, Michael Z. Lewin, Peter Lovesey, PawPaw Press 2006

The Sinking Admiral, edited by Simon Brett and written by members of the Detection Club, HarperCollins 2016

III: Edited Anthologies

The Black Cabinet: Stories Based on True Crimes, unlocked by Peter Lovesey, Xanadu 1989

3rd Culprit: A Crime Writers' Annual, edited by Liza Cody, Michael Z. Lewin and Peter Lovesey, Chatto & Windus 1994

The Verdict of Us All: Stories by the Detection Club for H.R.F. Keating, edited by Peter Lovesey; Crippen & Landru 2005; Allison & Busby 2006

IV: Tribute

Motives for Murder: a Celebration of Peter Lovesey on his 80th Birthday by Members of the Detection Club, edited by Martin Edwards, foreword by Len Deighton; Crippen & Landru 2016; Sphere 2016

V: Short Stories

By date of first publication in Britain and USA; some were retitled by *Ellery Queen's Mystery Magazine* and both titles are listed.

'The Bathroom', *Winter's Crimes 5*, Macmillan 1973; collected in *Butchers and Other Stories of Crime* and *Reader, I Buried Them and Other Stories*

'The Locked Room', *Winter's Crimes 10*, Macmillan 1978; collected in *Butchers and Other Stories of Crime*

'Behind the Locked Door' (retitled from 'The Locked Room'), *Ellery Queen's Mystery Magazine*, March 1979

'How Mr Smith Traced His Ancestors', *Mystery Guild Anthology*, Book Club Associates 1980; collected in *Butchers and Other Stories of Crime*

'A Man With a Fortune' (retitled from 'How Mr Smith Traced His Ancestors'), *Ellery Queen's Mystery Magazine*, November 1980

'A Bride in the Bath' (retitled from 'The Bathroom'), *Ellery Queen's Mystery Magazine*, August 1981

'Butchers', *Winter's Crimes 14*, Macmillan 1982; *Ellery Queen's Mystery Magazine*, mid-July 1982, as 'The Butchers'; collected in *Butchers and Other Stories of Crime* and in *The Staring Man and Other Stories*

'Taking Possession', *Ellery Queen's Mystery Magazine*, November 1982; collected as 'Woman and Home' in *Butchers and Other Stories of Crime* and *The Staring Man and Other Stories*

'Belly Dance', *Winter's Crimes 15*, Macmillan 1983; collected in *Butchers and Other Stories of Crime*

'Keeping Fit' (retitled from 'Belly Dance'), *Ellery Queen's Mystery Magazine*, March 1983

'The Virgin and the Bull', *John Creasey's Mystery Crime Collection*, Gollancz 1983; collected in *Butchers and other Stories of Crime*

'Fall-Out', *Company Magazine*, May 1983; *Ellery Queen Mystery Magazine*, June 1984; collected in *Butchers and other Stories of Crime*

'The Virgoan and the Taurean' (retitled from 'The Virgin and the Bull'), *Ellery Queen's Mystery Magazine*, July 1983

'Did You Tell Daddy?', *Ellery Queen's Mystery Magazine*, February 1984; collected in *Butchers and Other Stories of Crime*

'Arabella's Answer', *Ellery Queen's Mystery Magazine*, April 1984; collected in *Butchers and Other Stories of Crime*

'Vandals', *Woman's Own*, 20 December 1984; *Ellery Queen's Mystery Magazine*, December 1985; collected in *Butchers and Other Stories of Crime*

'The Secret Lover', *Winter's Crimes 17*, Macmillan 1985; *Ellery Queen's Mystery Magazine*, March 1988; collected in *Butchers and Other Stories of Crime*

'The Corder Figure', *Butchers and Other Stories of Crime*, Macmillan 1985; *Ellery Queen's Mystery Magazine*, January 1986; also collected in *The Staring Man and Other Stories*

'Private Gorman's Luck', *Butchers and Other Stories of Crime*, Macmillan 1985; *Ellery Queen's Mystery Magazine*, July 1985

'The Staring Man', *Butchers and Other Stories of Crime*, Macmillan 1985; *Ellery Queen's Mystery Magazine*, October 1985; also collected in *The Staring Man and Other Stories*

'Trace of Spice', *Butchers and Other Stories of Crime*, Macmillan 1985

'Woman and Home' (retitled from 'Taking Possession'), *Butchers and Other Stories of Crime*, Macmillan 1985

'Murder in Store', *Woman's Own*, 21 December 1985; collected in *Do Not Exceed the Stated Dose*

'Curl Up and Dye', *Ellery Queen's Mystery Magazine*, July 1986; collected in *The Crime of Miss Oyster Brown and Other Stories*

'Photographer Slain', *Observer*, 30 November 1986 (contest story)

'Peer's Grisly Find: Butler Dead in Bath', *Observer*, 7 December 1986 (contest story); printed as a separate pamphlet in 2001 as 'The Butler Didn't Do It', to accompany Crippen & Landru's limited edition of *The Sedgemoor Strangler and Other Stories of Crime*

'Brighton Line Murder', *Observer*, 14 December 1986

(contest story); reprinted as a pamphlet to accompany *Motives for Murder*, Crippen & Landru 2016

'The Poisoned Mince Pie', *Observer*, 21 December 1986 (contest story)

'The Royal Plot', *Observer*, 28 December 1986 (contest story); reprinted as a pamphlet by Crippen & Landru, 2008

'The Curious Computer', *New Adventures of Sherlock Holmes* (Carroll & Graf, 1987); collected in *The Crime of Miss Oyster Brown and Other Stories*

'Friendly Yachtsman, 39', *Woman's Own*, 18 July 1987; *Ellery Queen's Mystery Magazine*, May 1988; collected in *The Crime of Miss Oyster Brown and Other Stories*

'The Pomeranian Poisoning', *Winter's Crimes 19*, Macmillan 1987; collected in *The Crime of Miss Oyster Brown and Other Stories*

'The Zenobia Hatt Prize' (retitled from 'The Pomeranian Poisoning'), *Ellery Queen's Mystery Magazine*, August 1988

'Where is Thy Sting?', *Winter's Crimes 20*, Macmillan 1988; collected in *The Crime of Miss Oyster Brown and Other Stories*

'The Wasp' (retitled from 'Where is Thy Sting?'), *Ellery Queen's Mystery Magazine*, November 1988

'Oracle of the Dead', *Ellery Queen's Mystery Magazine*, mid-December 1988; *Best*, 3 March 1989; collected in *Reader, I Buried Them and Other Stories*

'A Case of Butterflies', *Winter's Crimes 21*, Macmillan 1989; *Ellery Queen's Mystery Magazine*, December 1989; collected in *The Crime of Miss Oyster Brown and other Stories*

'The Munich Posture', chapter in collaborative story *The Rigby File*, Hodder & Stoughton 1989

'Youdunnit', *New Crimes*, Robinson 1989; *Ellery Queen's Mystery Magazine*, mid-December 1989 and September/October 2001; collected in *The Crime of Miss Oyster Brown and other Stories*

'The Haunted Crescent', *Mistletoe Mysteries*, Mysterious Press 1989; collected in *The Crime of Miss Oyster Brown and Other Stories*

'Shock Visit', *Winter's Crimes 22*, Macmillan 1990; collected in *The Crime of Miss Oyster Brown and Other Stories*

'The Valuation' (retitled from 'Shock Visit'), *Ellery Queen's Mystery Magazine*, February 1990

'The Lady in the Trunk', *A Classic English Crime*, Pavilion 1990; collected in *The Crime of Miss Oyster Brown and Other Stories*

'Ginger's Waterloo', *Cat Crimes*, Donald L. Fine 1991; collected in *The Crime of Miss Oyster Brown and Other Stories*

'Being of Sound Mind', *Winter's Crimes 23*, Macmillan 1990; *Ellery Queen's Mystery Magazine,* July 1991; collected in *The Crime of Miss Oyster Brown and other Stories*

'The Christmas Present', *Woman's Own*, 24 December 1990; collected in *The Crime of Miss Oyster Brown and Other Stories*

'The Crime of Miss Oyster Brown', *Midwinter Mysteries 1*, Scribners 1991; *Ellery Queen's Mystery Magazine*, May 1991; collected in *The Crime of Miss Oyster Brown and Other Stories*

'Supper with Miss Shivers' (retitled from 'The Christmas Present'), *Ellery Queen's Mystery Magazine*, mid-December 1991; collected in *The Crime of Miss Oyster Brown and Other Stories* and *The Usual Santas*, Soho Press 2020

'The Man Who Ate People', *The Man Who . . .*, Macmillan 1992; *Ellery Queen's Mystery Magazine*, October 1992; collected in *The Crime of Miss Oyster Brown and Other Stories*

'You May See a Strangler', *Midwinter Mysteries 2*, Little, Brown 1992; *Ellery Queen's Mystery Magazine*, mid-December 1993; collected in *The Crime of Miss Oyster Brown and Other Stories*

'Murder by Christmas Tree', *Observer*, 20 December 1992 (contest story); printed as a separate pamphlet to accompany Crippen & Landru's limited edition of *Do Not Exceed the Stated Dose*

'Pass the Parcel', *Midwinter Mysteries 3*, Little, Brown 1993; *Ellery Queen's Mystery Magazine*, mid-December 1994; collected in *The Crime of Miss Oyster Brown and Other Stories*

'Murder in the Library', *Bath Evening Chronicle*, 6 October 1993 (contest story)

'The Model Con', *Woman's Realm Summer Special* 1994; collected in *The Crime of Miss Oyster Brown and Other Stories*

'Bertie and the Fire Brigade', *Royal Crimes*, Signet 1994; collected in *Do Not Exceed the Stated Dose*

'The Odstock Curse', *Murder for Halloween*, Mysterious Press 1994; collected in *Do Not Exceed the Stated Dose*

'Passion Killers', *Ellery Queen's Mystery Magazine*, January 1994; collected in *Do Not Exceed the Stated Dose*

'The Case of the Easter Bonnet', *Bath Chronicle*, 17 April 1995; *Ellery Queen's Mystery Magazine*, April 1997; collected in *Do Not Exceed the Stated Dose*

'Never a Cross Word', *Mail on Sunday*, 11 June 1995; *Ellery Queen's Mystery Magazine*, February 1997; collected in *Do Not Exceed the Stated Dose*

'The Mighty Hunter', *Midwinter Mysteries 5*, Little, Brown 1995; *Ellery Queen's Mystery Magazine*, January 1996; collected in *Do Not Exceed the Stated Dose*

'The Proof of the Pudding', *A Classic English Crime*, Pavilion 1995; collected in *Do Not Exceed the Stated Dose*

'The Pushover', *Ellery Queen's Mystery Magazine*, June 1995; collected in *Do Not Exceed the Stated Dose*

'Quiet, Please — We're Rolling', *No Alibi*, Ringpull 1995; *Ellery Queen's Mystery Magazine*, December 1996; collected in *Do Not Exceed the Stated Dose*

'Wayzgoose', *A Dead Giveaway*, Warner Futura 1995; *Ellery Queen's Mystery Magazine*, May 1997; collected in *Do Not Exceed the Stated Dose*

'Disposing of Mrs Cronk', *Perfectly Criminal*, Severn House

1996; *Ellery Queen's Mystery Magazine*, December 1997; collected in *Do Not Exceed the Stated Dose*

'A Parrot is Forever', *Malice Domestic 5*, Pocket Books 1996; collected in *Do Not Exceed the Stated Dose*

'Bertie and the Boat Race', *Crime Through Time*, Berkley 1996; collected in *Do Not Exceed the Stated Dose*

'The Corbett Correspondence' (with Keith Miles as Agent No.5 & Agent No.6), *Malice Domestic 6*, Pocket Books 1997

'Because It Was There' *Whydunnnit, Perfectly Criminal 2*, Severn House 1997; collected in *Do Not Exceed the Stated Dose*

'Ape', *Mary Higgins Clark Mystery Magazine*, summer 1998; collected in *The Sedgemoor Strangler and Other Stories of Crime*

'Showmen', *Past Poisons*, Headline 1998; *Ellery Queen's Mystery Magazine*, March 2000; collected in *The Sedgemoor Strangler and other Stories of Crime*

'A Monologue for Mystery Lovers' (verse), *Ellery Queen's Mystery Magazine*, February 1999; collected in *Reader, I Buried Them and Other Stories*

'The Four Wise Men', *More Holmes for the Holidays*, Berkley 1999; collected in *The Sedgemoor Strangler and Other Stories of Crime*

'The Perfectionist', *The Strand Magazine*, April–July 2000; collected in *The Sedgemoor Strangler and Other Stories of Crime*

'The Word of a Lady', *Ellery Queen's Mystery Magazine*, July 2000; collected in *The Sedgemoor Strangler and other Stories of Crime*

'The Sedgemoor Strangler', *Criminal Records*, Orion 2000; collected in *The Sedgemoor Strangler and Other Stories of Crime*

'Interior, With Corpse', *Scenes of the Crime*, Severn House 2000; *Ellery Queen's Mystery Magazine*, August 2001;

collected in *The Sedgemoor Strangler and Other Stories of Crime*

'Dr Death', *Crime Through Time III*, Berkley 2000; collected in *The Sedgemoor Strangler and Other Stories of Crime*

'The Problem of Stateroom 10', *Murder Through the Ages*, Headline 2000; *Ellery Queen's Mystery Magazine*, December 2001; collected in *The Sedgemoor Strangler and other Stories of Crime*

'The Amorous Corpse', *Mammoth Book of Locked Room Mysteries & Impossible Crimes*, Robinson 2000; collected in *The Sedgemoor Strangler and Other Stories of Crime*

'The Kiss of Death', published as Christmas pamphlet, Crippen & Landru 2000; collected in *The Sedgemoor Strangler and Other Stories of Crime*

'Away With the Fairies', *Malice Domestic 10*, Avon 2001; collected in *The Sedgemoor Strangler and Other Stories of Crime*

'Star Struck', *Death by Horoscope*, Carroll & Graf 2001; collected in *The Sedgemoor Strangler and Other Stories of Crime*

'The Usual Table', *The Mysterious Press Anniversary Anthology*, Mysterious Press 2001; collected in *The Sedgemoor Strangler and Other Stories of Crime*

'The Butler Didn't Do It' (retitled from 'Peer's Grisly Find: Butler Dead in Bath'), pamphlet, Crippen & Landru 2001

'Murdering Max', *Ellery Queen's Mystery Magazine*, September/October 2001; collected in *The Sedgemoor Strangler and Other Stories of Crime*

'The Stalker', *The Sedgemoor Strangler and Other Stories of Crime*, Crippen & Landru 2001

'Window of Opportunity', *Sunday Express*, 6 April 2003; *Ellery Queen's Mystery Magazine*, November 2004; collected in *Murder on the Short List*

'The Man Who Jumped for England', *Mysterious Pleasures*, Little, Brown 2003; *Ellery Queen's Mystery Magazine*, June 2005; collected in *Murder on the Short List*

'The Field', *Green for Danger*, Do Not Press 2003; *Ellery Queen's Mystery Magazine*, September/October 2004; collected in *Murder on the Short List*

'Second Strings', *The Strand Magazine*, June–September 2004. Collected in *Murder on the Short List*

'Razor Bill', *Sherlock*, issue 60, 2004; collected in *Murder on the Short List*

'Bullets', *The Mammoth Book of Roaring Twenties Whodunnits*, Constable & Robinson 2004; *Ellery Queen's Mystery Magazine*, September/October 2005; collected in *Murder on the Short List*

'The Case of the Dead Wait' (in three parts), *Daily Mail*, 24, 27, 28 December 2004; complete in *Ellery Queen's Mystery Magazine*, January 2007; collected in *Murder on the Short List*

'Needle Match', *Murder is My Racquet*, Mysterious Press 2005; collected in *Murder on the Short List*

'Say That Again', *The Ideas Experiment*, PawPaw Press 2006; *Ellery Queen's Mystery Magazine*, March/April 2007; collected in *Murder on the Short List*

'A Blow on the Head', *ID Crimes of Identity*, Comma Press 2006; *Ellery Queen's Mystery Magazine*, July 2008; collected in *Murder on the Short List*.

'Popping Round to the Post', *The Verdict of Us All*, Allison & Busby 2006; *Ellery Queen's Mystery Magazine*, November 2007; collected in *Murder on the Short List*

'Bertie and the Christmas Tree', *The Strand Magazine*, October–December 2007; collected in *Murder on the Short List*

'Agony Column', *Red Herrings*, May 2008; *Ellery Queen's*

Mystery Magazine, November/December 2018; collected in *Reader, I Buried Them and Other Stories*

'The Best Suit', *Ellery Queen's Mystery Magazine*, June 2008; collected in *Murder on the Short List*

'The Homicidal Hat', pamphlet for *Malice Domestic XX*, Crippen & Landru 2008; collected in *Reader, I Buried Them and Other Stories*

'The Deadliest Tale of All', *On a Raven's Wing: New Tales in Honor of Edgar Allan Poe*, Harper's 2009; collected in *Reader, I Buried Them and Other Stories*

'Ghosted', *Original Sins*, Severn House 2010; collected in *Reader, I Buried Them and Other Stories*

'Angela's Alterations', *Deadly Pleasures*, Severn House 2013; *Ellery Queen's Mystery Magazine*, July/August 2018; collected in *Reader, I Buried Them and Other Stories*

'A Three Pie Problem', *Ellery Queen's Mystery Magazine*, January 2013; collected in *Reader, I Buried Them and Other Stories*

'Reader, I Buried Them', *Guilty Parties*, Severn House 2014; *Ellery Queen's Mystery Magazine*, March/April 2018; collected in *Reader, I Buried them and Other Stories*

'Remaindered', *Bibliomysteries*, Mysterious Bookshop 2014; collected in *Reader, I Buried Them and Other Stories*

'The Tale of Three Tubs: George Joseph Smith and the Brides in the Bath', *Truly Criminal*, The History Press 2015; collected in *Reader, I Buried Them and Other Stories*

'Sweet and Low', *Ellery Queen's Mystery Magazine*, September–October 2016; collected in *Reader, I Buried Them and Other Stories*

'Lady Luck', *Mystery Tour: A Crime Writers' Association Anthology*, Orenda Books 2017; *Ellery Queen's Mystery Magazine*, March/April 2020; collected in *Reader, I Buried Them and Other Stories*

'The Bitter Truth', *Deadly Anniversaries*, Hanover Square Press 2020; collected in *Reader, I Buried Them and other Stories*

'And the Band Played On', *Reader, I Buried Them and Other Stories*, Soho Press, Sphere 2022.

'Formidophobia', *Reader, I Buried Them and Other Stories*, Soho Press, Sphere 2022.

'Gaslighting', *Reader I Buried Them and Other Stories*, Soho Press, Sphere 2022.

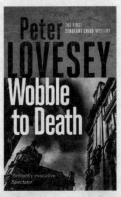

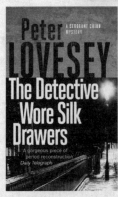

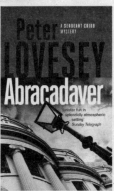

Discover Sergeant Cribb

'Lovesey has a special flair for re-creating Victorian
England with to-the-manner-born wit'
Saturday Review

'Sinister fun in splendidly atmospheric setting'
Sunday Telegraph

'Delightful Victorian mysteries . . . [A] fine picture of vice,
good mystery plotting, and fun'
San Francisco Chronicle

**The very first Peter Diamond mystery,
and Anthony Award-winning novel, from
the superb Peter Lovesey**

A woman's naked body is found floating in the weeds
of a lake near Bath, by an elderly woman walking her
Siamese cats. No one comes forward to identify her,
and no murder weapon is found, but sleuthing is
Superintendent Peter Diamond's speciality. A genuine
gumshoe, practising door-stopping and deduction:
he is the last detective.

Struggling with office politics and a bizarre cast of
suspects, Diamond strikes out on his own, even when
Forensics think they have the culprit. Eventually, despite
disastrous personal consequences, and amongst Bath's
rambling buildings and formidable history, the last
detective exposes the uncomfortable truth . . .

*

'A bravura performance from a veteran showman:
slyly paced, marbled with surprise and, in the end,
strangely affecting'
New York Times Book Review